THE
LOST
SOLDIER

THE DONAGHUE HISTORIES
BOOK THREE

C. JANE REID

SPINNING TALES PRESS

To Everyone who had to listen to me moan how this book would never be finished—

Here you go. It's finished. Enjoy. I'm celebrating with chocolate.

Lots and lots of chocolate…

CHAPTER ONE

Tuesday, May 28, 1782
Virginia's Eastern Shore

"This is a terrible plan, Shawn."

"I know it is."

"Then why are we doing it?"

"Have you got a better plan, Wallis? No?"

"We should've gone north from the first."

"I know it."

"I said it then. I said we should've gone north."

"I know it, Wallis."

"But no, there was nothing but for Trevor to go south. I told him, 'Your cousin won't be in Richmond, you blasted fool. Not since it burned.'"

"Enough, Wallis—"

"He was so certain. 'Molly'll be there,' he said. You remember him. Going on and on about the tall house and the kitchen and the fresh bread."

"For the love of God, Wallis—"

"And you know how I am about fresh bread, Shawn. When's the last time we had honest to goodness fresh-baked bread? Do you remember?"

"I swear, Wallis, if you don't shut it I'm going—"

"Did you hear that?"

Both men fell silent. Shawn leaned forward, as if the motion might help sound reach his ears. The darkness around him was complete, stealing away any chance to see, and over the lapping waves, it was nearly impossible to hear anyone approaching.

"I found a boat."

Shawn's knife was out of the beaded sheath hanging across his chest and in his hand before he recognized Trevor's voice.

"Balls, Trevor," Wallis said from next to Shawn, "you'll end up with a knife in your belly if you keep sneaking up on us like that."

"I made a sound to warn you," the small man said in his nasal voice. He always seemed on the verge of whining, and his quick-tongued Chesapeake accent didn't help.

"It's fine, Trevor," Shawn told him. "How far is the boat?"

"Not far."

"Is there anyone near it?"

"A cabin about three furlongs away. No lights burning."

"Dogs?"

"Didn't seem to be."

Shawn nodded, knowing his two companions wouldn't see it. Though, Trevor might. He had eyes like a cat. He had been the best scout in their company, and defeat and imprisonment hadn't dulled his senses. If anything, they'd gotten sharper.

Shawn sheathed the knife and checked the rawhide keeping the sheath hanging across his chest. He'd repaired it as often as he could, but now that he was down to only one length of rawhide, he was nervous of losing the knife. Again. Still, he kept the sheathed knife outside his shirt, the easier to reach it.

"Lead the way. Wallis, lean on me."

"I can manage—"

"Don't argue with me, man," Shawn snapped, his own Scots-Irish brogue, usually subdued into just a few words, thickened.

Wallis grumbled, but he found Shawn's arm and submitted to being helped. He moved stiffly, holding in a gasp, and Shawn feared his friend's ankle was more than just sprained. Bearing the bigger man's weight was going to be more difficult that Shawn anticipated, but it couldn't be helped.

Shawn felt his way cautiously out from under the trees through the scraggly underbrush, wincing as thorns tore through his worn clothing.

Not much farther, he told himself. Nearly there.

He'd been telling himself that for weeks.

The quarter moon was high in a clear sky beyond the canopy of knobby coastal trees. Shawn paused to allow his eyesight to adjust to the sparse light and saw Trevor standing only a few paces off, doing the same. The slight man stood with his shoulders hunched, as if preparing for a musket ball to strike him. He had their only musket cradled in his arms, ready to bring the bayonet to bear.

Shawn understood. He felt exposed, too, and would rather have kept to the trees.

The ground underfoot shifted from loam to silt to sand, and the trees fell back to bursts of beach grass. The smell of the ocean was welcoming, and the breeze would have been refreshing if Shawn weren't still chilled through. It hadn't been long since they'd had to swim to shore.

The boat rested high on the rock-strewn beach, overturned. It was flat-bottomed and wide and would hold the three of them easily. It was different than the boats Shawn had taken out on the Delaware River or on the creek behind his uncle's village. But a boat was a boat.

"This is still a bad plan," Wallis grunted in his ear. The taller man was huffing with pain and exertion.

"I'm open to a new one," Shawn whispered.

Wallis went quiet.

Shawn helped his friend settle on an exposed outcrop of rock. Sand pooled beneath it and beach grass fanned out along its sides, threatening to poke through clothing if Wallis shifted the wrong direction.

Together, Shawn and Trevor flipped the boat over. A pair of oars was braced inside the sloping hull, along with a long pole.

"Ever use one of these?" Shawn asked Trevor. "I'm not much for sea travel."

"It's not for open water," Trevor answered. "It's for poling in the channel."

"If you say so. You're sure one of the islands will be safe to land on?"

"I'm sure."

Trevor's voice was confident, but Shawn wasn't as certain. Still, there weren't many options left open to them. Not if they wanted to get home.

They pulled the boat close to the edge of the shoreline. The waves were calm, pulsing sedately onto the beach. It looked like the tide was going out. Shawn hoped that meant it would be easier to break away from shore.

Trevor held the boat while Shawn returned for Wallis.

"Do you know where this island is?" Wallis asked. His voice was tight with pain as he hobbled next to Shawn, clinging to him as they made for the boat.

"It's east of here."

"That's fairly vague."

"So is this whole plan."

Wallis fell silent as they reached Trevor. Shawn didn't want the other man to know how uncertain he was, but he wondered if Trevor had already heard them speaking. The man had ears like a cat, too.

With Wallis helping, Shawn and Trevor got the boat into the water. Shawn hadn't thought his boots could get any more damp, but the cold sea water seeping inside shocked him. He gritted his teeth and pushed past it.

Nearly there. Not much farther.

It took all three of them manning oars and pole to break away from the surf, mild though it was. The sky began to brighten on the horizon, back-lighting stretches of land across the narrow channel. Trevor aimed for that land, but their route wasn't direct. Crags of barnacled rock, snarls of sea plants, and strange tidal eddies pushed and plied them through the water.

It was exhausting work, and Shawn had been exhausted before setting out. Too many nights on the move with too little food, too little rest during the day, and constantly on edge lest they be discovered, had left all three men weakened. Wallis's injured ankle was only the latest in a litany of aches and pains they had all suffered. At least the knife wound Shawn had sustained was nearly healed, but his shoulder still ached from the strain of pulling on the oars.

The sun was well over the island as they neared a finger of land pointing out from a long stretch of coast. They'd been following the coastline for a few miles at least. Shawn couldn't judge just how many miles, but it was a sizable length of coastline.

They'd been eying the shoreline for the past hour, but the tides and the exposed shore hadn't encouraged them to approach. Trees, thicker than he'd expect so close to the ocean, rose gnarled and heavy-boughed from the strip of land that stuck out from the island.

"There," Shawn grunted.

Neither of the other men answered, but they worked with Shawn to urge the boat toward land. It wasn't easy. The current seemed to be heading away from the island. Shawn strained with the oar. The island promised safe haven after weeks of harrowing flight. He wanted to build a fire, dry out his clothing, forage for food, and sleep. He thought he might sleep for days.

As they neared the shore, they saw it wasn't beach, but rock rising several feet above the water. Gritting his teeth, Shawn urged his companions to follow the shallow cliff, looking for a landing point. The current grew stronger against them, and he soon saw the cause. A river emptied into the sea near where the strip of forested cliff met the rest of the island.

But the river also afforded a point of entry.

"There," Shawn called, gesturing with a nod toward the inlet.

"A river? Here?" Wallis was wheezing with exertion, but he found enough breath to sound dubious.

"Long enough island," Trevor said.

"If it's as wide as it is long," Shawn said, "we'll have no trouble finding a place to rest."

"Why don't we just build a hut and call it home?" Wallis said, his words twisting mockingly.

Shawn didn't answer. He was hoping no one had done just that or they would be in deeper trouble than they had been on the mainland.

The passage between ocean and river was a barrier of mingling waves and rushing fresh water currents. The plant life thickened, both above and beneath the water. The water didn't seem deep, but it was too bracken to see bottom.

"Smells like marshland," Trevor said.

Shawn kept rowing. It did smell like marshland, pungent with decay. The coastline they'd followed had been a mixture of sandy dunes and rocky shoals, so the marsh was unexpected.

The inlet broadened, expanding into salt marsh bordered by stunted trees. Farther up river, the trees grew denser, promising ground stable enough to make land, he hoped. Birdsong filled the air, many different than he'd heard before, though he recognized a few. The birds quieted as the boat passed beneath them, but beyond the river, they sang on heedlessly.

The river narrowed and then broadened again as it joined another branch.

"The trees are thicker here," Trevor said.

"Just on the one side," Wallis pointed out. "Still marshland on the other. I say we keep going upstream."

Shawn could barely hold onto the oar, let alone work it. "We're done in," he told the other two. "We keep trying to go onward and we'll likely get caught in a current and swept back to sea."

Neither argued against him.

"There," Shawn said, gesturing again with a nod.

With tired strokes, the men urged the boat to the riverbank. The water had cut down into the soil, but it was only a foot or so to the bank, and an exposed root made for a handy place to tie the boat.

Trevor did so as Shawn climbed out. He helped pull Wallis up as Trevor darted onto the riverbank, agile as a squirrel, but then his strength fled. The men lay on the damp ground, taking deep breaths. The sun tried to break through the leafy canopy but cast only dapples of light through the boughs. Still, what little light reached Shawn was warm, warmer than he'd felt in days.

"Camp," he managed to say. "And a fire."

"Sure it's safe?" Wallis asked.

"Safe or not, we need fire."

"Amen to that," Wallis muttered.

~*~

A fire. An assortment of roots and early spring berries. A single fish Shawn managed to catch in the river with the bayonet tied to the pole. And fresh water that only hinted at the bracken marsh farther downstream.

It took so little to feel like a man again. Shawn could have used twice as much of it all, plus a blanket, warm socks, and a drink that would make his throat burn, but for the first time since leaving the outskirts of Norfolk, he relaxed.

"You're certain no one's around?" Wallis asked Trevor for the third time. Shawn couldn't blame him. Wallis was sitting in his small clothes before the fire, his hairy arms and chest exposed, his shirt and trousers hanging over a low branch to dry out. He'd pulled his hair out of the twine holding it back from his face, and the ruddy locks were curling up around his thick neck and catching into his unkempt beard. He looked like a bear with mange.

The only answer Trevor gave was a nod.

"We'll need more wood before morning," Shawn told them. "I only found enough to start the fire."

"It's a good thing we still have that musket," Wallis said. "We need to find some flint, though, so we don't have to depend on the musket's."

"It's not good taking it out," Trevor said in a hushed voice. "We need it ready in case we're found."

"You said no one was around," Wallis complained.

"For now."

"Wouldn't much matter with only the few shots left," Wallis grumbled.

Shawn didn't like Trevor's paranoia after he'd been so eager to assure them the island would be safe.

"How's the ankle," Shawn asked, more to change the subject than anything. He'd seen for himself how swollen and bruised Wallis' ankle was when they'd wrapped it as best they could with cloth torn from the tails of their shirts.

"Fine," Wallis lied. Shawn could see the pain in his expression, no matter that his friend tried to hide it. "Wish we didn't have to tear up the shirts."

"No choice for it." Shawn sighed. "A clean shirt. I'd sell a year of my life for one. This one's only good for the rag bag." It was grimy and stained with blood and sweat and had a hole in it from where he'd been sliced by his own knife.

Wallis grinned. "When's the last time we got a clean shirt? After Yorktown?"

"Just before. I ripped the old one at the seam and Sergeant Gibbons gave me what-for. But he gave me a new shirt."

"That's right. I got one, too, seeing how he was giving them out."

"He wasn't too happy about that."

"No, he weren't." Wallis chuckled, then sobered. "Too bad about him. I liked him."

Shawn stared down at his feet. The last time he had seen Gibbons, the sergeant lay amongst the Yorktown dead, shot through the neck.

"I miss my coat, too," Shawn said to distract himself this time. "That was my favorite coat."

"That was a fine coat. Leather and water-proof and looked so warm—"

"Wallis," Shawn warned.

"Sorry. I'm just damned tired of being cold and wet."

"I know."

"Too bad the fellow that had your knife didn't have your coat, too."

Shawn nodded and touched the hilt to reassure himself that it was still belted at his waist in its beaded, fringed sheath. It had damaged his shoulder, but the wound had been worth it to get the knife back. And the soldier who'd taken it wasn't likely to hold it anytime soon until his fingers healed. Had his nose healed yet?

"Don't suppose you could spear up any more fish?" Wallis asked wistfully.

Shawn scratched at his beard, tired of the feel of it. "I could try. Though I'd hate to risk losing that bayonet."

"So don't lose it."

"Bad idea," Trevor warned. "We need that bayonet."

"He won't lose it," Wallis told the jumpy scout. "Shawn's been fishing creeks since he could walk. Isn't that right, Shawn?"

"Yeah, but usually with a hook and pole. Don't worry, Trevor, I'll be careful."

Trevor didn't look happy, but he said nothing more.

Shawn got to his feet, reluctant to leave the warmth of the fire. His boots didn't gush with water, but his feet were still damp, as was most of the rest of him.

Trevor curled up near the fire and closed his eyes, one hand wrapped around the musket, the other around the nearly empty shot bag that hung across his body. Shawn wondered it he would truly asleep. The little man had been sleepless ever since Yorktown.

Shawn nodded toward Trevor, and Wallis inclined his head in understanding. He'd look after him, so Shawn grabbed his makeshift spear and left camp.

The river was only about a hundred yards from where they'd made camp. They hadn't dared go any farther from their source of transportation. Shawn checked on the boat, double-checking that it was still tied securely since he'd cut a length from the painter. He returned to the little pool carved into the riverbank farther upstream. He could make out the dark shape of fish among the thin reeds growing along the edge.

He raised the makeshift spear, giving it a few shakes, then tightened the rope so that it caught in the groove he'd notched in the stout stick. He pulled the rope as much as he could, then shook the spear again. The bayonet was secure. Hungry or not, they simply could not risk losing it.

Moving carefully to the edge of the pool, Shawn looked for his chance. He'd only have a couple before the fish fled into the river. Or less, if they remembered his earlier attempts.

He stood poised, waiting. The forest around him seemed to hold its breath.

And that was when he realized the forest had gone still.

Shawn drew a steady breath to keep his heart from pounding in his ears. He turned on the balls of his feet, examining the area around him as he lowered into a crouch. He looked for the glint of sunlight off brass or iron, listening for the jostling of a buckle or the shift of underbrush, anything that might give away an enemy.

Nothing.

The bird song returned, just one or two birds at first, and then the chorus rose again to full strength. Shawn relaxed, though not all at once. He kept scanning the area around him until he was satisfied no one was there.

Unless Trevor had crept away to follow him. That might have quieted the birds. And Shawn wasn't likely to see Trevor if he didn't want to be seen, but the little man had no reason to follow him.

Shawn wouldn't know for certain until he returned to camp. But he wasn't going back empty-handed.

The shadows were growing longer by the time he'd caught two fish, one large enough to make a decent meal for two of them, and he carried them by the tails as he walked. And he hadn't lost the bayonet.

Small victories. He counted every one of them. Perhaps there would come a time when those victories outnumbered all the defeats.

The forest grew still around him again as he approached camp. Shawn slowed, feeling the hair rise on the back of his neck. Setting the fish down on a pile of fallen leaves, he readied the makeshift spear and sidled carefully forward. He could smell the campfire smoke, but he heard no voices.

A musket shot shattered the stillness, followed by a roar.

"Run!" Wallis shouted.

Shawn charged forward instead of retreating, but Trevor was suddenly there, eyes wide, face alight with terror, the musket smoking in his grip. If he saw Shawn, he made no show of it. He sprinted through the woods toward the river.

Wallis broke through the brush in a limping shuffle, wearing only his trousers, clutching his half-dried shirt and his boots. He didn't stop when he saw Shawn.

"Run, you fool!"

Another roar echoed through the trees, higher pitched, and a chorus rose up in answer. Chills raced up Shawn's back. He grabbed Wallis by the arm to help him, keeping tight hold of the spear.

"What are they?"

"Just run—"

Something dove out of the brush in front of them.

It was larger than a hound and bulky like a boar and was covered in patched, mottled fur. It rose up on its hind legs, coming to a height nearly to Shawn's head. It opened its maw and terrible thick tusks curved from its upper and lower jaw. They dripped with foaming spit as the beast gnashed at them, then lounged forward. Shawn pulled Wallis back just in time and remembered the spear, but the creature went sideways into a thicket before he could stab at it. Shawn heard it moving to get behind them.

"Was that a bear?"

"Just run, damn you," Wallis huffed, his voice shaking.

Shawn heard more beasts coming, and a keening wail rose in the air that sounded nothing like a bear. What was coming after them?

Heedless of his injured ankle, Wallis tore through the brush, pushing himself off trees and surging forward until his ankle failed. Shawn kept behind him, struggling to lift him when he faltered. He looked back to see the brush part to expose one of the beasts. Its head was narrow at the end and thick at the top and nearly hairless, with tusks like a boar and small, dark eyes but the mouth of a bear. The bear swiped at him with a twisted, overly large paw. Shawn skirted aside and jabbed back with the spear, marking it, and the snout pulled back with a grunt of pain.

Another musket shot shattered the forest just ahead of them.

"Damn fool." The words wheezed out of Wallis.

They came to the river to find Trevor loading the musket with desperation-fueled speed. A dark form charged from the trees to their right, and Shawn raised the spear, but the creature veered off at the last moment.

"Get in the boat," Shawn shouted. His own voice was weak and trembling.

"Behind you!"

Shawn whirled around at Wallis's warning, bringing the spear to ready. The bear froze, lips pulled away from its fearsome teeth as it growled.

"Get in, Shawn! You wait for him, Trevor—Trevor, I said wait!"

Trevor had sliced the rope holding the boat. Shawn turned and dove. He caught the gunwale with his free arm as the current caught the boat. Wallis grabbed hold of the back of his shirt and hauled him in clutching the spear, but the river soaked him from the waist down.

The current swept the boat back toward the sea. The forest had fallen silent once more, a dreadful silence held by that black form watching as Shawn and his companions were carried away.

"We cannot go back to that island," Wallis complained with Shawn began rowing the boat along the coast rather than back toward the mainland.

"We don't have a choice, Wallis."

"But the mainland—"

"Is no safer today than it was yesterday."

"Neither is that island!"

"We'll beach the boat and stay out in the open."

"And be exposed to any and all to see us? Trevor, tell him." Both men turned to Trevor, but he was curled in on himself, still clutching the musket.

"I don't think Trevor's talking just yet." Shawn studied the man worriedly. Trevor had never been completely sound in the head since Yorktown.

"Balls, what the devil's wrong with the man?"

"I don't know, but we can't stay in this boat."

"And we can't go back to that island!"

Shawn sighed. "Wallis, believe me, I don't want to, but you're in a bad way— No, don't argue, I can hear it in your voice. And Trevor is... I don't know what Trevor is and that's worse. I can't manage this boat on my own. I can see a beach. I think I can get us there."

Wallis looked skyward. "God help us."

Chapter Two

Thursday, May 30th

"What have you gotten yourself into, Ferny boy?"

Deirdre watched the lamb twist, a bramble branch caught firmly in the tight black curls of his wool. Tsking, she knelt down and put a gentle hand on the orphan lamb. "Don't be daft. You'll never be rid of it that way."

Deirdre pulled the little scissors from the huswife tied to her skirt and clipped the bramble out of the lamb's wool. She raised her arm to toss it away, then thought better.

"Most likely run right to it again, won't you?" she asked the lamb. He looked up at her with trusting brown eyes and bleated. Grinning, she gave the lamb a pat and stood, putting the scissors away before tossing the branch as far as she could.

"We're not getting many bayberries picked this way, you silly little goose," she told the lamb as she picked up her empty bucket. "Don't make me regret bringing you with me."

The lamb bounded away, his tail bobbing with each hop. At least he was heading away from the branch. Sighing, Deirdre followed him down the trail leading past the collection of broken crockery and animal bones that served as the village rubbish heap.

If she was lucky, she'd find enough myrtle berries in the thicket to make more candles. Great Aunt Clary had complained that they were nearly out of bayberry candles, and Great Aunt Clary did not like running low on supplies.

Deirdre understood why. They hadn't always had regular trade ships to the island when Great Aunt Clary was a girl. And in the past couple years with the war on, the ships had come much farther apart, too, like they had in early years. They islanders would be lucky to see a ship in a six-month.

This year had been better. They had iron for Conor's forge, and they had sugar again. Joseph said that was the most important supply to return, but her cousin had about the widest sweet tooth on the whole island.

The myrtle thicket was on the far side of the rubbish heap, just before the hog marsh took over along the river. Joseph wouldn't like that she'd gone without him, but she wasn't worried about the wild hogs. It was late enough in the day that the beasties would be taking to shelter.

"You don't know that for sure," Joseph would have said to her if he were there.

"I know because I listened to Uncle John, and he says they take to shelter when the sun hits the lowland trees," she would have answered back, and the discussion would end. Joseph wouldn't dare nay-say anything Uncle John had told her. Her uncle frightened him too much.

Of course, Joseph was a Donaghue, and Uncle John didn't hold with Donaghues. Except for her, but they were family.

Anyway, she'd have the berries, what she could find of them, and be back at the village before Joseph returned from the oyster harvest with his brothers.

"I could go oyster hunting," Deirdre said to the lamb gamboling ahead of her. Ferny stopped on rigid little legs to stare back at the sound of her voice.

"Don't look at me like that," she told the lamb. "I could do it. I don't see what all the fuss is about not letting us women out on the boats. Just because Grace fell out and nearly drowned doesn't mean I will."

Ferny gave no answer.

The towhees and thrashers were beginning to roost for the evening. Several of them jumped deeper into the thicket as she neared.

"You keep back, Ferny," she told the lamb. "I'm not going in there after you if you get stuck like last time." But the lamb seemed more inclined to pull at the tall grass nearby.

What berries were left this late in spring were deep into the thicket. She pulled off the lacy summer mitts running from her thumb to her elbow. Great Aunt Clary hadn't liked her going out without her short skirt, but it was a warm day. Deirdre had conceded to her great aunt's demands that she wear her fingerless gloves.

"You don't know what's hiding in the brush," her great aunt had told her sternly as Deirdre pulled on the hook-stitched mitts. Her great aunt tied a stitched kerchief, still smelling of wool oil, around Deirdre's neck and shoulders. "No fool ever died from being cautious."

It was her great aunt's favorite saying, borrowed from a saying of Deirdre's Great Grandmother Ailee: "Being cautious rarely gets you killed."

Deirdre preferred her great grandmother's way of saying it. She didn't think of herself as a fool, but then Great Aunt Clary tended to think that anyone younger than herself was closer to being a fool than not. And only three people on the island were older than Great Aunt Clary.

"An island of fools," Deirdre said to Ferny, "that's what we are." The lamb flipped his tail a couple of times in answer. Deirdre chuckled.

She tucked the mitts into her skirts and parted the branches to reach deep into the thicket. No thorns, at least. She worked for some while, not finding as many berries as she hoped but enough to scent a handful of candles. Aunt Daisy loved to make candles, so there'd be no difficulty asking her for help. Deirdre could surprise Great Aunt Clary with them next week just when they were using the last of what they had left. She'd have to put up with her great aunt's complaining about the emptying candle box until then, but that was easy enough when she knew it was a matter already remedied.

And Great Aunt Clary was the best person on the island to surprise. She went from sour to sappy in a heartbeat.

Deirdre set the bucket down and pulled a few loose myrtle leaves out of her hair. She should have braided it back, but she'd given it a weekly washing, and it hadn't dried.

Bare-armed, bareheaded, no kerchief, oh, yes, Great Aunt Clary had hit the rafters when Deirdre had tried to leave.

"And she thinks I'm with Deborah and Rosa. As though listening to Deborah moon over Marcos or Rosa go on and on about little Aileen was a pleasant evening spent. Much better to be out in a thicket."

Ferny made no answer.

"I think that's done it, Ferny," she said, looking for the lamb. Ferny wasn't there.

Deirdre heaved a sigh. "Ferny, where'd you get to now?" She circled the thicket, looking for the little black lamb among the meadow grass. "Joseph was right. I should tie a bell to your tail."

The lamb bleated from the far side of the thicket. Deirdre shook her head and hurried for him. "If you've got yourself caught again—"

Words failed her in the face of three unkempt, bearded men. One of them held Ferny by his wooly scruff. The burliest was leaning on a stout stick. The third held a musket.

She'd never seen them before in her life, but her amazement burnt away into outrage when Ferny bleated in fear.

"You put him down!"

The man looked startled, or at least she thought he did under that dark beard. "We meant him no harm." His accent was odd.

"Sure we did," the burly man with the reddish beard said. "We meant to eat him."

Deirdre stepped toward him, knowing the moment she did so that it was a stupid thing to do.

Fool, Great Aunt Clary would have called her.

The man with the musket raised it toward her. Deirdre froze, her heart thumping and her mouth going dry.

"Trevor," the man holding Ferny warned. "Don't."

"She's seen us."

"Put the musket down."

"But she's seen us."

"Why in the devil did we let him carry the damned musket?" the burly man asked.

"So I could help you get around. Trevor, put it down. She's no threat to us."

Deirdre wasn't a threat, but Uncle John would have their heads. She was wise enough to keep that to herself.

The man lowered Ferny to the ground, who bounded off toward Deirdre. The man with the musket, Trevor, startled to see the lamb bounce past, but the first man was on him before he could react, snatching the musket from his hands.

"But she's seen us!" the littler man said with a desperate look in his small eyes. "We don't know whose side she's on!"

All three men looked at her. Deirdre was at a loss for what to say.

"I'm… I'm not on a side." She had no idea which side they meant.

"You live here?" the first man asked, the one with the dark beard and the piercing gaze. His eyes were gray like a thunderstorm rolling in from the sea. She'd never seen their like.

Ferny was huddled against the back of her legs, almost hidden under her skirts. She couldn't run if she wanted to, not without leaving him behind. And she couldn't get away from a musket shot if she stopped to pick him up.

Unless she was clever about it.

"I do," she answered. "Easy Ferny, poor little lamb." She tried to make her voice soothing, but her words sounded trembling. "You frightened my lamb," she scolded the man.

He had the decency to look chagrined. "We didn't know he was yours."

"Whose did you think he was?" Deirdre asked as she knelt to comfort Ferny. She gathered him up into her arms and stroked him, trying not to look hurried though her heart was hammering.

"No one's. Just running wild."

"Running wild? A little lamb, all on its own? Is that what you thought?" Foolish notion, Great Aunt Clary would have said.

"I don't know much about sheep."

"That's obvious enough." She stood slowly as the man cocked his head at her.

"Where do you live?" he asked.

Deirdre tightened her hold on Ferny but worked the hand hidden underneath him into the folds of her skirts. She knew not to tell them. Uncle John had taught that lesson over and over. Do not trust strangers. Keep away from them.

"Over there, past the river," she lied, nodding toward her right.

Two of the men—most importantly, the one holding the musket—glanced that direction.

Deirdre took off running. She raced around the thicket, her skirts pulled indecently up to her knees, Ferny clutched against her. The grass was tall and dragged at her feet, but she kept from tripping, her only thought to get past the rubbish heap and start shouting for help.

Something caught her by the back of her shirt and kerchief, nearly pulling her over backwards. A wiry arm snaked around her, pinning her against a thin but iron-like chest. She fought against the man's hold.

"Don't hurt her, Trevor!" she heard the first man shout.

She tried to kick at the thin, stinking man holding her, but he was ready for that. She couldn't struggle and hold Ferny, too, so she tossed the lamb toward a mound of meadow grass just as the man with the gray eyes reached them. He took her by the arm, his grip careful but strong.

"Let go of her," he told the wiry man.

Trevor hesitated, but the gray-eyed man glared at him. Trevor set her down on her feet and released her.

"Run, Ferny!" she shouted, pulling at the hold on her arm. His grip didn't break, but the lamb startled and leapt backwards.

Trevor grabbed the musket from the man holding her and aimed it at the lamb, who was bouncing between grass heaps, uncertain and frightened.

"No!" Deirdre shouted.

"Stop that!" the other man shouted at the same time. With his free hand, he knocked the musket barrel downward. "Damn your hide, Trevor, what's wrong with you?"

Deirdre took the opportunity of his distraction to kick him in the shins.

"Ow!"

She tore out of his grasp and tried to run again, but he recovered faster than her cousin Joseph ever had when she'd pulled that same trick during their games as children. The man's arm was thicker and stronger than Trevor's had been when it wrapped around her waist, and he lifted her from the ground.

She kicked, trying to catch him in the legs or higher.

"Stop that," he snapped. "Everyone settle down for God's sake."

"You got her all right, Shawn?"

"No, I don't. Please, miss," he said to her, quieter, his breath tickling her ear. "We're not going to hurt you."

"He was going to shoot my lamb!"

The man grunted as her heel connected with some part of his leg.

"Please," he said again. "We need help."

It wasn't the words that made her stop struggling, but the way he said them. Plaintive, on the verge of hopelessness.

Deirdre stilled. He held her up from the ground, cradled against his chest in a way that no one ever had. At least no one who made her belly flutter when they held her. Before she could think of how she felt about that, he lowered her onto her feet and released her. She stepped away quickly but didn't run.

The gray-eyed man watched her warily, the musket grasped in his off hand. Trevor was looking at her with distrust, and the burly man stood as though in pain, leaning heavily on the stick.

"Who are you?" she asked.

"Shawn. That's my friend, Wallis. And this is Trevor."

She noted that he didn't add 'friend' as an introduction to the wiry man. If Trevor noticed, he made no sign of it.

"What are you doing here?"

"Looking for a safe place."

"From what?"

The man looked uncertain, then came to some sort of decision. "From the war."

"The war's over. My uncle John said so."

"Your uncle John isn't far wrong," the burly man, Wallis, told her. She could hear pain tight in his voice.

"What side are you?" Trevor demanded.

Now that he wasn't holding the musket, Deirdre lifted her chin to look at him in defiance. "I told you, we aren't on any side. We're on the island."

"That's good enough for me," Wallis said.

Trevor didn't look satisfied, but he kept quiet.

"Can you help us?" Shawn asked her. "Will you?" he added.

Deirdre hesitated. The three men had frightened her badly and had threatened to make a meal out of Ferny, and they smelled awful, but Great Grandmother Ailee would have helped them. Great Aunt Clary would curse them for fools, but she'd do it over a table laden with food to fill their bellies. And there was something about the gray-eyed man, Shawn. She was curious enough to put up with their stench to figure out what it was.

"Very well. But he can't carry that gun," she said, nodding at Trevor.

"He won't."

Trevor didn't seem to like that, but once again he kept quiet.

Deirdre took that as acceptance. "The village is this way."

~*~

"Think we can trust her?" Wallis whispered to Shawn as they followed the young woman.

"What choice do we have, Wallis?"

"She kicked you pretty good."

"I don't need you to tell me that."

"Think they know about the bears?"

Shawn grimaced. "I don't know. Probably."

"Should we tell her that Trevor shot one?"

"If it comes up."

"Think they'll feed us?"

"If they don't string us up first."

Wallis winced. It was a threat they'd lived with for too long, and Shawn didn't think it would come to that among these folk, but he wasn't completely dismissing the possibility.

His friend caught on to why. "What the devil was Trevor thinking?"

"I've no idea."

"We'd best keep an eye on him. Or maybe you'd rather keep an eye on the woman?" Wallis snickered.

"Shut it, Wallis."

Shawn didn't want to give credence to Wallis's teasing, but it was hard to keep his gaze off the young woman leading them. He thought her not yet twenty, only a few years younger than himself, but her youth was still gathered around her unblemished by war. Sunny brown hair fell loose and wavy down her shoulders, and bright green eyes glinted with a hint of laughter in their depths. She wore a nearly sleeveless shirt and plain corset and skirts, bereft of ribbon or lace except for the odd fingerless lace gloves and lacy kerchief tied around her throat, the red wool a striking contrast to the plain homespun clothing. She was the image of idyllic farm life, of carefree days spent under the sun. Of peace.

The bruises on his shins reminded him that she hadn't been afraid to fight, though. If she were the example of the type of folks this island bred, he and Wallis would need to tread carefully. And keep a sharp eye on Trevor.

The path she led them on met a wider lane of twin wheel ruts with a furrow of grass and spring wild flowers in between. She walked down one of the ruts, the lamb trotting and occasionally bounding at her side. Trees, a mixture of red maple, sweetgum, and scraggly coastal pines, began thickening to either side of them, though nowhere nearly as thick as the trees had been where they had first made land. He couldn't hear the ocean, so he suspected they were going deeper into the island.

He glanced at Trevor. The scout was watching the trees apprehensively, but he didn't look as though he'd bolt or do anything foolish.

Shawn smelled cooking fires. Voices reached them from around a bend in the lane, childish shouts and a few older voices calling out. A dog began barking. It was all so homey that Shawn's chest clenched with longing for his own hearth and family.

A dog bounded toward them, a white hound with dark patches. Only about knee-high with a slender nose and flapping ears, it stopped as soon as it saw them and gave a baying bark.

"Hush, Tippy," the young woman told it. Shawn realized he didn't know her name.

"Tippy!" a man's voice called. "Stop that yowling!"

"Who's that?" Trevor demanded of the woman.

She glared at him. "My cousin."

"Tell him to come out where we can see him."

"Trevor—" Shawn began, but the woman cut him off.

"You wanted me to bring you here, so either you're going to follow me or not. Your choice." With a sniff of annoyance, she continued around the bend.

"You brought that on yourself," Wallis told Trevor between clenched teeth.

Trevor's lip trembled as though it might curl. Shawn held out a cautioning hand. "What other choice have we, Trevor?"

The wiry man's shoulders slumped. He nodded tightly.

The trees thinned as they followed the lane and the framework of what would be a small cabin stood on the edge where the trees ended. The woman was speaking to a man near the same age. He stood with a hammer in his hand next to the wooden frame. He was dressed in the same casual homespuns and looked out with the same green eyes, but his hair was darker and caught back in a leather strip.

He was clean-shaven, a fact Shawn immediately envied. The man was staring at the young woman in shock, and with that same shock, looked past her to see Shawn, Wallis, and Trevor come forward.

"Are you beetle-headed?" the man tried to whisper to the woman, but his voice carried.

"Just go fetch Marcos," she told him.

"And leave you alone with them? Who are they? What are they doing here?"

"Joseph, stop fussing and go fetch Marcos." Her words were sharp, and the young man, Joseph, looked unhappy, but he set down his hammer. Or rather, he started to, thought better of it, and put it into the woman's hands.

She quirked her eyebrow at him.

"Stay, Tippy," he told the hound. Tippy lay down on the patchwork grass in a spot of sunlight.

"She'll be such a help," the woman muttered. Joseph frowned before he hurried off.

Shawn saw two other homes nearby, and more beyond them, scattered as though tossed across the clearing. Several trees shaded the homes, and kitchen gardens and outbuildings filled much of the remaining space. He heard more children and the distant ringing of a hammer on iron.

"I never asked your name," Shawn said to the woman, daring to draw a little closer. She looked at him and the musket, hefting the hammer in casual warning, and though he stood a few inches taller than she, she had a way of making it feel as though she were looking down at him.

"No, you didn't."

He liked the way she spoke, her accent close enough to his country cousins to be akin.

"Are you Irish? Scots-Irish?"

She blinked, clearly taken aback. "Why?"

"You sound it. My family is. I am."

"You don't sound it."

"I grew up in Philadelphia."

She didn't look impressed. "I've heard of it."

"Your name. Are you going to tell me?"

She opened her mouth to reply, but then a voice calling out interrupted her.

"Deirdre, come away." The voice belonged to an older man approaching with Joseph. The man's accent was strange, like an odd mixing of several, which was most likely the case, but he had the look of a Spaniard in coloring. Both Joseph and the Spaniard were grim, and the Spaniard carried an old saber in its sheath.

"The musket," Trevor hissed.

"No." Shawn put the butt of the musket on the ground and leaned against it, making it clear he had no intention of using it.

"Deirdre—" the Spaniard said again in warning.

"If they meant harm, it would've happened by now," she told him archly. "I found them by the myrtle thicket. That one's wounded."

The Spaniard approached, moving cautiously, looking at them each in turn with a wary gaze. "Who are you?"

"Shawn McClaren. My companions, Wallis Stewart and Trevor Danforth."

"Why have you come?"

"By accident," Shawn said, keeping his tone casual. "We were trying to make it farther north."

Keep it simple, he told himself. Don't give away too much. Not yet.

"Where did you land on the island?"

The way the Spaniard asked it put Shawn on alert. "A beach on the western shore. Saw some marshes, though."

Joseph and the Spaniard exchanged looks that Shawn couldn't read, and Deirdre shifted from foot to foot as though uncomfortable.

Shawn swallowed, uneasy. "I'm afraid we gave the young lady a fright," he continued. "I'm sorry for that. But she is right—my friend is wounded. Sprained his ankle. We could use a day or two to see it mended, maybe find a dry place to sleep and some food. We'd work for it," he added quickly. "Chop wood or mend fences, whatever you'd need doing."

"Don't let them near the sheep," the woman, Deirdre, whispered loud enough for him to hear. "They've no sense about them."

Shawn thought she meant for him to hear her by the look she cast him.

"Joseph," the Spaniard said, thoughtful, "tell the families. Ask that they to come to my house. Deirdre, best go to your great aunt. You men, come with me. But I will need that musket and any other weapons you carry."

Trevor stiffened, but Shawn didn't hesitate. He sensed that if he did, this man would see them cast off the island as quickly as possible. It hurt to give up his knife, hard-won as it had been, but he pulled the rawhide ties over his arm and head, wrapped it around the beaded sheath, and handed the bundle over.

The Spaniard accepted the sheathed knife and the musket, giving the latter a glance that spoke of his knowledge of guns. He cradled them with his saber in one arm, then held out his hand. Shawn accepted it.

"Marcos Fonseca." They shook. The man had a strong and calloused grip. Shawn guessed him somewhere in his forties. "Come with me, all of you."

Marcos Fonseca's home was a good-sized building of rough wood and split shingles, with a narrow front porch and glassless windows with plank shutters. The shadows had gotten longer with the coming evening and the shutters were open to catch the last light of the day. Shawn could hear a woman singing inside. She had a lovely voice.

"Take a seat," Marcos told them. He stepped to the doorway. "Rosa, water, if you will. And three cups."

Shawn saw Wallis into the chair on the porch. Trevor sank to his heels, leaning against the porch post. Shawn settled on one end of the wooden bench against the wall of the house. It felt good to sit on something crafted for that purpose and not on a rock or a fallen log or hard ground. Or worse, wet ground.

Weariness hit him like a musket shot. He tried to stave it off, sitting straight and not allowing himself to lean. Wallis looked like he was already falling asleep. Trevor, however, seemed ready to spring into action at the merest sign of trouble.

A young woman came out to the porch, carrying a clay pitcher in one hand and three horn and leather cups grasped by the rims in the other. She hesitated when she saw the three men sitting on her porch. Marcos gave her an encouraging nod. She looked to be the man's daughter, with his dark complexion and brown eyes, but her hair was fairer. She was probably of an age to Deirdre, and while she was pretty, Shawn didn't find her nearly as striking as the fair-haired firebrand of a woman.

Rosa offered Shawn a cup first, as he was closest. As she filled the cup, he remembered enough of his manners to thank her. It was hard not to guzzle it down. She refilled it for him without question and moved to Wallis.

"You men have been traveling some while," Marcos observed. He had a quiet way about him, this Spaniard. He still had the musket, but he'd set the saber and knife inside the house.

"We have," Shawn replied.

"On what business?"

"Just trying to get home."

"Where do you call home?"

Shawn hesitated. It was a risk, he knew, but then again, he'd already slipped and told the young woman. "Philadelphia."

"Are you soldiers?"

The man was too astute. It was the musket, Shawn thought. Too English, too new. They'd have been better off leaving it behind.

"We were."

The Spaniard said nothing more. Shawn wished he could read his mind, learn what he was thinking. The woman, Deirdre, had said they weren't on any side, but in Shawn's experience, everyone chose a side when pushed. It would be a great fortune if the islanders shared his loyalty, but Shawn wouldn't count on that. His fortune had been rotten of late. Like running into those twisted bears when they had cooked the first warm meal in days.

His thoughts were circling mindlessly. He was tired, too tired to think straight. He was going to make a mistake, one that might cost them everything.

"So it is true," another man said as he approached. Another Spaniard, a little younger, perhaps, than Marcos. Brothers? Cousins? Shawn couldn't be sure.

"The others are coming?" Marcos asked the newcomer.

"Soon. Bernardo had just sat to dinner. He won't be happy."

"I apologize for disrupting your evening," Shawn said to the newcomer.

The man waved the apology away like a bothersome fly. "I would ask many questions, but better to wait for the others or you'll be repeating them. And your friend looks done in."

Wallis did look asleep, relaxed in the chair as though he hadn't a care. He was worse off than Shawn had realized. It wasn't like Wallis to be so unguarded around strangers.

Then again, he'd been different before the war. They both had been. Wallis looked as though he was shaking off the soldier he had become, so relaxed he seemed.

A group of men approached, speaking quietly but falling silent as they came up to the porch. Joseph was among them, along with a couple more dogs, sleek-haired and brindled. They looked less like farm dogs and more like hounds kept for hunting.

Did they hunt the bears?

"Wallis, wake up," Shawn said quietly. Wallis's eyes opened blearily, but he roused when he saw the men coming to stand before the porch.

They were a collection of young and old, the eldest in his sixties and the youngest being Joseph. There was one other Spaniard among them, and a man who looked to have native blood.

One of the men approached Rosa and leaned in with a familiar manner to whisper in her ear. She gave him a look of disagreement but apparently heeded him, for she returned inside the house.

"Joseph did not exaggerate," the oldest said. "Strangers on the island. Is that the musket?"

"It is." Marcos stepped forward and held it out. "Brown Bess."

"So I see. Fine weapon."

"A soldier's weapon," said the man who'd sent Rosa inside. He and Joseph looked close enough alike to be brothers. Was everyone on this island related?

A hard-looking man with shorn, brown hair eyed Shawn with hostility. "Did you accost my niece?"

"No, sir, not exactly," Shawn answered.

"Just what exactly did you do?" he demanded. He was a big man, broad in the shoulders, though not as burly as Wallis. He had the air of someone not to be crossed, though, and Shawn feared he'd already done so if Deirdre was the man's niece.

This must be Uncle John who said the war was over.

"She came upon us rather suddenly, sir," Shawn explained. "I am afraid we might have over-reacted."

"If you put her in danger—"

"Deirdre seemed fine, John," Marcos interrupted. "I sent her home if you wish to see for yourself."

The man didn't look convinced, but he let the matter drop.

"I suppose the charitable thing to do would be to offer you shelter," the elder man said. His face was careworn, his fair hair thinning and going white, but his hazel eyes held a youthful gleam.

"Get some food into you."

Shawn waited for the "but." It never came.

"We'd be appreciative," he finally said.

"Give us a moment, then," the elder said, and he gestured for the other men to gather near. They spoke in low tones. John's raised once. "We need to keep them away from—" But Marcos interrupted him before he could finish, his words too low to hear.

Having come to some sort of agreement, the men faced Shawn and his companions again.

"We'll see you've a bed and food," the elder said. "And clean clothing, too. You'll stay with Marcos and Patrick," he said to Shawn. The man who had sent Rosa inside looked sternly at Shawn as if sizing him up. Shawn had the feeling if he stepped out of line by even a toe, the man would be all over him for it.

"Joseph and Daniel will see your injured man to their house. Their mother is our midwife and has a way with injuries."

"I'd be grateful for the help," Wallis said in a pained and exhausted voice.

"You'll come with me," John told Trevor.

Shawn tried to keep his breathing even, but panic settled over him. Split them up? The thought had never occurred to him.

"We don't want to impose," he said quickly. "A dry place in a barn would suit."

"Do you think we'd let strangers have the run of our village?" John asked crossly. "Leave you without watching over to do whatever you'd like?"

"Easy, John," the elder man soothed. "I don't think the boy meant harm."

"That's the whole point, Peter. We don't know what the boy means to do."

"I only mean to rest," Shawn told them, letting his weariness show. "And perhaps beg a bite of food. We're tired and far from home. We mean you and yours no harm."

"Then accept our hospitality as we'd offer it, son," the elder, Peter, told him, "and we'll see you rested and fed."

Shawn gave in. John gestured sharply for Trevor to follow him. The men had clearly decided on how to divide them. They must have seen something in Trevor to give him to the hard-eyed John. Both men were eyeing one another with distrust.

The scout glanced to Shawn.

"It'll be fine," he told him. "I'll see you come morning."

Looking ill at ease, Trevor followed John.

"Here," Joseph said, approaching Wallis. "Daniel and I will get you to our mother." The man next to him shared his same look.

Truly, all these people must be related, Shawn thought.

"I can manage," Wallis said, and he tried to rise, but his leg gave out. He caught himself with a curse. "Apologies," he said. "Mother always said my tongue would get the better of me."

"I think it's your leg this time," Peter observed wryly. "Let those boys help you, Mr. Stewart."

"It's just Wallis," he answered, "seeing as we're all friends here."

Peter smiled, and his lined face lit up. Shawn could understand why the men of the village listened to him. He was wise and clever with kindness to spare, but cautious, too.

Wallis submitted to being helped from the porch.

"Take care," Shawn called to him.

"Get some rest, Shawn. And stop fretting."

Shawn watched his friend limp down the path between houses, supported by strangers. It had been over a year since they'd been parted. Shawn didn't like it.

"Patrick, if you'll help with the pallet," Marcos said to the older version of Joseph, "we'll get our guest settled. Come, friend," he said to Shawn. "Rosa will make you tea and then we'll have a fine meal."

Shawn followed willingly. Nothing sounded better.

~*~

The house had been empty when Deirdre returned, which wasn't surprising given that it was lambing season. Great Aunt Clary had a gift when it came to lambing, and she was often called away if there was trouble.

Deirdre took the opportunity of her great aunt's absence to lean as close to the corner of the house as she dared, trying to overhear the conversation taking place on Marcos's front porch. Joseph had rounded up several of the men, including heads of families. Uncle Peter was there, who spoke for the Ballards, and her cousin, Patrick, for the Donaghues. Marcos spoke for the Fonsecas and Uncle John for the Guthries. The Smyths, MacGregors, and Lacours weren't present, but Deirdre was certain they would be if a family assembly was called.

And of course they'd call an assembly. There hadn't been strangers come to the island in years. Deirdre couldn't name the last time it had happened. Lennox was the newest person on the island, and that was through marriage, so he'd been made welcome. The families talked about what they would do if strangers landed, but Deirdre knew from experience that what's planned and what happens can be very different.

Like going out to pick bayberries and picking up three strangers instead.

The voices carried to her but not loud enough to make out the words. Deirdre fought the urge to move closer. The men wouldn't take kindly to her butting in. Patrick might come over later to discuss the matter with Great Aunt Clary since he stood for their family, and she'd learn more then. At least, that was her hope.

"Best see to supper," she told herself. But she lingered a moment longer. She watched the nasty, wiry man follow Uncle John away. If anyone could handle that little man, it would be Uncle John. Joseph and Daniel took the big bearded man, Wallis, toward the Donaghue House. Maybe the big man would turn her cousin Deborah's head away from Marcos, but Deirdre didn't think so.

The gray-eyed man, Shawn, went inside with Marcos. She wasn't sure how she felt about him being so close. Her stomach went funny, like she'd eaten an over-ripe fig.

"Deirdre Donaghue, are you eavesdropping?"

Great Aunt Clary came up from the river path. Her hair, iron gray ever since Deirdre could remember, was swept back into a tight knot under a hook-stitched headscarf, and a green-dyed kerchief was tied close under her chin. She wasn't an old woman, not like Aunt Lizzie, but she was one of the oldest on the island, having seen nearly sixty years. And she reminded Deirdre of that fact often, including her insistence that she be addressed as "Great" Aunt.

"In all my nearly sixty years, I've never seen a girl so keen on someone else's business." Great Aunt Clary stepped under the porch eave, looking tired and worn at the edges. She had energy for two, typically, so whatever she'd been called away for must have been bad. She'd removed her apron at some point and carried it wadded in one hand.

Ferny ambled closer to sniff at it, but Great Aunt Clary drew the apron out of the lamb's reach. "You don't need to be into that," she said in a gentle voice reserved for lambs and babes.

"Rough lambing?" Deirdre asked, offering to take the apron. Great Aunt Clary let her have it. Even wadded, Deirdre could see that it was soiled with more than dirt.

"Lost twins." Great Aunt Clary settled onto her favorite porch chair, the rocker her father had built for her mother, covered by a quilt she had made with her mother and sister. "Might lose the ewe, too. What was the fuss at Marcos's?"

"Strangers on the island."

The rocker squeaked as Great Aunt Clary sat upright. "Deirdre, what have you done?"

"Not a thing! Though I might have gone to the myrtle thicket."

"You said you were going to Daisy's."

"And I meant to, but then I remembered how last night you said the bayberry candles were nearly gone, and I knew there might be some berries left, so I thought I could pick them and then go to Aunt Daisy's and make candles with Deborah."

Great Aunt Clary leveled a look at her. She had a youthful face for an older woman, in odd contrast to the gray hair and careworn dark eyes.

"Tell me the whole of it."

Deirdre held in a sigh, then told the story of finding the men behind the thicket. She left out the part with the musket and trying to flee. It wouldn't do to have Great Aunt Clary decide they weren't to be trusted before she'd met them. Though Deirdre wasn't entirely certain they were to be trusted.

"What part of the island did they make land?" Great Aunt Clary demanded.

"A beach. Though they said they saw the hog marsh."

"Between the western point and the river, then." Great Aunt Clary nodded to herself. "What brought them here?"

"The war, they said."

"No war here."

"I think that's what they liked about it."

"Soldiers, then."

"I'm not certain." Deirdre chewed the inside of her lip. They hadn't looked much like soldiers, but she'd honestly never seen a soldier before. Soldiers didn't come to the island. They'd heard plenty about the war from the Fonsecas who sailed supplies to the island. Plus Joseph had brought news of the Yorktown battle the last time he'd traveled to Norfolk to see Iola, the baker's daughter. Britain had lost and given up, he'd said. Uncle John said that meant the war was done.

"So why run from it now?" she mused aloud.

Great Aunt Clary gave her a look.

"Uncle John said the war was over," Deirdre told her, backtracking her thoughts. Great Aunt Clary had grown accustomed to Deirdre's random observations and her need to catch listeners up. "So if the war is done, why run from it?"

"Maybe it's not as done as your uncle likes to think."

"Or maybe it's more than that. The war is an awfully easy excuse. At least, that's what you've been saying these past few years."

"It's the honest truth," Great Aunt Clary said with a sniff. "Can't make the usual trade, Captain Fonseca likes to say, because the war hurts the prices. Can't bring you any sugar because the war and the blockades. Can't come 'til the fall because the French and British ships fighting in the bay. Bunch of beetle-headed nonsense."

"So if the war didn't bring them here, what would?"

Great Aunt Clary looked out towards the river and the fig groves.

"No, that can't be it." Deirdre was shocked. "We've kept that quiet."

"Our families been on this island over sixty years, child. Lots of us going to the mainland to do trade and find husbands and wives. Not everyone lives out their days here. Kevin and Yvonne moved to Williamsburg. And Sheridan went to Norfolk. So did Catrina and Isabel with those German cousins they met. Just one of them tells a story to the wrong sort, and we get strangers on the island with a mouthful of lies and a musket full of shot."

Deirdre swallowed hard. "They wouldn't speak of it. They swore. They know what's at risk."

"Could be a few years off the island, they forget the risk. Start thinking it's just stories we old folk tell to keep you children in line."

"But Derry . . ."

"Derry McGregor was killed twenty years ago, afore most of you was born. Afore most of your folks were old enough to remember. No, child. The threat weakens with every year that passes, but the danger is true enough. It's just quiet, until something riles it again."

"Like strangers." Deirdre had gone cold.

Great Aunt Clary sat back. "If they came in by the hog marsh, then could be nothing. Could be it's like they say, and they're running from the war. Or running from something else. Still, best keep an ear out." She closed her eyes. "I'll have a word with Peter when we go to supper. You finish that bread pudding yet? Grace asked for it special and you promised her to make it."

"I was about to start on it."

"Well, turn that 'about' into a 'now.'"

Deirdre hid a smile as she went inside, tossing the soiled apron in the wash bucket by the front door. She didn't make it half way toward the hearth when she heard Uncle John's voice outside.

"Deirdre inside?" he demanded of Great Aunt Clary.

"Where else would she be?" Great Aunt Clary snapped back.

Deirdre shook her head. For eight years, Uncle John and Great Aunt Clary had been raising her between them, and the years hadn't improved their liking of one another.

She returned to the porch. "I'm here, Uncle John."

Her uncle's expression gentled when he saw her. "Walk with me a moment, Deirdre," he said, holding his hand out to her. Deirdre accept it and let him lead her from the house. She could feel Great Aunt Clary staring after them, but her great aunt never interfered with her time with Uncle John. The two of them would just argue about it later.

"I have to say," Uncle John began when they were out of earshot of Shaw House and Great Aunt Clary, "I'm not happy to hear you went away from the village on your own."

"It was just to the myrtle grove," Deirdre defended. "Nothing to worry me there." Uncle John eyed her and she blushed. "Usually," she added.

"These strangers are not to be trusted." Uncle John faced her and put his hands on her shoulders. "I worry what they're about. You need to stay clear of them."

Deirdre wanted to say they were no threat, but they had threatened her. Or at least the man, Trevor, had.

"Did you take one of them to the cabin?" she asked.

Uncle John frowned. "Spying again, niece?"

Deirdre looked down at her feet, trying not to smile.

"You have too much of your mother in you," he said with a heavy sigh. "Promise me you'll stay clear of the strangers?"

"Uncle—"

"I want your promise, Deirdre. This is for your own good."

"Like not going to Norfolk is for my own good?"

Uncle John pulled her into an embrace. "There will come a time for that, Deirdre. I've already promised you that."

"I know. It's just that Rosa married Patrick when she was eighteen, and I've not even had one suitor."

"Is that what worries you?" he asked, drawing back. "That you'll never wed?"

Deirdre half-shrugged. She wasn't as interested in getting married as she was to getting off the island. She loved her home and her family, but the island was feeling too small. Even with all the open spaces like the beach and the meadow, even with the ocean spread out to the Eastern horizon, she felt suffocated. She understood why Kevin and Sheridan had left the island, and why Yvonne and Catrina and Isabel had married after short courtships so they could leave faster.

Deirdre didn't want to wait for marriage to leave. How could she know if she wanted to marry or not when there was no one to court her?

"I don't want you to worry about marriage," Uncle John told her. "When the time is right, we'll find a man worthy of you."

He kissed her forehead, and she smiled. Uncle John was her closest kin, and he always wanted the best for her. She knew part of it was because of how much he'd loved her mother, his younger sister, and how he still grieved for her, but also because she was his only family left. He'd promised to raise her, even forsaking his own chance for a happy marriage.

"Now, promise me you'll keep clear of the strangers," he said.

How could she refuse him? "I promise, Uncle."

He gave her one of his rare smiles, the ones only for her. As he led her back home, Deirdre hoped she could keep her promise.

~*~

Deirdre followed Great Aunt Clary with a lantern held high. The sun had set, and while orange and red still streaked the clear sky, the shadows had grown long and dark. It was good she'd left Ferny shut up inside. She'd never have found him in the dark if he'd had a mind to run off.

They followed the path between the McGregor House and the Fonseca House. The kitchen gardens lining the beaten trail were already flourishing with early spring greens and last year's herbs. The air smelt pleasantly of wood smoke and sage, and the bee balm was already in bloom. It was Deirdre's favorite time of year, when new growth sprouted from the gardens and in the meadows, the trees leafed pearly pale green buds, and lambs bleated lustily. There were pups, a few calves, and piglets, too. Chicks were starting to cheep in the orchard, and Grace looked like she was going to have her baby any day, though Great Aunt Clary swore she had at least another month to go.

Deirdre usually liked to see the village by lamplight. The flickering light cast the village in a mysterious glow foreign to its daytime drowsiness. The mystery wasn't coming from the flickering lamplight, however. As she passed by the Fonseca House, she had to keep from craning her neck to see through the shutters to the stranger staying within.

What had Marcos learned? Would he share it tomorrow? Would she be able to sit in if the families met? She had found the men, after all. Great Uncle Peter would have to let her sit in to tell what had happened. She wished Patrick had come to speak with Great Aunt Clary. As head of the Donaghues, he had a duty to keep Great Aunt Clary informed.

"Don't dawdle, child," Great Aunt Clary snapped. Deirdre rushed to catch up, holding the lamp higher.

And then nearly dropped it when the light fell over the gray-eyed stranger.

He froze, uncertain. He was carrying a bucket in one hand and one of Mathilda's woven towels in the other, along with a cake of soap.

He recovered first and bowed. He made it seem natural, bowing to two women in the half-light on a dirt path.

"Aren't you fancy," Great Aunt Clary said drolly. The man blinked in surprise, and Deirdre suppressed an urge to giggle. She wasn't normally the giggling sort.

"You have a name, young man?" her great aunt asked.

"Shawn McClaren, ma'am."

"Good Irish name. Are you Irish?"

"Scots-Irish, ma'am."

"Scots-Irish?" Great Aunt Clary sounded impressed. Deirdre was amazed until Great Aunt Clary spoke again in a scathing tone. "You don't sound a lick of it."

"No, ma'am. My cousins tell me so, too."

"Do they now?"

"When I see them, which isn't often as of late."

"What's kept you from seeing family?"

"The war, ma'am."

Great Aunt Clary harrumphed. "Best time to make the chance."

"I can't argue with that, ma'am. I was on my way back home when we ran aground here."

"I see."

"I can't tell you how much your hospitality means to us."

"I'm sure you could if given enough time. Been to the river, have you?"

"I have."

"Marcos tell you not to cross it?"

"He did warn me. Said the hogs like to have the run of the fig grove on the other side."

"They do, and mostly at dark. You mind Marcos, young man."

"I will, ma'am."

Shawn bowed again as Great Aunt Clary walked past him. Deirdre hesitated.

"Is your friend better?" she asked him.

"He is. I thank you for that."

"Weren't any of my doing."

"You brought us here," he said simply.

"Deirdre, am I to feel my way down the path blindly?" Great Aunt Clary snapped from just beyond the lamplight.

Deirdre winced and hurried after.

"City born," Great Aunt Clary observed dryly to Deirdre as they continued to the Ballard House. "But he's not city soft."

"How do you mean?"

"You ever seen Lennox bathing in the river? Even just to sluice off after shearing or harvest?"

"Can't say I have."

"City soft. Told Briony before she wed him that he'd not take easily to island life. That first year, he was as miserable as a lamb caught in a thicket. He's gotten some better, but it took over a decade."

"Is that why he talks of moving to the mainland?"

Great Aunt Clary chuckled her raspy, dry laugh. "Child, I'm certain that man dreams of it nightly. But Briony won't have it, so he'll be here for as long as she is."

The Ballard House was still lit, though the shutters had been closed for the night. As they neared, the lamplight chased the shadows from the deep porch, revealing her Great Uncle Peter sitting on his chair, smoking his pipe.

"Clary," he said in greeting. "Come sit a while."

"I think I will at that." Great Aunt Clary settled in the second chair.

"Blair and Annabel are inside," Uncle Peter told Deirdre. "I don't think they'd mind company."

"The evening is so nice," Deirdre said, coming to sit on one of the two stools near the edge of the porch.

Uncle Peter merely nodded, the lamplight shining off his white hair. Great Aunt Clary would have insisted she go inside if they'd been home, but no one gainsaid another at his own home.

And good thing, because as fond as Deirdre was of her cousin Annabel, they had little in common. Annabel took after her mother, who'd been raised in the south, where keeping house, sewing, and knitting seemed to preoccupy women to an unnatural degree.

"Calling the families together tomorrow?" Great Aunt Clary asked.

"I am."

"What do you make of these strangers?"

"They've seen something of hardship."

"From the war?"

"Perhaps."

"The war hasn't touched us here, Peter. I'd like to keep it that way."

"Word is the war's nearly spent."

"John likes to think he knows something of the world saying such things, but it don't make him right."

"Captain Lachat said the same."

"A Frenchman would. They want to lay claim to the victory."

Uncle Peter smiled fondly. "Ah, Clary, always quick to see folks in the worst light."

"Being prepared and being contrary are two different things, Peter."

"And it's a line you like to walk, don't you, Clary?"

Great Aunt Clary sat back with a satisfied look on her face. "Someone has to."

"I don't think the war is coming to the island," Uncle Peter told her, "but I do think we need to help these men move on as quick as we can. Once the big one has mended."

"His name is Wallis," Deirdre spoke up.

"Wallis, yes."

"Can we trust them, though?" Great Aunt Clary pressed.

"Won't know until we try."

"That's a beetle-headed thing to say."

"I like to see the best in folks, Clary, you know that. And that young man, Shawn, spoke well for himself."

"Oh, he's got pretty manners, I'll give him that. City born for certain."

"You'd find fault if he were backwoods bred."

"That I would."

Uncle Peter chuckled. "We'll be cautious. And all the families will have a chance to speak their piece, as it's always been. You do realize," he said, leaning forward, "that your mother would've made them welcome."

"Just as soon as Father disarmed them, sure."

Deirdre held in a laugh, but Uncle Peter did not. He was still laughing when his son, Conor, stepped up onto the porch.

"What has Aunt Clary said now?"

"Just what we need to hear, like always. The men settled?"

"Aye. Daisy patched up the big man's ankle. Not broken, but a bad sprain. Told her he got it coming wrong out of a boat."

"So he's clumsy or they ran into trouble," Great Aunt Clary said.

"Big man like that, must be clumsy," Conor said.

"Don't assume so," Uncle Peter cautioned. "James McGregor could move quick as a snake, and he was a big man."

Deirdre sat up a little taller. She liked when Great Uncle Peter spoke of the folks who had passed. She didn't hear nearly enough stories of her Great Grandfather James other than "he was a kindly man."

"John has the little man in hand," Conor continued. "He looked nigh to jumping out of his boots when John let me in. Nervous fellow."

"Uncle John will keep an eye on him," Deirdre said.

Uncle Peter and his son exchanged looks, and Deirdre was surprised that she couldn't read the meaning behind the glances.

"Marcos likes their leader," Conor went on. "Said he's got manners to spare and got little Aileen to giggling something fierce. Rosa's taken to him, too, but not in a way that would make Patrick nervous."

"I suppose that's why he let the man wander unattended at night," Great Aunt Clary sniffed.

Conor stiffened. "You saw him wandering around?"

"He wasn't wandering," Deirdre said. "He was at the river to bathe."

Uncle Peter sat upright, but Great Aunt Clary waved him down. "Marcos warned him not to cross it, so just sit back."

"You're the one who brought it up, Aunt Clary," Conor groused.

"I guess that's all to be done tonight, then," Great Aunt Clary said, rising from her seat.

"Aunt Clary, I don't like you two staying alone in the house with strangers about, especially if they're wandering," Conor said to her. "Aunt Lizzie and Uncle Manny have room enough. You could overnight with them for the next few days."

"Be turned out of my house on a whim?" Great Aunt Clary glared at Conor.

"It's a precaution, not a whim."

"It's a whim. A man's whim, thinking us poor womenfolk can't mind ourselves."

"Aunt Clary—"

"You best stop speaking while you can, Conor," Uncle Peter said quietly.

"I'm only thinking of their safety."

"Of course you are. And I'm sure that's why Clary will keep Grahame's old musket loaded tonight and Deirdre will take Tippy and Blue into the house."

"Dogs in the house," Great Aunt Clary sniffed.

37

"Tippy has the best ears and Blue the best nose," Uncle Peter said patiently. "And both of them will raise Cain if they sense anything untoward."

"And raise it in my house," Great Aunt Clary argued. "Oh, fine, if it'll make you both feel better. Wouldn't want you menfolk spending a sleepless night fretting over us. Come along, Deirdre."

"I'll walk you—" Conor began, but Great Aunt Clary silenced him with a look. Without another word, she left the porch.

Deirdre grabbed up the lantern and hurried after, as proud as ever to be in Great Aunt Clary's care.

CHAPTER THREE

Friday, May 31st

"They've treated you well?"

"Shawn, I don't remember being this full, this dry, and this comfortable. I'm sure I must have been once, but I can't recall the last time it was."

"But have they asked you anything, Wallis? Wanted to know more?"

"Stop fretting, man. This is paradise."

"A paradise we'll be kicked out of soon enough."

"They don't seem like the kicking-out sort."

Shawn shook his head. "They don't know who we are, either."

"Then let's just tell them. What harm would it—"

"No!"

Shawn looked around to see if his shout had called attention. The older woman whose house this was had stepped out after seeing that the men had a pot of tea, leaving Shawn and Wallis to speak alone, but she had only gone to the porch with her daughter, Deborah, to spin wool, and Joseph was nearby splitting wood.

No one came in, however, so Shawn continued in a whisper. "We don't know who they're allied with or if they'd turn on us."

"You're starting to sound like Trevor."

Shawn sat back and rubbed his hand over his face before scratching at the beard he hated. "It's more than that. There is something they aren't saying. Last night when I wanted to go to the river to bathe, Marcos warned me not to cross to the other side."

"You went to the river? What if those bear things had been there?"

"I went to see if they were."

"By God, Shawn, you can't take chances like that."

"I didn't figure it a huge risk with the village sitting here."

"Did Marcos say why you shouldn't cross the river?"

"The wild hogs."

"Do you believe him?"

"I believe he was warning me. I'm not sure I believe it was because of hogs."

"Why do you say that?"

"Something in his tone. Like the way the sergeant would warn us about a hidden rebel."

Wallis's lips drew into a thin line, and he nodded. "I hear you."

"They're hiding something. And I don't want to let on that we might know what it is until they are ready to tell us. God willing, we can leave this island without anyone the wiser, both of where we came from and what we saw."

"You want to leave?"

"You don't?"

Wallis hesitated. "It isn't that I don't want to go home, but we've been running to or from some place for longer than I care to count. There's something to be said for holding still for a while."

Shawn sat back on the couch cushion. It was comfortable, sitting on downy cushions in a warm house, surrounded by handcrafted and well-loved furnishings. The place smelt of wood smoke, bayberries, and the herb tea in the little clay cup on the small table next to him. That morning's breakfast of ham and eggs and new greens had left him as full as he'd ever been, having eaten first with Marcos and his family, then arriving in time to be invited by Daisy to sit with her family and Wallis as they finished. They'd had the pleasant herb tea sweetened with honey, a luxury he'd not had in months, and berry jam for the fresh bread, and fig preserves. It was all he could do not to curl up on the couch in a stupor.

"It's tempting to stay," Shawn admitted. "But I need to get home. We still don't know what's happening in Philadelphia since Cornwallis lost Yorktown. I need to make sure my family is safe."

Wallis heaved a great sigh. "Yes, you're right. Like always. Fine.

When do we set out?"

"Once your ankle will hold your weight."

"Might be a few days for that."

"Then a few days. It'll give me time to trade work for supplies and sound out the boat."

"And those… things?"

"Keep it under your hat for now. Along with the other thing."

"If you think it's best, Shawn."

Shawn took leave of his friend, giving the ladies a courteous bow at the porch. He was sorry not to find Deirdre among them, but thankful as well. The young woman was a little too observant for his comfort, as was her great aunt. He suspected Marcos knew he was holding back, but so far the man hadn't pressed. How long that would last, Shawn couldn't say. Hopefully for the few days until they could leave.

Joseph was gathering an armful of split logs as Shawn approached. "Can I lend you a hand?"

The younger man eyed him with distrust. "I suppose."

Shawn brushed off the mistrust and gathered as much wood as he could carry. He followed Joseph to a wood room built against the wall of the plank house. "Good house," Shawn commented. It wouldn't hurt to try to win the young man's trust. He seemed close to Deirdre. "Large and sturdy."

"Not the largest. That would be Lizzie and Manny's house. The Fonseca House," Joseph added.

"The houses have names?"

"Some of them. The first ones do."

"What's this one?"

"The Donaghue House. My grandparents settled here when they first came to the island."

"Donaghue?"

"That's right. Why?"

"I know of a Donaghue family back north." It was more than that, but Shawn saw no reason to go into detail.

"Couldn't be the same. A Donaghue has never left the island. Well, we leave to visit Norfolk and such, but we always come back. A few members of the other families have left, like Ballards and Fonsecas. If Fonsecas didn't leave, we'd be overrun." Joseph laughed.

"So you are a Donaghue?"

"That's right. Me, my two brothers and sisters. Though Grace is a McGregor now, since she married Aiden. Aunt Clary is a Donaghue, too, my father's sister. And Deirdre, too."

"You're cousins?"

"More or less."

"I don't follow."

"My father was her grandfather's younger brother."

"Ah." Shawn said it like he understood, but he wasn't sure he would be able to keep it straight. There was more complications on this island than strange bears.

They unloaded the wood in a companionable silence.

"Do you think you might point the way to where my friend Trevor is staying?" Shawn asked as they finished.

Joseph hesitated. "Why?"

"I thought to see how he was doing."

"Of course, sure, it's just . . ." Joseph glanced behind him where a few houses sat, small outbuildings nestled between them. "John Guthrie's cabin is the one behind that. Your friend is there."

"Thank you. Deirdre said something about that being her uncle?"

"Her mother's brother. But I wouldn't mention family to John. Or Donaghues. I'd tread careful around any subject," Joseph warned. "John can be difficult."

Shawn recalled too well the hard-eyed man from last night's confrontation. "Thanks for the warning."

The Guthrie Cabin was small and roughly hewn, with no porch and only a single window in the front, still tightly shuttered though the sun was well up. A lone dog lay across the dirt patch before the door, with a tan coat and graying muzzle. The hound lifted its ears as Shawn approached but made no other move.

Shawn knelt down and offered his hand to the dog, who sniffed it a couple times before relaxing again. Taking that for a welcome, Shawn scratched the hound around the ears, earning a few weak tail thumps in response. "Good old dog," he said quietly.

He stood and rapped twice on the solid door.

"Who is it?" The muffled voice inside was hard.

"Shawn McClaren."

The door cracked open, revealing John Guthrie. The man's sharp gaze swept over Shawn. A pungent odor ebbed from inside, herbal but rank, like oil gone rancid.

"So they're letting you have run of the place?" John's tone was condemning. "What do you want?"

"I've only come to see Trevor."

The man eyed him before opening the door wider. Trevor stood beyond, his expression guarded.

"Trevor," Shawn greeted.

"Shawn."

The door shut.

Shawn gaped at it, surprised. He heard muffled voices, but the sound was too low to make out words. Gritting his teeth in frustration, he turned back for the Donaghue House.

No, he wouldn't tell Wallis of this yet. No need to worry his friend.

He changed course mid-stride, heading for Marcos's.

His path took him past the largest house he'd seen in the village, with a porch that wrapped around two sides, and the two front windows set with real glass. A group of women and girls sat on the porch with a brindle hound nursing a mess of puppies. The women appeared to be knitting, baskets of wool at their feet. Deirdre was amongst them, the little black lamb nibbling at a bowl of grain beside her chair.

"Ladies," Shawn greeted, sweeping into a bow.

The girls tittered in embarrassed delight. The oldest woman amongst them smiled guardedly. Deirdre arched an eyebrow in amusement. It was then he noticed that they held not knitting needles, but wooden hooks.

"You have crochets," he said, surprised.

The women stared at him blankly. He stepped up to the porch.

"The hooks. My mother uses one. A crochet."

"We just call them hooks," Deirdre told him.

"Grandmother Ailee had another name for them, too," the older woman said. "Something German."

"Hook is easier." Deirdre turned the one she held in her hand, looking speculatively at Shawn. "The way Great Grandmother Ailee spoke of it, few folks know about this sort of hook-stitching."

"Mother learned it as a girl. She taught my sister."

"But not you?"

He smile. "It wasn't the sort of skills for boys to learn."

The girls tittered again, but this time in amusement. He had a feeling it was at his expense.

"Everyone learns it here," Deirdre told him. It sounded as if she pitied him.

"Even the boys?"

"Even the boys. Even the menfolk who marry into the families."

"That seems a strange thing to do."

Deirdre lifted her chin in challenge. "Not for us."

"We could teach you," the eldest of the three girls offered. "'Tisn't hard."

"Oh, but Maggie, remember when Granny Lizzie tried to teach Lennox," the second one said with a flip of her dark braids. "She said he was all thumbs."

"I think you'd find me all feet at it," Shawn said. The girls laughed, but better still, he won a smile from Deirdre.

"Are you about some business?" Deirdre asked.

"Just returning to the house. I was visiting Wallis and Trevor." He grew solemn, still smarting over John's abrupt dismissal.

Deirdre pursed her lips. She set down her stitching—she looked to be making a lacy shawl of some sort—and stood. "I'll walk with you."

"Deirdre—" the older woman cautioned.

"It's just there, Mary Margaret. We'll not be out of sight for a moment."

The woman, Mary Margaret, didn't look satisfied, and she fixed Shawn with a warning gaze that spoke of retribution should he try anything untoward. The girls grinned and whispered between them.

He nearly offered his arm, the reflex ingrained, but he caught himself at the last moment. He recalled all too well that the last time he had taken hold of Deirdre it was to keep her from escaping, and he hadn't been gentle about it. He doubted she'd accept him walking close enough to touch her. Though it said something that she'd offered to walk with him.

"Has Marcos treated you well?" she asked. She walked slowly, and the little black lamb gamboled around them.

"Yes. I can't recall when I've been cared for so well."

"Are you getting enough to eat?"

"I could hardly move earlier. Rosa cooked a fine breakfast for us, and when I visited Wallis, Daisy insisted I join them, too."

"I'm sure she offered to tend any injuries you had."

"She did. Wallis says she's better than his family physician."

"Aunt Daisy tends to most of our hurts. Her uncle was an apothecary and her aunt a midwife."

"And her parents?"

"Her father was a blacksmith. My Uncle Coy apprenticed to him. My uncle said he fell for Aunt Daisy the first time he met her when she tended a burn he'd gotten. But he used to say it was her beauty that took away the hurt."

"That's a sweet tale."

Deirdre smiled. "It is. She needed one. Her mother died young, and her sisters too."

"I gather her husband, your uncle, has since passed."

"A few years back."

Sorrow tinged Deirdre's reply. Not wanting to see her grieving, Shawn changed the subject. "Did Daisy have to learn the hook-stitching when she came to the island?"

"Of course. But she's not as clever at it. She prefers spinning."

"She was spinning when I left."

"Deborah with her, I imagine. They're our best spinners. Though we're all getting more practice lately."

"Why is that?"

"The wool trades well on the mainland. Ever since the British cut off textile trading, there's more need for wool, both spun and raw. We trade in both."

Shawn fell silent.

"Before the war, we mainly traded in hog and figs," Deirdre continued as though she hadn't noticed his silence.

"You hunt the wild hogs? Marcos made them sound too dangerous."

"The men are cautious."

He noted the pause before she answered.

"It is a lovely life you've built here," he said, changing subjects again, but this time as a tactic. "I can't imagine the war ever touching you."

"We prefer it that way. The fewer folks who know of us, the better."

"Why is that?"

"We don't want to be governed by the mainland. They don't know enough about us to be making rules for us."

Shawn tried to suppress a surge of hope. "So you don't hold to the idea of states?"

"Doesn't affect us here."

"The Virginia Assembly might think differently."

"Still won't mean anything to us."

"It might if the states win the war."

Deirdre stopped walking, and the lamb bunny-hopped past them before tripping to a halt.

"I expect you hope that the states won't win," Shawn said, willing it to be true.

"As long as they leave us alone, it doesn't matter," Deirdre answered. "Anyway, Uncle John says the war is done. That it ended with Yorktown."

Shawn tried not to flinch. "Most likely. But nothing's certain until the treaty's signed."

She studied him a moment longer before speaking.

"Why are you running from the war?"

His mouth went dry. "I never said I was running."

"You said you wanted refuge. Isn't that like running?"

"I'm not... no. It isn't that simple."

"Sure it is. Great Aunt Clary says everything is simple in the end. We just complicate it all to make ourselves feel important."

Shawn admired Great Aunt Clary. "I'm just trying to get home."

"See, that's simple enough. Why couldn't your army or general or whoever's in charge of you get you home?"

"They weren't able."

"Why?"

"They just weren't."

She cocked her head, watching him, then continued toward the house. He had to take a couple quick steps to catch her up, the lamb following after.

"The families are meeting today," she told him.

"Concerning me and my companions, I expect. What might they do?"

"Take a vote."

"Over?"

"That's what they'll discuss. Vote to let you stay. Vote to send you away. Vote to keep you tied in the lambing barn."

He hesitated until she laughed. "They won't do that," she told him. "We've got ewes in there."

"What do you think they'll decide?"

"I wouldn't try to guess."

"What would you decide?"

She glanced at him, and for a heartbeat her expression was unguarded. He saw curiosity and compassion and a hint of bafflement before she smoothed her features into a wry smirk.

"You did try to shoot my lamb."

"Trevor tried."

"So maybe I'd only send him off."

A rush of apprehension swept through Shawn.

"What is it?" Deirdre asked, all trace of playfulness gone.

"It's nothing."

She quick-stepped to face him, making him halt. "It's something."

He glanced toward the porch of Marcos's house just a few paces away. No one sat outside except the dog, Tippy, who was stretched in a patch of sunlight. The lamb trotted to the dog and leapt over it. The dog barely flicked an ear.

"Tell me," Deirdre insisted.

"I went to see Trevor, but your uncle wouldn't let me speak with him."

"Did he say why?"

"No. He let me see him, then he shut the door. I was hoping Marcos could help."

"Marcos would be the best, yes, but I saw him making for the south sheep field. I can try. Uncle John listens to me, usually."

"I don't want to put you at odds with your uncle."

"Uncle John is usually at odds with nearly everyone. I feel a little left out." The wry grin was back.

Shawn knew he should refuse, but he couldn't find the words. Instead, he nodded.

"Come along, Ferny," she called to the lamb. It left off nuzzling the dog's neck and trotted after them.

"Does your uncle have a reason for his . . ." Shawn wasn't certain of the best word. Contrariness? Animosity?

"Bad blood?" Deirdre supplied. "He blames the Donaghues for my mother's death."

"What? Why?"

She half-shrugged. "Guess he has his reasons."

Shawn let the matter dropped, though he suspected Deirdre knew what those reasons were. They walked to her uncle's cabin in silence, the lamb tagging behind them. The old dog was still sprawled in front of the door, and the cabin was still sealed shut.

Deirdre paused. "That's odd."

"What is?"

"The shutters are bolted."

"I noticed that earlier."

She rounded on him with a suddenness he was unprepared for. "Is there something you aren't telling me, Shawn McClaren?"

"I—I don't take your meaning."

"Is there or is there not something you haven't said?"

There was a loaded question if ever he heard one.

"Deirdre?" The door had opened without either of them hearing, and John Guthrie filled the doorway.

"Uncle John." Deirdre started to go to him but hesitated. "Why are you wearing your cowl?"

John's hard gaze fell on Shawn then darted back to Deirdre. "Why are you with him?"

"He was worried for his friend."

The gaze hit Shawn again, piercing and unfriendly. "What has he told you?"

"I'm starting to think not nearly enough."

"Has Peter called the families yet?"

"Not yet. Paden let one of the ewes get out of the lambing shed, and Marcos and a few of the menfolk went to track her down."

"You get home," he told her. "Put your lace on."

"Uncle John—" Deirdre looked alarm.

"You put your lace on. Why did Clary let you outside without it?"

"I'm not leaving the village."

"That don't matter. You put it on, girl, straight away. And you," he said, pointing at Shawn, "you stay clear of her."

"Sir, I mean her no—"

But John was on him before he finished, kicking the old dog out of the way in his hurry. He grabbed the front of Shawn's shirt, and Shawn staggered in his grip. John reeked of the pungent herbal scent, and he was sweating from the thick woolen cowl twisted around his neck. "You stay clear of her," he growled.

"John, what's the trouble?" Marcos was striding toward the cabin, his son-in-law Patrick with him.

John glared at them, but he released Shawn. "You keep this man away from my niece, Marcos."

"I'm sure there is no reason to fret."

"Then you're a fool."

"Watch your tongue, John," Patrick warned. John leveled him with a withering glare.

"Deirdre, get home," her uncle demanded, and then he retreated to his cabin, closing the door on them all.

"What the devil's gotten into him?" Patrick asked.

"He does seem more riled than usual," Marcos said. "Come away, Shawn. Deirdre, your great aunt is looking for you."

Deirdre gave Shawn an odd look before hurrying away, calling to the lamb as she left. Ruefully, Shawn followed Marcos and Patrick back to their house.

"I meant no trouble," he told Marcos. But he couldn't shake the sense of foreboding that he had caused it in some way.

~*~

"Uncle John is wearing his cowl."

"Too hot for that. Did you ever finish that neckerchief?" Great Aunt Clary tossed a few choice bits of greens to Ferny as she worked in the garden.

"I gave it to him a fortnight back."

"He can't mean to take a boat to check the figs. Too early for fruit to take the chance."

"We haven't had trouble in the fig grove for years."

"No fool ever died from being cautious."

Deirdre would usually smile at this, but she couldn't shake the foreboding nipping at her. "I don't believe he means to check the fig grove. And it isn't like Uncle John to wear his cowl around the village. His shutters were still bolted, too."

"At this time of day?"

"And he was slathered in Bess's ointment."

Great Aunt Clary sat back on her heels, a handful of weeds in her grip. She tossed the weeds aside, and Ferny hopped over to lip at them. "Help me up."

Deirdre did so without comment, though it was an unusual show of weakness on her great aunt's part. Great Aunt Clary wiped her hands in her apron before removing it. She hung it on a peg set in one of the porch posts as Deirdre pulled on her summer mitts.

"Come with me."

Great Aunt Clary set a determined pace down the path toward the Guthrie Cabin. She rapped on the door with her bony knuckles, then stepped back and crossed her arms.

"Who is it?" Uncle John demanded through the door.

"Open the door, John."

The door opened, and Uncle John eyed Great Aunt Clary and then Deirdre. He looked around as if expecting find the stranger there.

"He ain't here." Great Aunt Clary looked him up and down. "What's gotten into you?"

Uncle John stepped out and closed the door.

"Is it that stranger you've got cooped up inside? Or did you come down with a fever?"

"There's danger coming, Clary," Uncle John warned her. "You shouldn't be letting Deirdre off on her own like she is."

"Deirdre's a woman of eighteen, not a girl of eight. She's surrounded by family. What d'you thinks gonna happen to her?"

Uncle John's jaw went hard and Deirdre ducked her head.

"There's plenty that goes on that no one knows about until it's too late."

"When are you gonna let that go, John? It's done and gone."

"Lizbeth was my sister."

"And Lizbeth was Deirdre's mother, but Bryant was her father. How do you think Deirdre feels when you keep dredging up the past like it's hateful?"

Deirdre kept her eyes cast downward, so she didn't see Uncle John come up to her until he cupped her chin in his hand and lifted until her eyes met his.

"You know I hold nothing of blame to you, don't you, Deirdre?"

She nodded, her throat tight.

"You're all the good that came out of that tragedy, and I thank God for you every day."

Deirdre fought against the urge to weep. "I know, Uncle John."

"But I tell you," he said, his tone hardening, "these strangers mean trouble, and I won't see you hurt by any action of theirs. Especially that bold one."

"I won't let that happen, Uncle."

She didn't think he believed her.

"I want you to come to the family assembly with me." His pronouncement was so sudden that Deirdre wasn't certain she'd heard it.

"You do?" She had never been allowed to join in one of the family meetings before.

"Yes. I want you where I can keep an eye on you."

Deirdre's pleasure deflated. "Oh." So she wouldn't be in the meeting, just at the house.

"Now don't be that way," he said, giving her a little shake, and she gave him a little smile. "You wait for me," Uncle John told her, and with a glance to Great Aunt Clary, he retreated into the house.

Great Aunt Clary shook her head. "That man."

"He means well," Deirdre said defensively.

"There's no doubt of his care," Great Aunt Clary told her, "but I wonder what he wouldn't do if it meant keeping you safe."

Deirdre didn't have an answer to that.

~*~

Uncle John walked next to Deirdre as they followed Great Aunt Clary to the Ballard House. Ferny trotted along beside her as she tied her kerchief around her shoulders. Great Aunt Clary was wearing her stitched kerchief as well, but then, Great Aunt Clary always wore a stitched kerchief, along with the spiral shawl pin of beaten copper curled into it, an heirloom from Great Grandmother Ailee.

Deirdre wanted to speak of her concerns about Shawn, but she wasn't sure what was bothering her. She was certain he was hiding something from them. He deflected questions a little too casually. And she knew Uncle John would immediately see danger in what was unsaid and demand that the strangers leave.

She didn't want it to be her suspicions that kicked the three men off the island. To hear Shawn speak with such gratitude about their welcome here had proven to her that they'd seen little in the way of hospitality for some while.

Uncle Peter stood outside the Ballard House with Conor and Patrick, listening to Marcos, who broke off as they approached.

"Call the others," Peter told Conor, who hurried away. "We'd best go inside," he told them.

Deirdre followed them in. No one said anything about Ferny following her because the lamb always followed her. In another week, half the houses in the village would have an orphan lamb or two.

The Ballard House was half a room larger than the house she shared with her great aunt. The half room had been added when Conor and Blair married, but Uncle Peter had moved into it after Aunt Elspeth had passed, leaving the larger bedroom to Conor, Blair, and their daughter. Annabel was in the front room with Blair, peeling potatoes for dinner. Deirdre crossed to them without being asked.

"Can I help?"

Blair glanced with concern at the lacy mitts Deirdre was wearing. "Is he calling the families now?"

Deirdre nodded.

"Guess we should take this outside. Too warm to cook inside today as it is. Annabel, get your kerchief."

Deirdre wanted to stay, but she didn't argue. She wasn't one of the heads of families or even in line to become one. She'd often thought that unfair given how she was related to every person on the island by blood or marriage. The only one who could claim it so, according to the family lineages Great Grandmother Ailee had kept.

But she knew what was expected of her, no matter that it chafed. She helped Blair and Annabel carry the potatoes and onions outside.

"Deirdre," Great Aunt Clary called as she left the house. "Stay near."

Deirdre nodded with a surge of hope, especially when Uncle John repeated it as she passed by him to leave the house.

The other men came in fits and spurts. Uncle Ian and Aidan first, then Lennox. Bernardo and Lucio arrived together, arguing about whether one of the cows should be bred to the Devon or the Kerry bull. Deirdre knew they'd ask Marcos and then do the opposite. Marcos knew it too, she suspected, and planned accordingly.

Elki trailed in. His hair, black as a crow's wing, was loose, as was his custom, and the look in his dark eyes was grim. He paused when he saw her and gestured her over. She left where Blair and Annabel worked, the lamb trailing and Annabel watching with the curiosity of a half-grown girl.

"Have you spoken with your uncle?" Elki's mixed French and

Iroquois accent, still as strong as the day he'd arrived on the island, couldn't mask the tension in his voice.

She nodded. "He's inside."

"These strangers I've heard spoken of, you brought them?"

It wasn't exactly an accusation, because Elki wasn't like that, but it was as close as he might come to one.

"They needed help."

Aiden came out. "Deirdre, your uncle wants you."

"Did he say what for?"

Aiden didn't look happy. "You're to stand with him." He disappeared back inside.

"Best come inside," Elki told her. "Leave the lamb."

Annabel swooped Ferny up into her arms without needing to be asked. Deirdre followed Elki, feeling the weight of Annabel's and Blair's stares. She tried to hide her excitement from them, but she was certain they saw it all the same.

Her excitement chafed, though, when she walk in on Aiden complaining.

"It's not done. She's—" Aiden stopped, looking to her as seeing her for the first time. Deirdre knew what he was going to say. She was a girl.

"She is of age," Elki said, unexpectedly coming to her defense. "She is directly of the family."

"But she doesn't carry the Guthrie name."

"So now the Donaghue name isn't good enough?" Uncle John challenged. "It was good enough when it was forced on my sister."

"John," Uncle Peter said in warning. "You insisted Deirdre attend and she's here. I see no reason why she shouldn't be." The last he said to Aiden, who went quiet, if sulky.

"Let's get to business," Great Aunt Clary said where she sat in the only cushioned chair.

Great Uncle Peter hesitated a moment, came to a silent decision, and gestured to a stool drawn over from the kitchen. "Sit yourself, Deirdre."

"Are we deciding whether the strangers stay?" Uncle Ian asked from where he leaned against the plank wall.

"I think there's a better decision to make," Patrick told them. "Whether we can trust them or not."

"Wouldn't that be one and the same? If we trust them enough, they stay. If not, they go."

"What do we know about them to say if we can trust them?" Lennox asked. "Or to judge what manner of men they are?"

"Daniel says the big man, Wallis, has been a good guest," Patrick said a bit grudgingly.

"As has Shawn," Marcos added.

"He's hiding something." The words were out of her before she thought to stop them.

All eyes turned toward Deirdre, but only Uncle John looked unsurprised.

"How do you mean?" Uncle Peter asked.

"There's something he's not saying."

"How do you know?" Marcos didn't ask it harshly but with concern.

"Why are they on the run? He won't say, just that he's trying to get home. How'd Wallis hurt himself? Why do they look like they've been sleeping rough for weeks and hardly had a mouthful in days? Why is the little man so twitchy?"

"The little man did seem a bit nervous," Marcos agreed.

"A bit? He pulled a musket on me!"

"Deirdre!" Great Aunt Clary leapt to her feet in shock and Uncle John stepped to her, but Deirdre pulled back before he could reach her.

She swallowed hard. "I'm sorry I didn't say it earlier. I figured I'd just startled them, coming across them like I did. But now I'm not so sure."

"Trevor said it was McClaren carrying the musket" Uncle John said darkly. He had an expression Deirdre hadn't seen before, as if anger wasn't good enough for what he was feeling.

Deirdre shook her head. "Not at first. Shawn took it from him when he pointed it at me."

"Has he said anything else to you, John?" Marcos asked. Her uncle didn't answer immediately, lost in thought.

"Not much. He's a nervous little man, like we've all seen. I shouldn't have left him alone." The last came out in a growl.

"I can go keep watch," Bernardo suggested.

"I already sent Joseph," Patrick told them. Uncle John glared at him, but Patrick simply shrugged. "I don't trust them."

"On that we find common ground."

It was the first time Deirdre had ever heard her uncle and her cousin agree on something.

"Where does that leave us?" Uncle Ian asked.

Uncle Peter rubbed his chin in thought. "Keeping them on means weighing what little we know of them against what they've shown of themselves and deciding if the risk of allowing them to stay is worth it."

"To send them away," Elki added, "would call for taking them off the island ourselves if we're to make certain they do not make land on another part."

No one in the room liked the thought of the men returning on their own.

"I say they go," Patrick said, crossing his arms. "If they are holding back, then we can't trust them."

"I agree." Uncle John's support was not surprising except that he was backing a Donaghue's.

Deirdre looked around at the men gathered there. She wished she hadn't have spoken, but to hold back her reservations to her family for a few strangers didn't strike her as wise. She needed to be on her family's side.

But no matter what concerns she had about Trevor or about what Shawn might be hiding, she didn't feel in danger. At least not from Shawn or Wallis. Uncle John would keep the little man in line, of that she had no doubt.

"They might have good reason for keeping quiet," Marcos pointed out.

"I see no reason to discuss it further," Uncle Peter said. "Let's have a vote."

One by one, the head of each family made their vote. Only Patrick and Uncle John voted against. Deirdre was surprised by how quickly it all went. They'd had their discussion, they spoke their votes, and the decision was made. This was the way it had always been done on the island, though at the beginning, everyone assembled, men and women, until the families grew too large, and it was considered too unruly to continue to meet as a community.

"We're decided, then," Uncle Peter said. "We let them stay."

"Til when?" Uncle John demanded.

"The next resupply ship, I think, should do it. That's only a couple weeks away."

"Weeks," Patrick muttered. "I hope we can at least expect them to pull their weight in work."

"They don't seem the shirking sort. Marcos, think you can find some tasks to keep them occupied?"

Marcos grinned. "I'm sure I can think of a few."

"But we keep an eye on them," Patrick warned. "They don't need to be roaming free on the island."

"True."

"And there's no call for them going across the river."

"In that, Patrick," Uncle Peter said, "we are all in agreement."

The men dispersed. Uncle John gave Deirdre a warning look as he left.

"C'mon, child," Great Aunt Clary said, rising from her seat. "We've our own work to see to."

Deirdre followed along, picking up Ferny as they left. She'd hoped to find Shawn and demand answer, but it looked like that would have to wait.

~*~

"What do you think they'll decide, Shawn?" Wallis asked.

"I couldn't say."

"Take a guess."

"I don't like guessing, Wallis."

"Do it anyway."

"Fine. They'll give us the boot, and we'll have to swim for the mainland."

"I don't care much for your guesses, Shawn."

"Then stop asking for them."

They sat in silence on the front porch of the Donaghue House. Shawn fought the urge to pace. He'd been on edge ever since the confrontation with John Guthrie. He hadn't spoken of it to Wallis yet, but Daisy and her daughter had been working within earshot until recently. They'd asked if the men needed anything before setting off to help one of the other ladies, leaving Wallis and Shawn alone.

He might not get another chance.

"I think Trevor's spoken to John Guthrie."

Wallis stiffened. "About what? About us?"

"Maybe. Or about what happened with those bears."

"You mean bears creatures?"

"They were bears."

"Never seen a bear like those. Have you?"

"I don't know." Shawn rubbed his head.

"What do we do?"

"I'm not sure."

Wallis leaned forward in his chair. "Shawn, there is something strange on this island. They don't talk about it when I'm near, but just before you came, I heard Joseph speaking with his brother. They're worried, and it has something to do with John Guthrie."

"Why?"

"I don't know. Maybe if Trevor is talking to Guthrie, he's told him about us and where we've come from."

"Why would he do that?"

"Trevor's first concern has always been Trevor."

Shawn sighed, fighting the sense of helplessness. "You're right. And Deirdre was upset. She wanted to know what I hadn't told her."

"Did you say?"

"No. I couldn't tell if she was asking about the war or when we first came to the island."

"They must know about those bears. They couldn't have lived on this island for generations and not come across them."

"What if we've done wrong, Wallis?" Shawn's voice was weak.

"How so?"

"By coming here."

"Then we make it right."

Shawn looked up at Wallis, and the big man's gaze bore into his.

"It's time to tell them the truth, Shawn. We owe them that much."

Shawn stood. "I'll find Joseph."

"He went to the lambing shed with Daniel."

"I don't know where that is."

Wallis pointed to the south, back toward Marcos's house. "They went that direction, if it helps."

"You're a fount of wisdom, you are."

He got a thin smile from his friend, but it faded quickly.

Shawn followed the path toward Marcos's house, hoping to run into someone who looked approachable. A group of young ladies were gathered outside the house sitting a ways behind the Donaghue House. They were enjoying the shade cast from a nearby tree. Their spinning wheels were grouped in a circle, and they were speaking with forced gaiety while four children played nearby with a few puppies.

He recognized the three younger ladies sitting at spinning wheels as the girls who had sat working with the crochets with Deirdre. He also knew Rosa, Marcos's daughter and Patrick's wife. The other young woman he hadn't seen before, but he could tell even from across the yard that she was heavily with child. Deirdre wasn't there nor her great aunt, but an old woman was. She sat amid the young women apparently napping in a spot of sunlight.

"There he is, Grandmother," the youngest of the three girls said.

"Quiet, Nola, he'll hear," the eldest hushed.

"He can't be surprised by our curiosity." The old woman spoke without opening her eyes. The sunlight made her gray hair look silver and highlighted the deep lines of her face. She spoke with an English accent as familiar to him as the Scots-Irish lilt most of the villagers had. "Invite the gentleman over, Grace."

"Aidan mightn't like it," the fair-haired pregnant woman said.

"Aidan isn't here to gainsay me," the old woman told her, finally opening her eyes.

To save the young woman from discomfort and from having to rise, Shawn turned his steps toward the group. "Ladies," he said, trying to sound gallant, but the word came out stiff and formal. "Mrs. Donaghue," he said to Rosa.

"Mr. McClaren."

"Shawn, isn't it?" the old woman asked. "We don't keep to formalities here."

"Marcos has said. He warned me I might have three replies to one greeting."

The old woman smiled, and it brightened her face. Her eyes were cloudy with cataracts. "Lizzie Fonseca." She held her hand out to him. Shawn stepped forward to take it and bowed. The girls tittered with delight.

"Shawn McClaren. It's a pleasure."

"You're kind to say so. I do hope you are finding your stay with us restful."

"Honestly, I would be willing to do more work and less lying about." Shawn was finding it difficult to keep his tone casual.

"You sound troubled."

He blinked in surprise. "I—I'm trying to find the lambing shed. I was told I might find Joseph there."

"That is simple enough. Help me stand, young man."

He did so, and she took his arm afterwards, tucking her hand into the crook of his elbow with easy familiarity.

"Follow the trail behind Marcos's house."

"I don't wish to trouble you. Directions would suit, ma'am."

"It is no trouble. My husband Manny says I should walk more, so we'll walk. Shall we?"

Shawn took slow steps, but she moved well for her age and seemed to know the trail by feel. He was not so much guiding the old woman as escorting her.

"Are you Marcos's mother?" he asked her.

"I am. Manny and I were blessed with seven children, and we were even more blessed to see them all wed. Catrina, Javier, and Isabel left the island, but my other children are here with their wives and husband, and their children. We lost Alva, Rosa's mother, but life is like that. Death comes whether we are prepared for it or not."

He felt the weight of her words.

"You know somewhat of loss, too, I think."

"As you say. Life is like that."

"Family?"

"A sister and brother to sickness."

"Ah, it is difficult when they are young. Few things can break your spirit faster than burying a child. I'm sorry for your mother's sake. We have our fair share of little graves here, too."

Silence fell between them as they passed behind her son's house.

"Tell me what troubles you."

Shawn glanced at her, but she was staring ahead, milky eyes unfocused. Her touch was light, and she smelt of herbs and woolens. He wondered if his grandmother would have carried the same scent, or walked with the same cautious steps, or worn the same care-lines in her face.

"I'm a long way from home." The words came from him without his meaning to speak.

She didn't answer. He thought she was waiting for more. He stopped walking, and she stopped next to him, patient.

"Miss Lizzie, ma'am—" He stumbled for the right words. "I haven't been honest with Marcos." He almost said Deirdre's name and thought better at the last moment.

"Go on."

"Have you heard why we've come?"

"I have. Seeking refuge from the war. A war my countrymen lost, as I hear."

"They have. We have." The memory of that final battle bowed his shoulders. "Wallis, Trevor, and I—we were part of the Queen's Rangers."

"Loyalists." She didn't say it unkindly.

"Tories." His own voice was a whisper. "I still believe in our cause, but since Yorktown, I know it's a lost one."

"Yorktown was months ago, or so we were told. Have you been fighting all this time?"

"No, ma'am. We were taken prisoner with the rest of the British forces at Yorktown. The officers were ransomed or released, but the men were held."

"Go on."

"We escaped on the day they were marching us north. We'd heard stories about what's happening to British patriots in Philadelphia. Wallis and I have families there. Trevor only wanted to be free. He didn't do well under guard. So we planned our escape. We nearly made it clean, too, but . . ."

"But men died?"

"I hope not. But we injured two soldiers. They left us no choice." He could still feel the burn of the wound across his shoulder and the sticky slippery blood on his knife when he wrestled it free.

She patted his arm. "Marcos tells me you seem like a good man. I think I see why he believes that."

"I haven't told you the whole of it."

"I thought not. But I thought you needed a little encouraging."

He nearly smiled, but the urge left him quickly. "We didn't land by the hog marsh. We came upriver first, through a larger marsh, and made camp in the forest beyond."

The old woman's face went still, and Shawn realized it wasn't which side of the war he had fought on that would concern the villagers. It was what had happened on the other side of the island.

"Bears attacked Wallis and Trevor at camp. Trevor shot one of them."

She closed her eyes and her lips moved silently.

"I know something is going on with this island," Shawn hurried to say. "I thought I was seeing things at first, but now… what were those creatures?" He wanted to hear her say they were bears. He needed to hear it. Anything else would be madness.

"Bears. We simply call them bears."

Shawn nearly sagged with relief, but he caught himself and pressed onward.

"Wallis doesn't think they are bears."

"Oh, they're bears, just bears gone off. Bred wrong, see. Too few on this island."

Shawn nodded, though of course she wouldn't see.

"They mostly keep to the lands on the other side of the river. We call it the truce."

"The truce?"

"Nothing formally signed, naturally." She chuckled in a dry way. "Just seems to be an understanding. Those bears, they learn, understand, and somewhere along the way, they learned that this side of the river wasn't safe. And we've learned that their side of the river tisn't safe for us. Mostly because of the wrong ones."

"Wrong ones? The ones inbred?"

"That's the ones. They don't look much like bears, or so I recall. Odd noses and twisted paws and patchy fur. The first one that we came upon killed a man." She patted his arm. "I say we, but I mean they. My step-father and those traveling with him. They built our lives here. I guess you could say they were looking for refuge, too. Theirs just came with some ugly, misshapen bears."

So did ours, Shawn thought. "So they are dangerous."

"That they are, if you rile the wrong ones. Those, though, they aren't so good at swimming the river. At least, that's what my Manny believes. The others, well . . ." She trailed off and turned her face upward as though looking for guidance from the blue sky. Shawn remained silent, wondering if she would say more. It was having a history lesson about a very small community and he found himself intrigued.

"It started with Ailee Donaghue," Miss Lizzie finally said. "She and Marjorie Monigal were the two womenfolk who first came. It was Marjorie's husband that was killed. Ailee, Lord bless her, taught the way to keep them and us safe, but she had some particular ideas about the bears and those have been passed down."

"What kind of ideas?"

Miss Lizzie smiled. "That they're demons in bear form, or fae beasts, and only sheep wool and the oil we boil out of it can protect us from them. And it is true," she continued before Shawn could find any way to respond, "they don't seem to care much for the sheep. Manny thinks it's something in the brush the sheep graze. They do have a different taste than sheep off the island, and their wool is coarser, but we've no idea what kind of sheep they are anymore."

"Inbreeding, like the bears?"

"We aren't so backwards as that, young man." Her words were sharp, but her tone was playful. "We bring in ewes and rams to keep the stock fresh. It's showing, too, but in those early years the sheep were an oddity."

"So, the rest of the town thinks the bears are evil spirits that sheep can protect them from."

"When you say it like that, it does sound mad, doesn't it?"

"As you say, Miss Lizzie."

"Not everyone believes it," she assured him. "It's mostly the older folks who grew up with the stories and teachings. Nothing much wrong with it, as it keeps us safe and keeps the children away from the river. When Derry died, though, it brought it all back. One of Marjorie's sons," Miss Lizzie explained before he could ask. For a mostly blind woman, she had an uncanny knack of reading him. "She remarried after her first husband was killed. A good man, James was. It was a tragedy, what happened to Derry, but one of his own making. He knew better than to cross the river when the figs are ripe. The bears love those figs and they don't take well to trespassers."

"They killed him?"

"That they did. He was one who swore the bears were just beasts, so he wasn't wearing his stitching, and most everyone was sure that was why he died."

"Stitching?"

She tugged on the crochet lace around her shoulders. "Everyone on the island has stitching to wear. The thicker the better with the bears. Of course, they'll get a mouthful of wool, won't they, and I can't say any creature would care much for that? Still, that's the reasoning. Me, I like to wear it. Manny says it brings out my eyes."

She grinned, and Shawn had to chuckle.

"I confess, Miss Lizzie, that is the most unusual tale I've heard."

"That it is. But it's best you know what you're up against," she said, sobering. "Killing one of them, even being on their side of the river, will be looked at as riling up the bears. Peter and the other heads of the families will take that seriously."

"What do I do?"

She turned her face up towards him. "You go to the Ballard House. The families are meeting now. You tell them the truth, young man."

"I'll take you back—"

"I've been walking these paths for longer than you've drawn breath. You go, Shawn McClaren. You go now."

The family gathering had already ended when Shawn, breathless, reached the Ballard House. Shawn stopped a few paces away to see Marcos and Patrick come out. Patrick gave him an unfriendly look and walked in the other direction, but Marcos came toward Shawn.

"I was hoping to find you," Marcos told him. "You and your friends are welcome to stay until the resupply ship arrives in a few weeks. That should see Wallis healed and the lot of you fattened up some for your voyage."

"My thanks." He looked around. "Is Peter here?"

"He's gone to rest. He isn't a young man anymore. Did you need something in particular?"

Shawn didn't want to speak to just anyone, even though he was coming to trust Marcos. The older man had been straightforward, generous, and honorable.

"I'd like to talk to him first chance I can," Shawn said.

Marcos studied him and Shawn kept himself still, not actively trying to hide anything, but not wanting to let on to the depth of what he needed to say.

"I'll let Conor know. He'll send word as soon as his father is awake. In the meantime, do you mind lending a hand? There's always much to be done in the spring."

"I'm happy to do so."

"Good. Let's see what we can find for you."

Shawn glanced back at the Ballard House as he followed Marcos. It felt as though the seconds were ticking faster, counting down the minutes until the truth was out before he had the chance to claim it.

~*~

Deirdre had spent the rest of the day at her work, which kept her hands busy but her mind free. She puzzled through how she would approach Shawn to learn what he was holding back. What could it possibly be? She didn't know enough about life off the island to piece much together.

Which only made her frustration grow. Once again, her lack of experience was showing itself.

Uncle John wanted her to stay away from the strangers. Deirdre wasn't certain if it was because he didn't trust them or he didn't trust her. Did he think she'd try to run off with them? He said often enough that she was too much like her mother, impulsive and prone to not considering the consequences of her actions.

Deirdre had never gotten herself into much trouble, though, no matter her temperament. Nothing truly dangerous. Even running into the strangers hadn't turned out wrong, no matter what they might be hiding.

"Deirdre."

She stopped folding the shirt she'd just taken from the line at the sound of Uncle John's voice. He came up to her, his expression pensive.

"Have you stayed with your great aunt today?"

"Mostly. She got called to another lambing."

He nodded and glanced around as though he was looking for someone. Deirdre could guess who.

"I haven't spoken to him. Them," she amended quickly. "The strangers."

Uncle John's expression hardened. He stepped closer and lowered his voice when he spoke.

"They were hiding something," he told her. "I just had it from the little man."

Deirdre's eyes widened at her uncle's dark tone.

"McClaren, the leader," he said, "killed one of the bears."

Deirdre's heart thudded against her chest and her mouth went dry. "That can't be right."

"They landed on the far side of the island and got the bears riled. When one of them charged, McClaren had the musket and he fired."

"What if it was the little man instead?" Deirdre was desperate for it not to have been Shawn. "I don't trust him, Uncle John. He might be lying to you."

"Could be, but can we take the risk? Deirdre, there's been a death each generation from the bears on this island. Another's due."

"That's not how it works." But Deirdre had her doubts. First Shaw, then Derry... "It skipped a generation."

Uncle John studied her, unspeaking.

Deirdre didn't want to voice it. She knew the stories, that it hadn't been an accident that her father drowned, but that it had been the bears. Great Aunt Clary didn't gainsay it, though she didn't spread it, either, but Miss Lizzie said it was foolishness, that if it had been the bears, it wouldn't have been by drowning. Still, the stories circled for months after her father's death.

She knew Uncle John believed them. That was why he was so insistent that she wear her kerchief and mitts, and the heavy cowl in the winter.

"Danger's coming," Uncle John said. He put his hand on her shoulder as though to steady her. "It's coming, Deirdre, and we must take care. You must promise me to take care. Stay away from the strangers."

"Uncle John—"

"Deirdre, Aunt Clary needs you." Joseph walked up to them, took one look at how they were standing, and went on his guard. "What's happened?"

"Nothing that concerns you." Uncle John glared at him. Deirdre would usually stand up for Joseph, since he hadn't ever done anything to Uncle John except by being born a Donaghue.

Uncle John squeezed her shoulder. "Remember what I said."

"I will."

He left them, casting Joseph an ugly look as he passed him by.

Joseph watched him walk away. "John seems more wound up than usual."

"It's the strangers." Deirdre wanted to talk to Joseph about what her uncle had just told her, but at the same time, she wanted to get at the truth first. She needed to talk to Shawn.

"Your aunt needs you," he repeated to her.

"Where is she?"

"The lambing shed. She needs you to bring her birthing herbs."

"Not another ewe?"

"Could be. Does Ferny need a little brother or sister?"

"That's not funny, Joseph."

Joseph looked abashed. "I know it isn't, but everyone is so grim around here lately. There's something in the air. A tension. Ever since you brought those men here—"

"So now you're blaming me for it?"

"That's not what I meant."

Deirdre called Ferny over, and he bounced three steps to reach her. She lifted him up and thrusted him at Joseph. "Ferny can't go to the lambing shed. You watch him for me. Maybe remember what he was like after his mama died."

"Oh, Deirdre, that's not—"

Deirdre didn't wait to hear his apology. Why was she so sensitive all of the sudden?

Thinking on her parents, that's why. It always put her in a strange turn. She needed to shake it off, especially if she was going to help in the lambing shed.

She was nearing the shed when she saw Shawn helping Elki wind rope. She stopped, wanting to cross to him and demand answers.

Elki looked up to see her watching.

"Deirdre." His accented voice carried across the short distance to her. Shawn looked up at the sound.

"Elki. Shawn." She didn't like that her voice sounded cold, but if the something he'd been holding back had to do with the bears, whether he shot one or not, she had every right to be angry. That was a large omission, lying about where they landed on the island, even without encountering the bears.

Shawn frowned, but even frowning he was handsome. She wondered what he'd look like without the beard.

"Are you going to the lambing?" Elki asked.

"What? Oh, yes. Great Aunt Clary sent for me." She lifted the small satchel of wrapped herb packages.

"Best hurry. Death waits for no one, even ewes."

Deirdre cursed herself for her delay and rushed off, but Elki's phrase stayed with her. Death waits for no one.

That evening, though, it paused, and the ewe, and her twin lambs, survived.

~*~

It had been a long afternoon of labor, and Shawn had reveled in it. How long had it been that he'd done honest work? Not simply surviving day to day, running from his crimes of desertion and imprisonment, or marching, endless marching only to wait, endlessly wait, for battle to begin?

How long had he even done a hard day of labor? It wasn't something typical for him back in Philadelphia. His parents were fairly affluent, and he had been on track to follow his father's footsteps in politics. He hadn't thought twice about it. But he'd preferred the time he spent in Beryl's Hollow with his cousins and aunts and uncles and extended family. Working fields, hunting, tending the homes and teaching the boys. He'd learned to bargain with the local natives, even picking up common words to make the conversations easier.

If he were honest with himself that was why he'd joined the war. The natives. His parents supported the Tory cause, being Tories themselves. They were loyal to Britain and the King and prided themselves on it, even while they worked to ease some of the restrictions and taxes the crown had imposed.

Shawn, though he hadn't admitted it to anyone else, had joined to support the native land. The crown didn't want any further expansion west, which meant no more encroaching on tribal land. Shawn had the utmost respect for the natives, envied them at times, and he was in full support of the Proclamation Line. He supported it not only because it would stretch resources in men and supplies to continue moving west and expecting the crown to protect the settlers, but because it would increase tension with the natives, leading to more raids, more deaths, more misunderstandings. Shawn was confident there was a way for them all to live in peace.

He knew now that it had been an inevitability that the colonies would continue to move westward. Even if the crown won the war and brought the colonies to heel, there would still be expansion. The men that the crown could send to try to enforce the proclamation were just too few to police the length of the colonies. They would creep westward, force the natives to defend their land, and lead to another French and Indian War.

Shawn sat back on his heels. He'd stopped by the river to wash the sweat and dirt from his face and arms. The water was cool and not brackish, as he'd expect from it passing from the bay, through a swamp and back around the island.

He'd untied the laces of his shirt and rolled his sleeves. He'd had to restrain from pulling his shirt off altogether, an act he never would have considered doing back in Philadelphia. Even visiting his cousins, he wouldn't join them half undressed at the riverside. It had been too ingrained in him to remain clothed in public. But after four years at war among men, many who didn't have such upbringing, he'd loosened up. It had become necessary if he'd wanted to be clean.

He was far too aware of the local womenfolk on the island, though. And far too aware of one in particular. Deirdre's uncle was already set against him. Shawn didn't need to do anything more to antagonize him such as appearing in undress out of doors.

"Shawn McClaren."

Shawn turned on his heel to find the very woman he'd just been thinking of standing a few paces away, her arms crossed, her face a storm of anger.

It was not a look he wanted to have focused on him. He'd suspected that under her sweet exterior was the heart of a fire brand, but he hadn't seen it in its full fury.

She was disheveled, her hair falling from its stays and sticking to the sweat on her tanned cheeks and brow. Her apron was stained, her lacy gloves and tucked into the apron strings. She'd drawn her skirts up, too, on either side, to tuck into her apron strings, and at his kneeling vantage, he caught the curve of her shins, the delicate ankles and small feet.

She was barefoot.

Shawn smiled.

It was entirely the wrong thing to do.

Deirdre glared at him. "Proud of yourself? Of what you've done?"

He decided that remaining on his knees was probably the best thing under the circumstances. She could glare down at him better.

Also, it gave him a moment to try to puzzle which part of his crimes she had learned.

He let out a long sigh. It was going to come to this sooner or later. He'd just hoped to be able to speak with Peter before it had come out.

"You'll have to be more specific," he said quietly.

Deirdre's brow wrinkled in confusion, then smoothed above her green eyes.

"You mean there's more than one secret you're hiding?"

"Men have secrets, Deirdre. I'm no different. I'm sure you have your own."

"Mine don't put the village in danger."

Again, she could have learned of either of his crimes—allowing the bear to be shot or running from imprisonment and possibly leading the militia to the island.

They really should leave. It only now struck him how much danger he could have brought upon the peaceful village.

Shawn finally stood. Deirdre's gaze followed him, then moved downward to the open collar of his shirt, his rolled sleeves. Her face turned red.

He had to stop from smiling. She had such an innocence among that ferocity. The pair was too becoming, and too distracting. He'd never been so drawn to a woman, and that was as dangerous as his other faults.

It didn't stop him from wanting her. Wanting to know her better. Wanting to spend time with her and learn her habits and faults and strengths. To hear what her voice sounded like in the morning and how she felt in his arms at night.

Stop it, McClaren, he cursed himself. She's not for you.

If only she could be.

"You've learned about the bear," he guessed. It would be the closest in importance to her.

"I have. Uncle John told me."

Shawn's mouth tightened. If John Guthrie knew, then it was through Trevor. And Trevor would tell the tale in a way that would protect Trevor and cast blame elsewhere.

Shawn was the most likely choice. "We were in danger."

"You shouldn't have been on that side of the island."

Shawn's ire spiked. "Maybe you should hang warning signs, then. It isn't as though we knew anything about the island when we made land."

Deirdre winced, and Shawn cursed his harsh tone. She recovered quickly, however. "It's a marsh," she challenged. "What fool makes land in a marsh?"

"Desperate ones."

Her expression softened. "I hadn't thought of that."

Shawn shrugged. He didn't want her pity.

Good thing, because he didn't seem to have it.

"Still, why is it the first thing you think to do, shoot what scares you?"

"Deirdre, it was a bear. A strange, misshapen bear. We didn't see a choice."

"They aren't fast, those bears." But she didn't sound as certain.

"Fast enough for tired, hungry men."

Deirdre's arms dropped to her sides. She realized that her skirts were drawn up, blushed, and Shawn expected she'd pull the two corners loose to cover her legs, but she didn't. Instead she raised her chin.

"Why didn't you tell us?"

"It didn't seem—" Shawn stopped. He had kept it back. It wouldn't have been difficult to mention the bear. This island belonged to these people. To withhold what had happened could be seen as poaching, something Shawn abhorred. "I wasn't sure how you'd take it," he finally admitted. "Deirdre, we were desperate. You can't know how long it's been since we've had rest and comfort and safety."

She took a step forward. "I wish you'd told us, though. The bears, they—" She pursed her lips as if to keep the words in.

He sighed. He'd hoped maybe Deirdre would side with Miss Lizzie about the bears, but it seemed she believed they were some sort of demon let loose on the island that the villagers must be wary of.

"I'm mean to tell Peter," he told her. "I was washing up so I could find him."

She nodded, then studied him but this time, not in shock or awe, but in consideration. "What other secret are you hiding?"

Shawn hesitated.

"Very well, answer me this, then, and keep your secret," she said. "Will it put my family in danger?"

He hesitated again, trying to find a way to reassure her while confessing that it might. But his hesitation must have been answer enough.

Deirdre shook her head, and he heard her mutter "Men" under her breath. "If you won't tell me the truth," she told him crossly, "then be man enough to tell my great uncle. Or you'll only prove my Uncle John right."

"That you should stay away from me?" He didn't like the sound of that.

"No. That you should be sent from the island."

With that, Deirdre whirled and stalked away.

Shawn rubbed his hands over his face, feeling old and tired. He wanted nothing more than to tell Deirdre everything, to assure her that he'd let no harm come to her village. He wanted her to understand why he'd done what he done, starting with why he'd joined the Queen's Rangers and ending at this very moment. He wanted her forgiveness. He wanted her to care.

Shawn made his way to Marcos's house. Rosa was there, and Shawn realized that he hadn't tied his shirt closed, but she didn't look askance. She must be accustomed to it.

Patrick wouldn't like it, though. Thank goodness he wasn't there.

"I've just come to change," he told her, but quietly, as little Aileen was asleep on her small pallet nearby. "If my own clothing is ready?" He was in borrowed clothes, a pair of Marcos's pants and one of Patrick's shirts.

Rosa tutted at him. "Those are in the rag bag, but we've another set for you."

Shawn's chest tightened and he felt his eyes prick. Brought close to tears from new clothing. This was what his life had become.

"Thank you." His voice was thick.

Rosa gave him a gentle smile. "We take care of our own."

"But I'm not—"

She interrupted him. "You are while you're on this island." Rosa handed him a set of folded clothes.

Shawn changed in the next room, ran his fingers through his hair and tied it back again, and hoped he looked presentable enough. If he was going to confess his sins to the elder of the village, he should at least look as though he'd dressed with respect.

Rosa said nothing as he left the house, but she was busy with supper. His stomach growled from the smell of fresh bread and roasting mutton.

The walk to Peter's house was entirely too short, as all walks are to face fate.

Blair and her daughter were on the front porch combing wool into the neat little rolls he'd seen the women at his cousins' village make. He stopped to admire their skill.

"Have you never seen a rollag?" Blair asked. The older woman was sweet-natured with a round face and pretty brown eyes. Her daughter favored her father's look, sharper and hazel eyes, but she'd be a lovely young woman in a handful of years. Wallis was right, this island was like paradise.

"I have," he answered Blair. "And I've always been struck by how you do it."

"We can teach you," her daughter offered with a shy grin.

Shawn held back a sigh. He wouldn't win any favor by allowing the local girls to flirt.

"No, thank you," he said politely, but distantly.

The girl's face flushed, but she got over it swiftly.

"Is Peter inside?" Shawn asked.

"He is. And drinking his coffee," Blair added in a whisper. "Don't let on to Conor. He doesn't like his father to have it."

Shawn assured her with a smile that he wouldn't say a word and went into the house.

Peter was at the kitchen table sipping from a clay mug. He started when he heard Shawn enter, moving the mug to hide under the table, then chuckled.

"Shawn, welcome. I fear you caught me at one of my vices. Join me?"

Shawn crossed to the table and sat. "Thank you."

Peter poured him a cup. "Sugar?"

Shawn nodded, trying not to look too eager, but Peter's clever gaze caught it.

"Not had much of it, I expect."

"No, sir, I haven't."

Peter waved him off. "It's only Peter," he said.

They drank in silence for a few moments. The coffee was hot, sweet, and heavenly.

Peter set down his mug. "I expect you've come to talk to me of something of import?"

Shawn set down his mug. "I have."

"There's no need."

Shawn started. Peter continued.

"All that matters to me is that you're a good man. Are you a good man, Shawn McClaren?"

"I hope so."

Peter nodded.

"But I wouldn't be," Shawn finished, "if I didn't admit to a few events."

Peter studied him. "Have you done the best you can?"

Shawn sat back. "Sir?"

"Have you done the best you can with what you've got and with what you've known?"

"I hope so."

"Then, the past is past."

Shawn lifted his mug to cover his frustration. Peter was wise, there was no doubt about that, but he'd lived his life sheltered on this island among peaceful friends and family. Life could be boiled down to good men, bad men, good intentions, bad intentions. Shawn knew better.

"Dad," Blair said from the doorway in warning.

Peter stood quicker than Shawn would have imagined of a man his age and took his mug to the wash basin. Shawn drained his mug and handed it over.

Peter was rinsing the mugs when Conor walked in. He stopped, frowning unhappily at the scent of coffee, and crossed to the table.

"Father—"

"We've a guest, Conor," Peter said. "You wouldn't deny him a small comfort, would you?"

Shawn didn't want to get involved in a family squabble. "Thank you for your hospitality," he said to both men. "I should return. I wouldn't want to insult my hosts by being late to dinner."

"Good man," Conor said approvingly.

Shawn took his leave, Conor's words ringing in his ears. Good man.

Was he?

He hoped so.

CHAPTER FOUR

Saturday, June 1st

Deirdre left the house early, making a quick breakfast to leave for Great Aunt Clary when she rose. Even Ferny was still sleeping, and she left the lamb behind.

It was clear morning, lovely with a brightening sky empty of clouds. Deirdre's favorite time of day was dawn and dusk, when the sky changes and life seemed to be holding its breath.

She smiled to herself. She was feeling poetic, maybe to offset the deed she needed to do. It was never easy to face her uncle in disagreement.

Shawn had never denied shooting the bear, but she didn't believe it was him. There was something gentle about him. Driven, yes, and protective, which meant he'd take the blame of one of his fellow's failings. She could see that about him. And she suspected who had actually fired the shot and lied about it.

Shawn was a good man. She believed that as well. She was beginning to understand why her uncle was against him, and she didn't want lies compounding it.

Plus, she liked Shawn.

More than liked Shawn.

He felt so familiar. He was easy to speak with. He was handsome, too. Her face heated to remember how he'd been partially undressed at the river. His forearms were strong and corded with muscles, dusted with fine, light hair. His chest, what she had seen, was equally firm looking with the same light hair, not too much, though. Just enough, she thought. It had been ferocious, that gut wrench of attraction. Even in her anger, she'd barely held it back.

She definitely more than liked him. And that was dangerous. Her uncle would never agree to anything between them. And Deirdre wasn't sure that Shawn would even feel anything for her. He was so worldly compared to her. What fine women he must know. Why would he want a village girl raised on a secluded island?

Deirdre lifted her chin in defiance. There was nothing wrong with her upbringing. If anything, she was even better suited to making a home and raising a family. She could do whatever a household required, be a true helpmeet and equal to her husband. She wouldn't be surprised if she could be more than equal.

With that thought she arrived at Uncle John's cabin in time for the door to open. Trevor stepped out.

He froze when he saw her. She wrinkled her nose at the pungent smell coming off of him, a mixture of Bess's ointment and something that smelled off. Wrong somehow. The little man was wrapped in one of her uncle's thick cowls and was wearing a coat. He was sweating, lines of it running down his cheeks and under his collar, which was drenched. If he stayed so clothed as the day warmed, Deirdre though he'd most likely pass out from heat stroke.

"Good morning, Master Trevor," she said with a bob of a curtsy. She felt foolish and bold at the same time.

"M-morning." He clutched a water bucket in front of him.

"Is my uncle within?"

"No." His voice grew stronger. "He was called away."

Deirdre sighed, somewhat dismayed. However, the source of her annoyance was standing in front of her, and it was a chance she didn't want to let pass.

"Fetching water?"

He nodded warily.

"I can lead you to the pump."

"John pointed the way."

"Then I'll walk with you. It's such a lovely day for a walk."

Trevor looked as though he wanted nothing more than to argue, but he kept his lips pressed closed, so Deirdre walked with him. He didn't head to the water pump, though, but toward a stream that broke off from the river near the closest sheep field. Deirdre found it odd, but maybe her uncle didn't want Trevor mixing with the townsfolk. That would be like him.

"We haven't seen much of you," Deirdre told him, choosing her words carefully. "Your friends have made themselves useful."

"They aren't my friends." Trevor's voice was sharp.

"Oh?"

He didn't rise to the bait.

"Uncle John isn't happy to keep you all on the island."

Trevor said nothing. She noticed his mouth was tight and he walked with his shoulders hunch, as though preparing for an attack. And there was a curious sound she found was a bell attached to the bucket.

Strange.

But he was a strange little man. And not entirely all together.

It might be foolish to be alone with him.

Deirdre reconsidered her plan. They were out of sight of her uncle's cabin, the one farthest from the village. She could hear the stream gurgling through its entrenched furrow through the tufts of heavy grass.

"I've nothing to say to you," Trevor said, stopping beside the stream. He fixed his hard gaze on her. His eyes were wide, too wide. He was unsettled, and unsettling.

Deirdre backed up a step. "Very well. I'd best get to my work."

"You do that."

In that moment, his disdainful snarl in her ears, she truly thought she hated the little man.

Deirdre didn't turn away from him to go straight back to the village. Instead, she walked along the stream where it led toward where the rams were fielded. The stream curved so her back wouldn't be entirely to Trevor. She just couldn't trust him. When the stream straightened, she leapt over it and glanced back the way she'd come to mark how far she'd gone . . .

And stumbled into a shallow hole.

Deirdre caught her balance and leapt out of the exposed dirt. It was a strange place for a hole. It didn't look natural, dug in among the grass as it was. She circled it, for it was a good meter round, and tripped again as short branches tangled between her feet.

No, not branches.

Bones.

She knelt down and fingered one of them. They weren't fresh, having been picked free of flesh, but they hadn't been exposed long enough to bleach out white. They looked like hog bones.

No one slaughtered hogs here, and she hadn't heard of the wild hogs straying this far east on the island. It certainly could be a hog wallow. The ground would be moist this close to the stream, easy for them to roll into, but the hole didn't look right. It was too even.

She let the bone fall back to the ground. She should go back and tell Great Aunt Clary what she found, or tell Patrick. Or both. Someone had to know what it was. If it was just the hole, she wouldn't think twice, but the bones around it made it unusual and this close to the river, unusual wasn't good.

She leapt back over the stream and pointed her way back toward Uncle John's cabin.

That's when she heard the scream. High-pitched, hair-raising, heart-stopping, and coming from the direction she'd left Trevor.

~*~

Breakfast had been as delicious and filling that morning as every meal he'd had so far on the island. Rosa was an excellent cook, and sitting around the table with the family, even with Patrick watching him as if he expected Shawn to turn into a murderous madman, was as close to home as he'd felt in far too long. He enjoyed listening to Marcos's stories of the island and had learned a great deal more about the people who lived there. All five generations of them.

"My father, Manolo—"

"Manny," Rosa corrected. Marcos rolled his eyes, but he looked fondly on his daughter.

"He served aboard the *Senhora do Mar* under my grandfather, who brought the first families to the island. That was back in 1722."

"And then he stayed?" Shawn asked.

"Not at first."

"Not until he met Grandmother," Rosa said with a grin. The tension coming from Patrick always eased when his wife smiled, but when she grinned, he looked as though he worshiped her.

Shawn envied them.

Rosa shifted Aileen, their two-year-old, on her lap and offered the girl another bite of biscuit. "When Grandmother came over from

Norfolk, he fell in love, but she wouldn't have anything to do with a sailor."

"A Portuguese sailor at that," Marcos said, "even if he was going to inherit the ship."

"Every time they made land with supplies, Grandfather would bring her a treat or a trinket. But it didn't work."

"Then how did he win her?" Shawn asked.

"He promised that he'd sell his stake in the ship to his younger brother," Marcos said, "and stay on the island. And that was enough for her."

"So they became one of the founding families?"

"No, those families were already here. The Donaghues and Ballards and McGregors. But the Fonsecas became the newest family and next oldest." Marcos said it with pride.

"And were much welcomed," Patrick added, still looking fondly at his wife.

"It is a lovely story," Shawn admitted. "But I haven't seen much of this life that doesn't seem idyllic."

"We have our troubles," Patrick told him, his expression shifting when he looked at Shawn.

"All men do," Shawn agreed. "But after growing up in the city, I can see the appeal of living this life."

"Do you?" Patrick's question was loaded.

Shawn didn't answer at first. He swirled his tea in his mug, then drank it. "It isn't a decision to be made lightly," he said carefully, "to change one's future plans."

"Have a good life waiting for you back in your city?" Rosa asked.

"I thought once I did. Now, I'm not so sure. I've had time to consider other possibilities. But it will be good to get home, if I can manage it."

Nobody asked after his plans, or his home. He helped clear the table, then stood back to watch Patrick take Aileen from her mother so she could wash the breakfast dishes. Patrick held the girl so gently and with such fondness. He was an attentive and devoted father and husband. Shawn hoped he knew how fortune he was.

"Let's walk," Marcos said, clapping Shawn on the shoulder.

Shawn followed him outside. Marcos held out a slender object to him wordlessly. It was Shawn's knife.

He took it. "My thanks."

"I haven't seen beadwork like that," Marcos said, gesturing at the beaded sheath. "Or worn in such a way."

"It's Iroquois. A gift from my Uncle Finley. He saved an Iroquois warrior's life and the warrior gave him this knife in return. And Uncle Finley gave it to me. He had no sons," Shawn added. It had been more than that. His Uncle Finley had been like a second father. He looped the rawhide ties over his head and arm. He felt more himself with his knife against his chest.

"It's a fine knife. And a generous gift."

"Yes, it was." Shawn swallowed past the lump of grief. What would his uncle think of him and his choices? He'd asked himself that question too often in the past few years.

They walked past the houses. Shawn didn't know where Marcos was taking him, but he found he wasn't concerned. It was enough to take in the morning and the sounds of the peaceful village and solitude of the island. A man could make a fine life here. Especially with a wife he loved.

The word made him stumble to a halt.

Marcos turned. "Shawn?"

Shawn shook his head. "It's nothing." But Marcos didn't look convinced. "Can I ask you a question?"

Marcos nodded.

"Why did you stay?"

"On the island." Marcos considered. "I left, for a time. Traveled. Even served aboard my uncle's ship. That's how I met my wife, my Alva." His look turned wistful. "In port at Norfolk. She'd just come from Germany and looked so lost. She was a sweet, innocent thing and I fell for her. Courted her, then married her. But I wanted to give her a life as gentle and sweet as she, so we came to the island. She loved it here." He gazed up at the sky as if seeking her out. "There's not a day I don't miss her."

"I'm sorry for your loss."

Marcos smiled at him. "Ah, don't be. I had a wonderful life with her. I lost her too soon, yes, but I'm thankful for that time we had. I'm the better man for it. And she gave me our Yvonne and Rosa."

"Yvonne?"

"Our eldest. She married one of the McGregors and they moved to the mainland." Marcos shrugged. "The island doesn't hold us all here. The young men and women, they often want more. But they returned when they can to visit. Many settled in Norfolk. They can't leave the island entirely." He winked at Shawn. "Come."

"Marcos."

John Guthrie approached, his expression determined.

Shawn sighed and braced himself.

"Good morning, John."

"Has he told you?"

Marcos looked puzzled. "Has who told what?"

John gestured with a nod of his head toward Shawn. "Him. About killing the bear."

Marcos took a step sideways to look at Shawn. "What is this?"

Shawn gathered himself to explain, expecting that he'd be sleeping rough that night. But before he could draw breath, Miss Clary came up to them, looking cross, Deirdre's little black lamb leaping after her.

"Have you seen that girl?" she demanded of John.

"No." John looked worried, and he turned as though the girl, who Shawn was certain was Deirdre, would appear.

"She's supposed to be plucking that chicken I butchered, but I've not seen hide nor hair of her since I woke."

"I'll find her," John swore.

"Send her to the house when you have." Miss Clary walked away, shaking her head, the lamb following after.

"We'll help," Marcos offered.

"I think you've more to tend," John said with a pointed glance at Shawn.

John hadn't gone five paces when they heard the scream. It came from beyond the village to the east, but it was desperate and terrified enough to raise the hair along Shawn's arms and neck and send his heart pounding.

"Deirdre!" John tore off in the direction of the sound.

Marcos clapped Shawn on the shoulder. "Go. I'll bring muskets."

Shawn darted after John, clutching his sheathed knife.

"Shawn!"

Shawn didn't slow, running the direction the scream had come, but he glanced behind him. Joseph was running toward him.

"It came from behind the Guthrie Cabin," Joseph told him, keeping pace as they sprinted around buildings. John had already outstripped them, moving with a speed that spoke of his fear for

Deirdre.

They ran past the Guthrie Cabin. Shawn didn't know where Joseph was leading him, and he didn't care, as long as they made it in time.

"Deirdre!" John's shout carried in the open air. Shawn sprinted faster.

And nearly tripped at the sight that opened before them.

Deirdre was backing away from a black shape lumbering toward her. It was one of the bears.

John swore. Shawn tripped and caught himself, managing to keep his feet under him. The scene was from a nightmare. Deirdre was retreating, waving her arms as though to distract the creature.

It was his first clear look at one of the bears. Its fur was patched, missing entirely in places. It walked as though its legs weren't right, its shoulders too thick, and its hips too wide. The hollow of its sides didn't look like starvation, but it was still unnatural. And its head—

Shawn would dream about that head for the end of his days, nightmare dreams that would send him waking in sweat. It was furless, with a flat brow and pig-like ears, and an elongated nose with teeth that didn't fit entirely in its mouth. It was horrible and gut-churning and heading straight toward Deirdre.

Shawn's stomach lurched and his knees buckled. He'd never felt such utter terror before.

Joseph looked on helplessly, empty hands clenched. Shawn was the only one with a weapon.

He didn't hesitate. He pulled the blade free. "Here!" He ran toward the bear, shouting and waving his arm while keeping the knife ready. The beads at the end of the fringe clattered together and caught the bear's attention. It turned from Deirdre toward him.

"Shawn!"

He glanced behind him. Marcos held up the musket, then tossed it at him. Shawn dropped his knife to catch it and found it loaded and primed.

He lifted the barrel and took aim.

A growl rolled from the creature. It raised up on its hind legs, standing taller than Shawn expected, enough to glare down at him.

He shuddered at the look in the bear's eyes. Hunger, rage and madness.

"Shoot!" Joseph shouted.

Shawn leveled his aim.

"Don't!" Deirdre yelled.

He hesitated. The bear lurched forward back onto all fours, maw opening. Someone whistled shrilly, distracting the bear. And then a scream came from the direction of the river, where the woods thickened. The bear turned on its misshaped legs, and moving faster than Shawn would have thought possible on those twisted limbs, raced toward the woods.

"Shoot it!" Joseph yelled again.

Deirdre reached her uncle, her face pale under the sweat, her breath heaving. "Trevor."

"Did it hurt you? Are you hurt?" John grabbed her by the arms.

"No. No. But Trevor—"

"Trevor? Where's Trevor?" Shawn demanded.

She nodded toward the woods. "Two more," she managed to say. He realized her breathlessness wasn't exertion, it was fear.

Shawn exchanged glances with John, his expression was hard, then he turned for the trees.

"Don't—" he heard Deirdre begin, but he tore off towards the trees. "Wait!" Deirdre shouted after him.

"No, Deirdre, stay here," her uncle demanded.

"He can't go alone! They'll kill him."

Shawn wasn't sure if he was touched by her concern or offended by how weak she thought him.

He heard movement behind him, coming fast and prayed it wasn't Deirdre, but he saw Joseph instead. He was carrying Shawn's knife.

"What's ahead?" Shawn asked without stopping.

"The river. This way."

Once again, Shawn followed Joseph, but not for long. Shawn wasn't the tracker that Trevor was, but he wasn't without some skill. He picked up the bears trail quickly. The bears had charged through the underbrush and scraggly bushes, darted around trees, not quite in a straight line for the river.

Where did Trevor think he was going? Why wasn't he heading back toward the village? Was he trying to lead the bears away to save the others? Shawn wouldn't have thought the man likely to do so.

More likely, Trevor was panicked and running with no thought to where he was going.

Heart pounding, Shawn hurried after them, pausing to listen every now and then, Joseph now following. The river was closer—he could hear it readily. The rest of the forest was eerily still. The birds had quieted, the smaller creatures had vanished.

A cry of fear followed by a splash gave him a rush of speed and his bearing. He heard Trevor cry out again, but this time his cry was cut short. The keening whine of the bears set Shawn's teeth on edge and raised the hair on his arms.

Together, Shawn and Joseph darted around a stand of trees and reached the river. Shawn stumbled to a halt, grabbing Joseph before the younger man surged past him.

The bears were clustered at the river's edge around a struggling shape, legs splashing in the river in an attempt to get away.

The bears were growling and pushing the weakly struggling shape deeper into the river.

His mouth went dry. They were holding Trevor under the water as he struggled against their weight.

Shawn lifted the musket and aimed at the nearest bear. He fired, the power of the musket kicking against his shoulder, the smoke and stench of black powder filling the air as the noise echoed through the trees.

One of the bears howled in pain, but all three of them leapt into the river and made for the far side.

Trevor's body floated to the surface, facedown, unmoving.

Shawn leapt forward, or would have if Joseph hadn't wrapped lean, strong arms around him.

"Wait," Joseph hissed in his ear.

One of the bears, the largest of the three, stopped partway across the river, then started back toward Trevor's lifeless body.

Shawn broke free of Joseph and raised the musket like a club.

"No!"

The bear drew back. Once again, Shawn got a full look at the hideous face. It looked so wrong that Shawn's mind didn't want to process the sight of it, rebelling at the odd shape and unnatural conformation.

The bear swam after its fellows. Shawn watched bleakly as the three bears climbed the far shore and lumbered away, growling, one limping heavily. Shawn hoped it would suffer a painful death.

~*~

"Are you hurt?"

"No, they didn't touch me. Please, Uncle John." She watched as Shawn reach the tree line.

"What happened?"

"We have to help Shawn." Deirdre pulled against him, desperate.

"Stop!" His grip was bruising. "You are not going after him. I will not lose you because of that man's folly."

"Oh, Deirdre, thank God." Marcos limped over to them, breathing heavy. Deirdre looked around for Joseph and saw him sprinting after Shawn.

"What the devil's going on?" Daniel hurried to them, Elki and several other of the men following after.

"The bears—" Deirdre began.

"By God, did you say bears?" Daniel looked shocked.

"I warned you about the strangers," Uncle John began.

"Will you listen to me!"

The men stared at her in shock.

"Shawn went after the bears and the bears went after Trevor. That way." She pointed toward the tree line, the thin border separating the village from the nearest sheep field. The trees led to the river. Shawn had already disappeared.

Joseph met her gaze. She could see the fear shining in his eyes and tightening his jaw. He swallowed hard, came to a decision, and gave her a nod.

Without a word, he sprinted toward the trees.

"Joseph, are you mad?" Daniel called after his younger brother. "Joseph!" Gritting his teeth, Daniel set off after him.

"Wait, Daniel." Patrick reached them carrying the old Ballard musket. The match was lit. Daniel took it and hurried after his brother.

"What's happened?" he asked.

"Take Deirdre to Peter," Marcos told John. "Patrick, go warn the others that the bears were near the village." He followed after the younger men.

Patrick stared after him, shocked.

Deirdre didn't want to go to Uncle Peter. She wanted to follow, to help in some way like her great grandmother would have done. But Uncle John did not relinquish his firm hold on her arm, so she had no choice but to let him take her to the Ballard House.

Word had already reached the house.

"You can't go after him." Great Aunt Clary stood in the doorway, arms crossed, expression stern.

"Great Grandmother would have."

"Child, you're brave, but you're not Ailee Donaghue."

"I'm her grandchild."

"And I'm her daughter, but I'm not foolish enough to hie off into the woods after those bears."

"Joseph and Daniel went."

"I'll not hear another word on it."

Deirdre threw her summer mitts onto the table in frustration. Blair wrapped her arm around Deirdre's shoulders.

"Come lie down. You've had a terrible shock."

"I don't want to lie down."

"I'll take her back, Mother," Annabel offered.

"Go on, child," Great Aunt Clary told her. "We'll wake you with any news."

Blair nodded encouragingly. Annabel held out her hand.

Heaving a sigh, Deirdre allowed Annabel to lead her into the back room.

Annabel closed the door. Deirdre fought the urge to kick at the bed frame.

"Did they really follow the bears?"

Deirdre nodded mutely. Where had Ferny gotten off to? Was he still at the house?

"I need to find Ferny."

"Your lamb? I haven't seen him. Not since earlier with your great aunt."

"He was at the house."

Annabel looked concerned. "I could go look."

"No!"

The girl froze, shocked. Deirdre tempered her voice.

"If the bears were to come back..."

"Then you shouldn't go, either."

"He's my lamb, Annabel. I'm all he has." Deirdre hated tricking the girl like this, but she was desperate.

Annabel looked torn. "Well, I suppose if you went out the window—"

"Thank you!" Deirdre hurried to the single window in the room and unlatched it. She opened the shutter slowly, peering out as she did so.

No one was nearby.

"You'll make excuses for me?" she asked the girl.

Annabel nodded. "But hurry."

"I will."

Deirdre hefted herself out the window. She closed the shutter and crept to the edge of the house to look around the corner.

Elki and Lennox were speaking in hushed voices outside the house.

"Elki!" Tate shouted from his doorway. "What news?"

The two men went over to Tate's cabin. She waited until Elki's back was turned. He had sharp eyes and if anyone would see her, it would be Elki. Tate was engrossed in listening to the two men, so Deirdre sneaked as quickly as she dared to the little stand of trees, then hurried toward the Guthrie Cabin. She had just gotten around to the back and toward the woods when she heard Elki's voice.

"Deirdre." Elki stood behind her, his musket in hand.

"I was, ah . . ." She had no excuse, and they both knew it.

He studied her, then stepped aside and gestured toward the Ballard House. Deirdre cast a glance toward the tree line, but the trees told her nothing. With a weary sigh, she returned to the house.

"Where is she?" Uncle John's voice came from the room on the other side of the window, angry and stern.

"I—I—" Annabel stuttered.

"I'm here." Deirdre pulled open the window shutter. Uncle John stood in the bedroom scowling. Great Aunt Clary and Blair stood behind him. None of them looked pleased.

"I wanted to fetch Ferny." She might as well try to keep the ruse going, though Elki could counter it easily. Thankfully, he hadn't followed.

Her explanation didn't seem to help.

"A lamb?" Uncle John was furious. "You risked yourself over a lamb?"

"Ferny would have been fine," Blair added. Uncle John cast her a dark look.

"She knows that."

"She's had an awful fright. I'm sure she's just not thinking

86

clearly."

"I'm thinking perfectly clear," Deirdre defended.

"No smarter than her father," Uncle John muttered as he turned away from the window.

"There's no call for that, John," Great Aunt Clary snapped. "Deirdre, you come around through the front door. Now."

Sighing, Deirdre did so. Most of the houses were shuttered and barred. She didn't see anyone else out. It was eerie.

And here she was, calm and centered.

"Why is that?" Deirdre asked aloud. "I should be faint with fear. They all expect it. Why aren't I?"

"Because you haven't the sense God gave a goat." Great Aunt Clary met her on the front porch. "I raised you better."

Her great aunt's words stung. "I don't think—"

"That's right, you don't." Uncle John stormed out of the house. "From here on out, you're staying with me."

"She's safe enough here," Great Aunt Clary told him.

"Is she? She got out under your nose. I don't think you're up to watching her proper. First she goes off beyond the village with no one knowing and runs into those strangers. Then she gets herself attacked because of those same strangers."

She remembered suddenly there was one more stranger in the village and he might not know what was happening. "Wallis!" Without thinking, Deirdre darted off toward the Donaghue House on the other side of the small orchard. She made it halfway before her uncle caught up.

"Deirdre!" He grabbed her arm, wrenching her to a halt. "What do you think you're doing?" Uncle John looked incredulous and enraged.

"No one's told Wallis what's happened. He needs to know."

"You get back to the house at once."

"But Wallis—"

"Let someone else deal with it." He began dragging her back toward the Ballard House.

Deirdre wrenched her arm from his grip. "No. I'm telling him now."

"Deirdre—"

"Uncle John, I know you're trying to protect me, but I'm doing all right on my own. You don't have to keep fussing."

He stared at her as if she'd struck him.

"I'm just going next door," she said, softening her voice. "Come with me."

He drew back. "No. You come back with me."

"Uncle—"

"John!"

It was Elki's voice, coming from the Ballard House. Deirdre didn't need further urging. Elki rarely sounded so alarmed.

He was standing before the porch. Daniel was with him. Neither Shawn nor Marcos was in sight. Neither was Joseph.

The fear hit her the way Great Aunt Clary had wished, but it wasn't for herself.

Joseph.

Shawn.

She'd never felt so helpless.

~*~

"They drowned him?" Joseph approached the body cautiously, as if the obviously dead man might sit up.

"They were holding him under."

"Good God."

Shawn knelt down next to Trevor. He'd seen death. Lord knew he'd seen plenty of death. But not like this.

Swallowing against a surge of queasiness, he rolled Trevor over. It wasn't easy to move the dead weight of a still body, especially one so water-logged.

Trevor stared up at him sightlessly, his mouth slack and opened, his skin tinted with a bluish cast. It was ugly for such a bloodless death. Shawn had seen men missing limbs, with pieces torn from them, with holes where no holes should be. He'd seen them bleed out from bayonet wounds, watched the life leave their eyes, heard that final gasp that was half prayer and half plea. They haunted him still, those deaths.

This death would haunt him, too.

"By God." Daniel stopped well short of where Shawn knelt.

"The bears—" Joseph couldn't seem to find the words through his horror.

"What did they do to him?"

Shawn took his hand from Trevor's chest. "They killed him."

The men were silent, each lost to their own dark thoughts. Shawn stared across the river, trying to see if any of the bears were watching. He couldn't shake the sense of gazes upon him, marking each movement and action.

"They didn't drown him," Shawn said, still watching the far side. "He was trying to get away. They caught him and were trying to get at him. Their weight pushed him under."

Marcos approached. He said nothing, simply bowed his head when he saw Trevor.

Prayers. Shawn felt as though something should be said, but none of the proper words would come.

"We need to take him back," Marcos said at last. "Daniel, go find Elki. He is at the village standing watch. Best find John, too, and give him the news."

Daniel was off like a shot.

The older man came to kneel next to Shawn.

"I am sorry for your friend."

Shawn nodded, throat tight. Marcos held his hand out to Joseph, who handed him Shawn's knife.

Shawn turned it over in his hands, feeling the familiar weight, before tucking it into the beaded sheath across his chest.

"I should have told you all about the bear," Shawn said.

"Yes, you should have."

He looked at Marcos. The man's brown-eyed gaze was fixed on him. From the corner of his eye, Shawn saw Joseph frowning down at him.

"We escaped from a military prison," Shawn said, his voice tight. He didn't look away from Marcos. "We were captured at Yorktown."

"You are a loyalist."

Shawn didn't answer.

Marcos sighed. "Will they come for you?"

"I don't know. Likely they don't know where we've gone."

Marcos nodded. He stood and extended his hand to Shawn. "We will take your friend back to the village and see him tended. Then we will discuss what is to be done next."

Shawn couldn't argue with him, though there was much he could have said, such as how Trevor had never truly been a friend. Or how none of them should be considered guests after causing such strife on the island. How he just wanted to go home.

Would leaving end this? If he and Wallis were to go, would the bears and the militia leave the village in peace?

He didn't know.

Daniel returned with Elki and a couple of woolen blankets. Thankfully, John Guthrie wasn't with them. Shawn couldn't have taken John's condemnation at the moment.

They laid out the blankets and shifted Trevor's body onto them. Joseph and Shawn took the corners at Trevor's head, with Elki and Daniel taking the corners at his feet. Marcos led the way, finding the easiest path and carrying the musket.

The village was a welcomed sight. A small cluster of men stood near the Guthrie Cabin. Two of them broke off to hurry forward, taking hold of the blankets to help carry the load of the dead man.

No one spoke. Marcos led the way behind the village to a shed set beyond the last garden. Inside was a long table that, in the gloom, looked coated with dust. Garden tools lined one wall, hanging from pegs set in the wood or set upon shelves. Dried plants and seeds rested in baskets, and sacks were stacked on a trestle against the opposite wall. Coiled rope and buckets stood against the third wall.

"We tend for our dead here," Marcos told him as Joseph and Daniel left the shed. "It seemed fitting given that it is also a place to plan for the life to come in the gardens and fields."

It did seem oddly fitting. And peaceful. No shallow pits dug to fill with the dead and cover quickly to ward off animals. No hasty words of prayer before the next march or much-needed foraging party. After a battle, the dead had been a necessary task to handle quickly. It would never do to dwell on death when muskets might be waiting around the next hill.

This shed was a place for kindly ministrations, a final moment to share with the departed with love and grace.

Trevor might have someone who loved him. Shawn had never asked after parents or a wife, and Trevor had never offered. He'd only known about the cousin in Richmond.

Shawn would get word to her, if he could.

"We can see to him, if you wish it," Marcos offered.

"No. Wallis and I will do it. He was one of us." Shawn tensed. "Wallis—has anyone seen him?"

"He is being told," Elki assured him. "But yes, you should go.

Bring him here. We'll be ready. The others are bringing a winding sheet."

Shawn left the shed, expecting it to have grown dark since he'd entered, but the sun was still well in the sky. Only mid-afternoon. Was it possible?

Word had spread that the bears had left, for he saw folks beginning to gather as he crossed through the small village toward the Donaghue House. They fell quiet as he passed, then began speaking once more. He heard clips of words but focused on his path and kept an eye out for John Guthrie rather than eavesdropping. There was little doubt what they spoke of, and he didn't want to learn if the people he had come to think well of were turning against him. He wouldn't blame them if they did.

"Shawn!"

His chest constricted at the sound of Deirdre's voice. She hurried from one of the groups gathered in front of the Ballard House. Oddly, her lamb wasn't with her.

She drew up a few paces from him. He couldn't read the expression on her face except to see tension there.

"I heard about Trevor. I'm sorry."

"You weren't hurt, were you?"

"No. They weren't after me."

"Your lamb?"

"At home. Great Aunt Clary kept him locked in the house instead of following her around." She seemed touched that he'd asked and drew closer. "Daniel said that your friend… that Trevor was drowned."

Shawn nodded mutely.

"Good God." She wrapped her arms around herself as if to ward off a chill.

"It isn't like you think—" Shawn began.

"Did you shoot the bear?"

"I think I marked one, but it followed the other two."

"Not those bears. The first bear." She asked it with an intense look in her green eyes.

Shawn sighed, but gave her the truth. "No."

"No."

"Swear it to me."

"I can't."

Her expression grew hard. "Why not?"

"Because I'm the one who insisted we come to this island. I brought Trevor here, and he shot the bear. I'm as guilty as he was."

She drew in a ragged breath. "You didn't force him to shoot."

"Deirdre, if I'd been in that camp when the bears came, I would have been the one to fire."

She didn't look like she believed him. "Are you going to speak to Wallis?"

"I am. He needs to know about Trevor."

"Conor told him."

"I need to tell him, too."

Silence fell between them.

"You should get back home," Shawn told her. "I don't think your uncle would want you out."

"No, he wouldn't. Shawn," she called as he turned to leave. "I don't think you would've fired."

He didn't look at her. "I'm a soldier, Deirdre. We defend our own."

She didn't answer. He could feel her watching as he walked away, and it was an effort not to glance back at her.

Wallis was standing outside the Donaghue House alone, staring toward the river. He glanced to Shawn.

"I heard."

Shawn came up to stand next to him. "We brought his body back."

"Why did they drown him? Do animals even do that?"

"He was trying to swim away. They caught him and pulled him under trying to get at him." Shawn couldn't shake the sense of doom. It wasn't just the bears. He didn't know why they attacked when everyone seemed so certain they wouldn't cross the river. He didn't know if the militia would learn where he and Wallis had escaped to and follow. There was too much uncertainty, and he was tired of it.

"What do we do, Shawn?"

"We leave."

"And go where?"

Shawn didn't answer.

"Good God, man, you don't want to end it, do you? Give yourself up? Because that didn't work out so well for us last time."

"This isn't remotely like last time."

"No, it'll be worse." Wallis stared down at him.

"Wallis—" But Shawn couldn't argue. It was the truth. "The best thing we could do now is to leave."

"These people know how to handle themselves."

"You don't want to leave?" Shawn studied him. "I can see it in your eyes. You don't want to leave."

"Of course I don't want to leave. This place is like paradise. Except for those beasts, I could spend my life here and count it a fine living. This is exactly what we were fighting for—a community like this of families going back generations. Did you know Marcos's wife was German? And he's Portuguese. Elki is half French and Iroquois. It's a colony of its own, taking in newcomers who are willing to do their share of the work."

"It isn't quite the same—"

"It's what I was fighting for," Wallis cut him off. "It's what made Philadelphia great before all the politics got involved."

"Wallis—the militia—"

"I know, the militia." Wallis looked like he was struggling with the idea.

"They'll come after us," Shawn said quietly.

"We don't know that for certain."

"This island isn't completely separated from the mainland, no matter what they'd have us believe. Supply ships. Family in Norfolk visiting. Word that strangers have settled here will get back and as soon as the militia hear, they'll come for us."

"Not if enough time passes." Wallis gripped Shawn's shoulder. "Once the war is over, truly over, we're nothing to them."

"I don't believe that. You know how hard we've fought. They won't let Tories alone just because they've won. They'll fear an uprising backed by the crown."

"Yes, but no one has to know we were Tories."

"Wallis "

"Your friend might be right."

The two men turned to see Peter approaching. Joseph was with him.

Peter came to stand next to them. "I am sorry for your loss."

"Thank you," Shawn answered.

"We'd like to offer him a resting place among our own."

"That's kind of you."

"Daniel and Aidan have started on the grave. We'll hold a service, with your blessing."

"Trevor was Anglican," Wallis said. Shawn hadn't even realized it.

"So is Lennox. He will lead it."

"We appreciate it." Shawn hesitated. "How much did you hear?"

"You were prisoners?" Joseph looked shocked, and that answered Shawn's question.

"Since Yorktown fell. Wallis, Trevor and I escaped when they were going to move us north. A couple guards we didn't anticipate tried to stop us and were hurt." Shawn closed his eyes, the guilt still eating at him.

"Did you kill them?" Joseph demanded.

"No. At least, I don't think so."

"We couldn't stop to find out," Wallis said, and Shawn heard his regret too.

"We stole what we needed as we went," Shawn continued. "Word spread that we were on the run. They might have learned we stole that boat and start thinking to search the islands. I can't risk it."

"They might search the islands whether you're here or not," Joseph said darkly.

"Not if I turn up elsewhere."

"Enough." The single word from Peter silenced them. "The war has never touched us and we're fortunate for that. I have no desire for it to do so."

Shawn nodded, considering the matter settled. He would leave.

"The families are meeting," Peter told them, "after the burial. We have much to discuss. But we'll make you comfortable beforehand."

Meaning that Shawn and Wallis were not invited.

"I can save you the time," Shawn said. He looked to Wallis, who sighed, but nodded. "We'll leave. If you'll help us return to the boat we brought over—"

Peter interrupted. "Ah, but I'm not entirely sure that's the best course of action."

"But—" Wallis looked confused. "You just said—"

"I know what I said," Peter interrupted, but not unkindly. "This is why we call together the families—to hear various ideas and suggestions. It's rarely failed us."

Wallis let out a breath. "If you think it best."

"I do. Will you consider abiding our decision?"

"I will," Wallis assured him. Shawn didn't answer.

Peter didn't miss his lack of response, but he let it pass. "We'll speak again soon." The elder man left them, but Joseph stayed.

"I'll help, if you'd like," he offered. "With your friend."

"That's kind of you, but we can manage. Do you think we should leave?" Shawn asked him before he could turn away.

Joseph looked at him gravely. "I think it's too late for that now."

Shawn was afraid he was right.

~*~

They lowered Trevor into his final resting place as the sun touched the tops of the trees. Lennox led them in service, though he was a nervous speaker.

The words spoken, the hymns sung, the dirt thrown over the pine wood coffin, the villagers left the graveyard. Deirdre tarried, watching Shawn and Wallis shovel the dirt into the grave. Joseph offered to help, but they politely refused, so he crossed to where she stood near her mother's grave. Ferny roamed near the grave of Great Grandmother Bess, nosing at the tall grass.

"You haven't come out here for a while," Joseph said.

"Neither have you."

"I find Father speaks to me in other ways. Like whenever I don't replace a tool, I can hear him nagging me not to leave it lying about."

Deirdre smiled, but it faded quickly.

"You're worried."

She nodded. "I don't want anyone else buried like this."

Joseph was uncharacteristically silent.

"What is it, Joseph?"

"You saw them."

She who she meant. Deirdre tried not to think about the way the bear had look, misshapen and stunted and wrong. "I did."

"Only Grandmother Ailee has been that close to one and lived."

"They weren't after me." She didn't how she was so certain.

"You can't know that. Deirdre," he said when she didn't answer, "did she tell you how she did it?"

"What do you mean?"

"What did she do to keep them back? Besides teaching us about the stitching and sheep wool and wool oil?"

"I don't know."

"She didn't tell you?"

"I know you think Great Grandmother shared some magical knowledge with me, but she didn't. She told me once that when it came to protecting her family, there was nothing she wouldn't do. So of course she'd face the bears."

"When you put it that way . . ."

"I understand what she meant now." Deirdre looked out toward the sand dunes, seeing the blue ocean water beyond them. The rise of the graveyard was one of the loveliest places on the island because of the view, which was why it had been chosen as the final resting place for their loved ones. "When those bears were after Trevor, I wasn't thinking about saving him. I was thinking about how to make the bears stop without making it worse. Maybe I should have thought about how to save Trevor, but if I could have stopped the bears instead, all this would be over and we'd be safe again, them and us."

"By God, you do sound like her."

"That's what Great Aunt Clary said."

"Aunt Clary isn't often wrong."

"Don't I know it." They both chuckled.

"The families are gathering," Joseph said. "We'll figure out what to do next."

"Will we?" Deirdre looked to where Shawn and Wallis were finishing filling the grave. Would they have to dig more? Would it be Shawn or Wallis laid to rest in the next one? Her chest constricted painfully. How had she come to care so much what happened to them in just two days?

Had it truly only been two days? That just wasn't possible.

"Deirdre?"

Joseph had asked her a question, and she'd missed it. She felt her cheeks color and couldn't say why.

"Are you ready? We should return," he told her.

"Just another moment." She knelt before her great grandmother's grave. Hollyhocks and foxglove grew behind the headstone, a flat-fronted rock with "Ailee Donaghue, July 10, 1702 - September 12, 1781" carved into it.

She brushed her fingers along the carved letters. "What would she do?"

"If you don't know, then no one does."

"That isn't true. You spent about as much time with her."

"Then I think she'd go talk to the bears," Joseph said. He was grinning.

Deirdre frowned. "But what would she tell us to do?"

"Sit tight and don't fuss. Wear your stitching. Eat more greens."

"I'm serious, Joseph."

"So am I." He knelt next to her. "She'd do what she thought was best, regardless of what the others said. She'd protect her family, just like you said."

"We're finished," Wallis called to Joseph.

Joseph rose and walked to where the two men stood. Deirdre rose, too, but she returned to where her parents had been laid to rest. Her mother was only a name and a few stories to Deirdre. She'd died a day after Deirdre was born. But her father walked and talked in her memory. Bold, full of laughter but with sorrow lurking behind his eyes. She remembered only kindness and love from him and not a hint of the treachery her uncle often claimed of him.

"Your father?" Shawn had come up behind her unawares.

"Yes."

"He died young. Illness?"

"He drowned."

Shawn drew back, shocked. "The bears?"

"No, no, of course not. He was harvesting figs from the grove."

"The one across the river? I thought you never went there."

"We don't go on land. But there are trees within reach from the river. So we take a boat, tie it, and use a basket and a long pole. It's simple, really, but only the men are allowed to do it."

"Did he fall in?"

"The boat capsized, we think. He hit his head when it did." It didn't sting as much to say aloud as she expected, but the grief was still sharp.

Shawn was frowning, deep in thought.

"It wasn't the bears," Deirdre told him. "It was an accident."

"You're certain."

"They've never done anything like this before. But . . ." She hesitated. "Great Grandmother always believed they were clever."

"I heard she convinced the bears to leave the village alone."

"That's the story. But she didn't talk to them or have power over them. It was the sheep and the wool oil."

"I've heard that, too."

Deirdre didn't hide her surprise.

Shawn smiled. "I happened upon Miss Lizzie. She's quite the woman."

"That she is. She told you the stories?"

"A few." Shawn looked away and Deirdre had the feeling he was purposely avoiding her gaze.

"Miss Lizzie doesn't believe in the bears the way most of the village does."

Shawn only nodded.

"Anyway, it's the wool oil that keeps them back. And sheep in general it seems. It's poison to them."

"That's why you aren't worried about the sheep roaming free."

"They don't bother the sheep."

"And you wear the knitting—"

"Stitching."

"—that you make with the crochets."

"We spin the wool raw, too. And make ointment out of the wool oil to wear."

"Was that the smell coming from your uncle's cabin?"

"It was. They were both covered in it." Deirdre paused and found Shawn staring at her meaningfully. "Trevor was covered in it," she said slowly. "But it smelled off."

"Off how?"

"I don't know. It was familiar, but—" She sighed and rubbed the bridge of her nose. Exhaustion was setting in, but the day was long from over.

"Do you believe?"

Shawn's question was quiet, as though he wasn't sure he wanted to ask it.

She didn't have to ask what he meant.

"I don't know." It was the first time she'd ever given voice to her doubts. "They do sound like fairy stories, don't they? If I'd never seen one before, I'd say they were told to keep children from trying to cross the river. But today . . ." She shuddered.

Shawn put his hand on her arm. It was warm and larger and oddly comforting.

"They're hideous," she whispered.

"They're wrong, but not because they're devils or demons.

They're trapped on this island."

Deirdre thought about what Shawn was saying. "When my great grandparents came to the island, the only thing here were sheep, bears, and wild hogs. And a few of these houses. No people. There weren't so many sheep then."

"How many bears?"

"No one knows for certain." She crossed to another grave, her great grandfather's, and ran her fingers over his name. Grahame Donaghue.

"My great grandfathers mapped the island, but the only details are on this side of the river. They circled the rest by boat. They didn't see the bears, but they didn't dare make land in the marshes or the woods on the west side."

"So no one has scouted that side?"

"Derry tried. A relative of mine," she added. "He was killed."

"By the bears."

Deirdre nodded.

Shawn turned toward the ocean. "It's beautiful here."

"Yes, it is."

"But there is something wrong on this island, Deirdre." His stormy gaze caught and held hers.

"You don't think it's the bears?"

"Do you?"

Deirdre faced away, back down at her great grandparents' graves.

"We should get back," she said at last. "The families are gathering."

"I know. Peter doesn't want Wallis and me there."

"The women aren't allowed, either."

"You were at the last one, weren't you?"

"That was different. I was the one who found you."

Shawn chuckled. "I suppose that will be a story passed down."

"Most likely. Come with me." Unthinking, she took hold of Shawn's hand. It was larger gripping her smaller one, with rough palms and strong fingers. A tremble ran up that arm and through her.

"Where are we going?" He didn't fight as she led him from the graveyard.

"Back to the village. There will be a meal shared between all the families to celebrate Trevor's life. At least, normally there would be. Most likely the families will take it in their own houses in case the bears return."

"If there is so much concern, we should set watches."

Deirdre looked at him. It was easy to forget he'd been a soldier. "Do you think we should?"

Shawn shook his head. "The houses should be safe enough. And there are enough dogs around here to wake an army if they sense danger."

She laughed. "That's the point."

CHAPTER FIVE

Sunday, June 2nd

Patrick had left for the family meeting with a warning look at Shawn as he passed him on the porch. Shawn had already sworn to stay out of the house until Patrick or Marcos returned. He knew Patrick didn't trust him enough to be alone with Rosa, and Shawn, raised as he'd been, wouldn't be caught alone with a woman, even a married woman, inside without another present. Little Aileen notwithstanding.

So he was reclining in the chair on the front porch, trying to enjoy the cool evening breeze that carried the smell of ocean and sand and fields, when Deirdre approached, her little black lamb trotting behind her. The dying sunlight cast her hair into a reddish hues and she walked calmly toward him with none of the ire she'd approached him with before. She carried a work basket with her.

He stood and bowed, though it felt like a silly thing to do given the informality of the island folk.

Deirdre chuckled. "I expect that looks fancier in a coat and breeches and a beaver hat in your hand."

"I expect it does." He smiled.

"Is Rosa inside?"

He tried not to let his smile falter. Of course she'd be here to see Rosa. "Yes."

Deirdre stepped onto the porch and passed him for the door. He caught the scent of herbs and wool as she went by.

Shawn settled back onto the chair. He thought he might go speak to Wallis.

He heard the women's voices but not the words. Little Aileen tottered out the door, surprising him as she made straight for the single step down off the porch. He saw her beginning to topple and swooped in to catch her before she did.

"Goodness," Rosa said, coming out. "Thank you, Shawn."

Aileen weighed next to nothing, and she didn't fret but gripped his shoulder with her small hand.

Deirdre stepped out behind Rosa. "She likes you."

"I suppose so," Shawn said, his face heating unaccountably.

"Oh, she's been taken with him from the first," Rosa said. "We should get going. They'll be waiting."

Rosa stepped back inside the house as Deirdre crossed over to Shawn.

"Do you have any?" she asked.

Shawn jerked in surprise. "Children?"

Deirdre nodded, not quite looking at him. Her color had gone pink.

He tried not to smile, suspecting that maybe she was asking a different question altogether.

"No. No children. No wife. Yet." He didn't know why he added it. The word just came out.

Deirdre's green-eyed gaze met his and they stood looking at each other for what seemed like hours.

"Do you mind carrying her, Shawn?" Rosa asked, stepping out and closing the door behind her. She had a larger basket with her.

"No, not at all. If she doesn't mind." He focused on Aileen. "Do you mind, little miss?"

Aileen grinned and tucked on his hair.

The women both laughed.

Shawn followed them from the house, Aileen in his arms. She rested against him, twirling her fingers in a lock of his hair. It was oddly soothing until she pulled.

"Ow!"

Rosa looked back at them. "I should've warned you."

"It's fine. She just caught me off-guard."

"Women will do that, if you aren't careful," Rosa warned with a teasing smile.

Shawn had no response to that.

They ended at the large tree near Miss Lizzie's house, the largest house on the island. It looked as though all the women and children were present, spread under the tree with their spinning wheels and crochet and a couple knitting. The children were nearby, running circles and playing with toys. Aileen struggled against him, eager to join them.

"You can put her down," Rosa told him. "Annabel and the older girls watch over the children."

Shawn set the girl on her feet. She tottered a moment before finding her balance and then rushed as fast as her little legs could take her, stumbling only a few times. Annabel met her and swept her up into a twirl as Aileen giggled. It was the sweetest sound.

The lamb must have thought so, too, for it bounded away from Deirdre to join the children.

"Join us," one of the women told Shawn. Rosa and Deirdre had spread out blankets and joined the other women. Several had brought out chairs and the others sat on more blankets. The women spinning had stools.

Shawn hesitated. There were no other men present, and the oldest boy he saw, playing with the others, was the same age as Aileen.

"Sit with me, Shawn." Miss Lizzie patted the empty chair next to hers. She was facing toward him as though she knew exactly where he was standing.

Shawn took a steadying breath and crossed to the chair.

"Thank you," he said to her. The old woman gave him a gentle smile.

"Good to see you're secure enough in your manhood to sit among the lady folk," one of the other women said, a darker-skinned woman who looked as though she shared native blood. The other women chuckled.

"Mathilda," Miss Lizzie chided.

"I mean no offense," the woman said to Shawn. She smirked. "You don't see any of the other men here. I think they are frightened of us gathering altogether."

"They should be," another older, graying woman said without looking up from her crocheting.

The women chuckled. Even Shawn smiled, though he felt out of place. And, if he were honest, a little frightened.

"Are we all here?" Miss Clary asked. Shawn saw her sitting in a chair near where Deirdre and Rosa had spread their blankets. Deirdre was sitting on hers, legs splayed out in front of her, shoes off, a skein of wool in her lap as she started on a new crochet piece. She was so young and lovely and free.

Deirdre caught him staring and blushed. He glanced away, feeling his own face grow hot, and looked straight into Rosa's eyes.

She smiled a knowing smile.

Shawn chided himself. He needed to be more careful. No matter how attracted he was to Deirdre, there was no future with her. He couldn't stay and he couldn't ask her to leave, not with the danger surrounding him.

"We're all here, Aunt Clary," one of the younger women said.

"Then let's not be sitting gawking at the boy. What do we know?"

Shawn shifted, but the attention left him and he relaxed. It seemed as though he'd fallen into a meeting of the townswomen. Did their husbands and fathers know? They were at their own meeting. Is this what women did when men were at their own work?

He felt as though he'd fallen into a secret world. Or been allowed inside.

"Elki says the bears won't return," a steady, older woman assured them. She had beads on her dress and was spinning using a long pole instead of a wheel.

"And we've been told all our lives that they'd never come here to begin with," another challenged.

Miss Lizzie leaned toward Shawn. "That's Mary Margaret, my son Lucio's wife," she whispered to him. "And the one before is Elki's wife, Roberta. They don't get along so well. Never have, even as girls."

"There's been sightings," the older, graying woman said. Shawn recognized now her accent as Irish.

"Caitlyn McGregor," Miss Lizzie said. "Ian's wife. Marjorie and James' son. He speaks for the McGregors. Caitlyn speaks whenever she has a mind to."

Shawn had to smother his chuckle and glanced down to see Miss Lizzie grinning.

"Not that story again," Mathilda said with a roll of her eyes.

Caitlyn drew herself proud, and Shawn could appreciate what a beauty she must have been in her youth. "You weren't on the island then, Mathilda."

"So we are going to break down into who was born here and who was brought?"

"Enough of that," Miss Clary snapped. "Caitlyn's right. There've been sightings. And yes, Derry was fool enough to follow after one."

"Clary—" Caitlyn said in warning, her tone sharp.

"Don't deny it, Caitlyn. What became of him was a tragedy and we're all the worse for his loss, but he knew better."

Miss Lizzie shook her head, her expression pained. "Ian never believed that Derry would be so foolish."

"This is an old argument," another woman said in a gentle voice. He recognized Daisy Donaghue.

"Your friend is staying with Daisy, isn't he? Her husband, Coy, was Clary's youngest brother."

Shawn nodded to Miss Lizzie, forgetting she wouldn't see. There had to be at least a dozen women here and he'd never remember all the names and connections, but it was kind of Miss Lizzie to try. And the few he did remember might be useful.

He hated thinking like that.

"Daisy's right," Miss Clary said. "We aren't going to get into all that past with the bears. It's what the menfolk are deciding now that we're here for."

"And the strangers." The woman who spoke from her spinning wheel cast Shawn an apologetic look. "Not that you're to blame for anything."

"Of course he isn't," Deirdre said before Shawn could answer.

"I think they are good men," a young woman near Deirdre's age added, though shyly.

It must have been unusual for the young woman to speak because all eyes turned to her. She flushed bright red and stared into her lap where her stitching rested unnoticed.

"I swear, Hetty." The woman who spoke Shawn recognized as Daisy's daughter. "You haven't been coming round my house to visit me, have you, but to visit a certain guest of ours."

"Leave off, Deborah," Deirdre warned.

"Because you haven't been coming around my house to visit me," Rosa added, "but a certain relative of mine."

It was Deborah's turn to go bright red, but she didn't lower her face. Instead, she lifted her chin boldly.

"I'll not argue it."

"She's sweet on Marcos," Miss Lizzie told him. "Daisy's daughter is."

"Marcos?"

Miss Lizzie chuckled quietly. "Quite the scandal, wouldn't you say? He being twice her age. But I think she'll have him yet. Once he notices."

"The bears," Caitlyn said, bringing the matter back around.

"What will the men decide?" another of the young women asked. She shared Mathilda's coloring, but not, it seemed, her disposition.

"Mona," Miss Lizzie whispered," Elki and Roberta's oldest. She's sweet on Joseph, but the girl's bound for disappointment."

"Patrick wants them hunted," Rosa declared. All eye focused on her. She looked unhappy. This was the first Shawn had heard, but he'd caught Patrick and Marcos speaking alone and hushing quickly when they noticed him last night. "Father, too."

"Bernardo feels the same," Mathilda said.

"And Lucio," Mary Margaret added.

"The Fonsecas have never agreed with the truce," Caitlyn accused.

"But they've abided by it," Miss Lizzie said for all to hear. "Me and Manny, too."

"Grandmother Bess said that Grandfather Thom abided it but never quite agreed to it."

Miss Lizzie sat up straighter. "When did she say this, Briony?"

"When she was ill." Briony shifted on her chair. She wasn't young, but she wasn't old either. One of the third generation, Shawn thought, and then realized he was starting to think in terms of generations. Did they do so, too?

"This is the first I've heard of it," Miss Lizzie accused.

"Bess never liked to go against Mother and Father," Miss Clary said.

Miss Lizzie sighed and sat back. "True. Mother always felt beholden to them for letting her come to the island. And to Thom for bringing her."

"And Thom would never have gainsay Father," Miss Clary added.

"So where does this leave us?" Daisy asked.

"Where did Coy stand on it?" Miss Clary asked her.

"He never said." Daisy smiled sadly. "You know Coy. He kept his thoughts to himself."

"Unlike his sons," Mathilda chuckled.

The rest of them laughed.

"So the Fonsecas and the Donaghues will vote to hunt," Miss Clary counted. "The Ballards?" She looked at Blair, who Shawn recognized as Conor's wife and Peter's daughter-in-law.

Blair sighed. "Dad will want them let alone. And Conor would agree."

"Ian too," Caitlyn said.

"I've never understood that," Mathilda told her. "Derry was his brother."

"And Ian doesn't believe the whole story of it," Caitlyn retorted.

Mathilda opened her mouth, but Roberta laid her hand on her arm. "Let it go."

"Please," Mary Margaret added.

"It don't matter much the whys," Miss Clary said. "If Ian takes the McGregor vote against."

"Briony," Daisy said to the woman, "what will Lennox decide?"

"I'm not sure." Briony twisted her fingers into the wool on her lap. "He doesn't tell me much of those things."

"He'd keep you on a shelf wrapped in wool if he could," the woman sitting next to her said with a wide grin that showed her crooked front teeth.

The ladies laughed again and Briony blushed, but she wore a sweet smile that spoke of her devotion to her husband.

"Lennox looks to Tate," the woman continued, "and Tate will side with his father, so the Smyth vote will probably be against."

"Nessa, you should tell Tate to let Lennox make up his own mind," Caitlyn chided.

"Lennox speaks his mind when he has something to say," Briony told them. "He doesn't follow Tate blindly. He trusts him."

"Fair enough."

"And Elki?" Caitlyn asked Roberta. Mona, their daughter, sat up and watched her mother carefully.

"You know Elki doesn't hunt unless there's the need," Roberta said, "but now he sees a need. But not all of the bears," she said quickly. "Just the ones that are the most dangerous."

"The evil ones," Mary Margaret said with a shudder.

Miss Lizzie's mouth went tight. "Silly girl," she muttered.

"Which leaves the Guthrie vote," Caitlyn said.

Shawn stiffened.

Everyone looked to Deirdre.

"He doesn't tell me his mind," Deirdre defended. "Unless it has something to do with me."

"The bears nearly got you," Roberta reminded her.

"It wasn't like that."

"It was close enough." Shawn didn't flinch as all the ladies turned to look at him. Deirdre, however, glared at him.

"What do you think should be done," Caitlyn asked him, calling him out.

Shawn came close to brushing aside the question, but Miss Lizzie put her wrinkled hand on his arm and squeezed.

Speak your mind, that grip seemed to say.

So he did.

"I'm not of your village, and I don't have the whole of the history, but I've seen something of these bears, the ones that hardly fit the name. Tell me, are there bears not so ill built?"

"Yes," Roberta said. "Elki, Lennox, and Tate stood watch near the hog marsh to see them."

"They did what?" Briony looked stunned and beside her, Nessa looked angry.

"Elki wanted a count of their number," Roberta explained. "They took the safest measure."

"Wild hogs and the bears?" Nessa shook her head, clearly displeased. "I don't call that safest. Either could've had at them."

"Elki is better than that," Roberta defended.

"Of course he is," Mathilda agreed. "My brother could follow a mountain cat at six paces and not be caught."

"I couldn't say that about Tate and Lennox," Caitlyn said wryly.

"Ladies," Miss Lizzie warned.

"How many did they count?" Shawn asked Roberta. She looked startled that he addressed her, then embolden.

"A dozen or so."

They were silent.

"At least half were the sickly ones. The rest were normal, he said."

"How long ago was this?"

"A couple years," she admitted.

"Does anyone know how long they live?" Shawn's question was met with blank expressions.

"If they're devils, they can live as long as they want." One of the women who hadn't spoken yet shuddered.

"Grace," Miss Lizzie said sternly, "they live and die like any beast."

"They aren't like any beast, though, Miss Lizzie."

"Beast or not," Shawn said, "they can be hurt and killed."

The women stared at him. Shawn looked to Deirdre. She was tight-lipped, but she nodded.

"We killed one," he told the women, "when we first made land on the island. It attacked us."

He waited for Deirdre to speak up and claim it was Trevor that killed the bear, but she was curiously silent.

"We made land past the marsh at the far side," Shawn continued. No one spoke, they simply looked at him. "We had no idea they were there, or what they were. I don't have any other excuse . . ."

"Except that you were exhausted, hungry, and desperate," Miss Lizzie said for him. "And that's reason enough."

"But you upset them!" Mary Margaret's look was anxious and frightened. "They followed you here!"

The women burst into talk, their voices vying with one another.

Shawn sat back, worn out and sick at heart.

"Don't fret so," Miss Lizzie said, patting him on the arm.

"How can I not?"

"Shawn?"

He looked up to find Deirdre standing before him

"Walk with me." She turned before he could answer.

"Best go," Miss Lizzie told him when he didn't move. "That's not a young lady to keep waiting."

Shawn chose not to read anything into the old woman's words as he rose and followed Deirdre.

~*~

Deirdre took the long way around the village, keeping well away from who might see her with Shawn. Specifically her uncle. Her stomach was abuzz with unease. She was still shaken from her confrontation with the bear, but she was also too aware of how near Shawn was walking. She couldn't ignore his closeness, from the occasional brush of his sleeve on her arm to the scent of him, all man and sweat and wood smoke.

"Does that always happen?" Shawn asked as she led him toward the stream that cut between the sheep field and the village. Deirdre started, wondering if he was as aware of her as she was of him.

"Does what always happen?"

"The women gathering as they did."

"Of course. Nothing would get done properly otherwise."

He laugh. He thought she was joking. She stopped to face him.

"The men think they know what's best, and usually they are close, but it's the women here who have kept the island in peace and growing. You don't have all the answers, you know."

Shawn took a step back at Deirdre's forceful tone. She calmed herself.

"I didn't mean you personally."

"No, I think you did."

"Shawn—"

"I'm not arguing, Deirdre."

She liked the way he said her name.

"What did you bring me out here for?"

"To see this." She led him to the stream and leaped across it. Shawn followed with a long step rather than a leap.

Deirdre hunted around to find the shallow pit. "When I was coming along here, I found the oddest thing. There's been no time to tell anyone else, and I wouldn't know how to describe it. Since you're here, I thought you might have a look."

She found it, nearly stumbling into it again, but Shawn caught her by the arm and steadied her.

"Thank you."

"You're welcome."

He didn't release her right away. They both realized it at the same time. He dropped his arm, and they both took a step back.

"What is this?" Shawn noticed the pit at last. He circled it.

"I thought maybe it was a hog wallow, but they don't come this far to the village. And the sheep don't make these."

Shawn knelt down to study the ground. "It's too even to be an animal," Shawn said.

"And then there's these." Deirdre held up one of the bones.

Shawn stood and took it from her. "You needn't hold it."

"Why?"

"Well . . ." He seemed at a loss.

"It's only a bone." She bent and picked up another. "I can't tell for certain if they are from sheep or hogs. Maybe both."

Shawn turned it over in his hand, then walked the ground, looking for more. He picked up what he found, and Deirdre was shocked when he returned with easily ten bones.

"They all look like they're from the same part of the animal," Shawn told her, holding one up. It had bleached white.

"What are they doing here?"

"You'd be better for that answer, seeing as I've not seen this part of the island."

He said it with a smile, and Deirdre laughed. "True." She sighed. "I should take this to my uncle."

"Or Peter," Shawn said hastily.

"You don't care much for my uncle, do you?"

"I'd like to claim that I don't know him well enough to say either way, but I think we both know that would be a lie."

"He doesn't much care for you either."

"I had noticed that. Do you know why?"

Deirdre faced away. "It's because of my mother. My uncle accuses my father of leading her astray, which led to her coming into a family way, which led to their marriage and to me. But that killed my mother."

"I'm sorry for that, Deirdre."

Deirdre shrugged the sentiment away. "My uncle has always blamed my father for her death. And the Donaghues in general for allowing it all to happen."

"Did your father love her?" He asked it tentatively.

Deirdre faced him. "Oh, yes. My father was devoted to her. Even after she passed, he never thought to take another wife. And when he spoke of her." She sighed again, but this time with fondness. "He loved her."

"Your uncle fears I'm going to lead you astray."

He said it calmly, but Deirdre tingled with the words.

"Yes."

"I'd never do that."

Deirdre looked away, biting her lip. It was foolish to be disappointed. She would never want to bring about the same hard feelings and strife between families as had happened with her parents.

"If I liked a young lady," Shawn said quietly, "I'd court her proper."

She opened her mouth to ask how but closed it again.

Silence built around them. Deirdre tried to think of something to say, but all she could wonder was how Shawn McClaren would court a lady, and if she would ever know what that was like.

"Tell me about what happened to Derry."

"Derry?"

Shawn nodded.

"He went after the bears and they killed him."

"And that's it?"

Deirdre nodded.

"There seemed to be another story the women knew."

"Oh, that. Well, there were rumors." Deirdre shook her head. "Not rumors, not really, more like whispers, especially from Uncle Ian."

"What were these whispers?"

"Why?" she challenged.

"I'm not sure," he admitted. "I just have a feeling that there's something more underneath all of this."

Deirdre wanted to tell him that she was starting to feel the same, but she wasn't sure that she should be admitting it yet.

"Word is that Derry was in love with my grandmother, Hattie Ballard, but she married my grandfather, Alistaire Guthrie. When she died, word is that Derry blamed it on Alistaire. She died of illness, but Derry accused Alistaire of hurting her in some measure and that had killed her."

"Was it true?"

Deirdre shrugged. "No one could say, but my grandfather was heartbroken when my grandmother died. Even my uncle will tell you how her death destroyed Grandfather."

"And Derry?"

"He mourned her too and never married. And then, several years later, he was killed."

"How many years?"

Deirdre frowned. "Ten, maybe?"

Shawn nodded, his mouth tight.

"What are you thinking, Shawn McClaren?" she demanded, crossing her arms.

"There seems to be a few deaths surrounding your family that strike me as odd."

"What do you mean?"

"Your grandmother and the rumors. Derry and the rumors. Your father—"

"What about my father?" Her voice was hard.

Shawn winced. "I'm out of line. I apologize. Truly, it's no business of mine."

"No, it is not. I should be getting back before Uncle John comes looking for me.

Shawn winced again. "I might stay and have a look around."

"Fine."

Deirdre knew she was being childish, but she hurried away all the same. Why was she so bothered by what Shawn had said?

And who should she tell about the bones and the pit?

Uncle John and Great Aunt Clary were the ones she'd normally rush to, but for some reason, she was hesitant to do so.

Shawn had suggested Uncle Peter, but she hesitated.

Then who?

The name came to her as if the past was whispering in her ear.

Uncle Ian.

~*~

Deirdre thought the men would be finished with their meeting, so she went directly to Uncle Ian's home, but when reached the McGregor House, but no one was in. The men must have gotten into quite the discussion or were arguing. Either was just as likely.

She knew where they were meeting. She should sit on Uncle Ian's porch and wait, but then again, she might be able to overhear something useful if she happened near an open window where the men were meeting. It couldn't hurt to walk past. Perhaps they were already finishing and she could walk Uncle Ian home.

She knew, even as she made for the Ballard House, that she wasn't simply going to walk by an open window.

Thankfully, the little apple grove separated the Ballard and Donaghue Houses. The young men who weren't old enough to attend the family meeting gathered there. Joseph would probably join her, but the others, like Ewen and Claude, would probably call her out if they saw her sneaking around.

The outside of the house was clear except for old Patch, who was dozing in a patch of sun, his namesake. The dog was stone gray but had always found a patch of sunlight to doze in. Laziest dog on the island. And the quietest. Ferny could jump back and forth over him and on him, and he didn't so much as flick an ear. He wouldn't wake when Deirdre approached. Still, she was glad Ferny was playing with the children.

She stayed low, creeping to stand under the window. This was not allowed, and if the men caught her, she'd be in the worst trouble of her life.

It was worth it.

"It's time to rid the island of them." Uncle John's voice carried through the window she crouched under. He spoke as though daring the other men to gainsay him. Uncle John was typically outspoken, but this time his tone was determined and refused to be dismissed. Not that many on the island would.

"How do we do that?" Marcos asked. "We have only a few muskets between us." Deirdre had expected him to agree outright given what Rosa had said.

"We set traps if we must. Elki has experience with them."

"We have no idea how many we'd be facing," Marcos said.

"Yes, we do." Lennox's gentle voice barely reached her. When he didn't say anything more, Deirdre could imagine him looking to Tate to continue.

Tate didn't disappoint. "Elki and the two of us scouted them out sometime back."

"That was foolishly done," Uncle Peter chastised.

"We took care," Elki told him calmly. Little flustered him.

"How many did you count?" Marcos asked.

"A dozen. I suspect there are more. The elders that can't cross to the marshes to hunt."

"They came in groups," Tate said. "A couple of them together that looked usual, then a few more of the same in singles. Then a mass of the others, the ones that are, well . . ." He trailed off.

"Wrong." Elki declared.

"A dozen plus more," Patrick said. He also had a determined sound to him.

"Guess work," Uncle Peter told them. "No, it's too dangerous."

"We've stood by while they've held half the island against us." Uncle John spoke fiercely. Deirdre couldn't remember the last time she'd heard her uncle so upset. "We've allowed them to kill our own. And now they've come into our village. How long until they come into our homes?"

"They know how to hurt us, even while wearing the wool oil." Lennox rarely spoke, so to hear him a second time showed how serious this was to him. "John says Trevor was wearing it. He's still dead."

"Derry, too." Tate added.

"They got Derry by the leg," Peter said quietly. "No protection there. He bled out."

"That could have been bad luck," her cousin, Aiden, said.

"It could have been planned." Uncle John stated. He was followed by silence.

"Are you suggesting they can reason?" Marcos finally asked.

Deirdre shivered. What if they could? Were they intelligent?

She hadn't gotten that sense when she'd faced the one. No, she'd gotten the sense of barely held madness, fury controlled by the thinnest thread of sanity. Can something so wrong reason?

"They've understood to stay on their side of the island," Uncle Peter answered. "They've kept to their own and only bothered us when we went across the river."

"That isn't true," Patrick challenged.

"We'd newly come to the island," Uncle Peter told him. "What happened to Shaw Monigal was a tragedy, but an accident."

"Like Derry was an accident?"

Like Father? Deirdre added silently.

"Derry was no accident." Uncle Ian's voice was stern. Deirdre had to keep herself from rising to look in so she could see what was happening when no one responded.

Patrick broke the long silence first. "We need to end this before anyone else is killed."

"We could all be killed trying," Uncle Peter said. "You might have forgotten, but I remember Father's stories of first coming here. How all the houses stood empty. How only sheep roamed the meadows."

"I've heard those stories, too," Uncle John said. "Even Thom Ballard would admit that no one knew what happened to those first-comers."

"But we've seen what the bears can do. We can guess what happened."

"Even more reason to hunt them and rid the island of them."

"John's right," Patrick agreed. "They've come across the river now. The wool oil didn't stop them. The truce, however it was gained, didn't stop them. How soon before they come again? What if they go after the women and children out in the fields?"

"We keep them closer to the village until we know it is safe," Uncle Peter argued.

"And who will mind the sheep and lambs? We only have so many hands to go around, and we need all of them this time of year."

Another silence.

Deirdre's gut sank. She knew what the vote was going to be, and she knew she couldn't stop it. If it had only been Uncle John to dissent, she might have had a chance. But with arguments like Patrick was making, how could she argue?

This was wrong. It was going to end in disaster and death.

"We can't be rash in this," Uncle Peter finally said.

"We can't afford to dilly dally over it, either," Patrick answered. "I'm sorry, Peter, but I have to agree with John. We've been cowering on this side of the island long enough."

"And what do you think is on the other side worth fighting for?"

"The fig grove for one. More trees for building. There could be meadows, too, where Grandfather Grahame and Manny couldn't see to draw their map. The point is, we don't know. We've let fear hold us back."

"Nothing wrong with a healthy dose of fear." The sound of Great Aunt Clary's voice shocked Deirdre. She was allowed to be present as one of the first born on the island, but why had she left the women's gathering to join the men? "Nothing wrong with keeping to our own lands," her great aunt continued. "We've plenty here to live on. More than enough. When's the last time you went hungry, Patrick Donaghue? When's the last time you went without a fire or planks? When have our animals ever starved? Or maybe you're planning on opening up the island to mainlanders—selling off parcels like the assemblies do inland."

"This has nothing to do with the mainland." Patrick sounded offended. "This is about us."

"Yes, it is. All of us. You, your wife, your children. The decision you make today will affect us all. There'll be no turning back from it."

Murmurs followed Great Aunt Clary's stark pronouncement. Deirdre forced her thoughts back to her confrontation with the bear. Why hadn't it attacked her? Why hadn't it attacked the others? Shawn had a musket, true, but how would the bear know what that was?

Something more was at work here. Had it something to do with Trevor? Were they only after him for killing one of their own? What would happen if the men went across the river to try to kill them all? Muskets only fired so fast, and they only had a couple on the island.

"We all know what's at risk," Uncle John said with an eerie calm. "We can talk about it for days or we can call a vote."

Deirdre hit the ground with her fists. Why was no one speaking everything she was thinking?

The decision came and forced her into action before she reconsidered. She stood and spoke through the open window.

"Why didn't the bear attack me?"

She couldn't see everyone inside in the shadows of the room, but she could feel their gaze fall upon her and feel the tension in the room change to anger.

"Deirdre—" Uncle John rumbled her name in warning.

"Trevor was covered in wool oil and stitching," she continued over her uncle's protest. "They still attacked him, but not me, and I barely had anything on to protect me. None of you did," she said, wishing she could find Marcos in the room. "They could have attacked us and killed us and been away before anyone knew otherwise, but they didn't. They only went after Trevor."

"We came at the bear as a group," Marcos said. "That was probably enough to scare it off."

"Then why didn't it run as soon as you came up?" she argued. "They've always known how to kill us, haven't they, if what you say about Derry is true. They could have gotten to us at any time. But they never had cause. Trevor shot one of them—"

"McClaren shot it!" Uncle John stormed into view. "Don't let him lead you astray with lies, Deirdre."

Deirdre stiffened at his suggestion that she was so easily swayed. "Shawn didn't shoot it. Trevor did. Shawn didn't argue against it because he felt responsible."

"That would make sense to me," Marcos said. "I've come to know something of the man, and it would be like him to take responsibility for the actions of the men he leads."

"It doesn't matter which one of them killed it," Uncle John said, but he sounded unhappy to be told it wasn't Shawn. "The bears crossed the river. They killed a man. That should be enough."

"They didn't hurt me." Deirdre repeated. "That has to mean something."

"It doesn't change the fact that we need to reclaim this island," Uncle John said.

"Reclaim? It was never ours to begin with." Great Aunt Clary reminded him sternly.

"It should be ours. Or do we have to wait for another person's child to be killed?"

"Derry was no child," Great Aunt Clary reminded them.

"But he was my brother." Uncle Ian spoke in a thick voice. "I won't let his death be bantered about like this."

Silence.

"That's two of our people they've killed," Patrick said quietly. "We can't let it be more."

"If we do this, it could very well be our death," Uncle Peter told them darkly.

Deirdre started. She didn't believe her great uncle was speaking of their deaths, but the island's death.

Why would the island die?

The secret of the bears. They'd been keeping it for five generations. It kept those who left the island from speaking of where they came from. It kept the ones still on the island from encouraging visitors. If the bears would gone, how long would it be before the island became just another piece of the mainland, ruled over, settled, changed from what it was to what the mainland would have it? It would be the end of their way of life.

"I call the vote," Uncle John said.

Uncle Peter let out a long sigh. "Very well."

"I vote that we remove the threat of these creatures from the island by whatever means necessary."

"The Guthrie family has voted for. Speaking for the Ballard family, I am against," Uncle Peter said. "How do the Fonsecas vote?"

Deirdre held her breath. Marcos had sounded as though he was arguing against it early on. Had that changed?

"For."

It had.

"McGregor?"

"Against." Uncle Ian said determinedly.

"Ian—" Patrick began, but Uncle Peter cut him off.

"The time for debate has passed. Smyth family?"

"Against," Lennox said.

"Lacour?"

The pause was long, and Deirdre had time to hope. Two for and three against.

"For," Elki finally answered. Deirdre sighed. The votes were going the way the women said they would. And since Uncle John had voted for…

There was only one family left, and Patrick had made his position clear.

"Donaghue."

"For."

"Against."

Patrick and Great Aunt Clary answered at the same time.

Great Aunt Clary could vote? Deirdre straightened, trying to see deeper into the room. Great Aunt Clary sat in her usual chair, glaring at where Patrick stood with his arms crossed. He glared back, though his surprise was evident.

"I'm the elder," Great Aunt Clary said harshly. "I have the vote."

"I'm the man of the family," Patrick argued. "The vote is mine."

Great Aunt Clary stood. "Man of the family?"

"Aunt Clary, you know how we all respect you, but that is the only reason you are allowed to attend these gatherings."

"Allowed?" Great Aunt Clary's voice shot up an octave.

"Patrick—" Uncle Peter said warningly.

Patrick didn't heed him. "It has always been the man of the family to hold the vote. Even Grandmother recognized that."

Deirdre waited for someone to argue against his claim. The villagers had all had a voice at the beginning. But no one spoke.

Deirdre wished she could go to her aunt. Her well-worn face had gone pale. She stared at Patrick, then looked around the room. No one spoke out in support of her, not even Uncle Peter, even when it was Great Aunt Clary's vote that would stop the madness. Deirdre wanted to scream at them all.

Slowly, her great aunt gathered her shawl around her shoulders.

"Come along, Deirdre."

Deirdre wanted to argue, but she didn't dare. Not now. Emotions warring inside of her, the tension of the room pressing at her even through the window, she backed away to join her great aunt at the front of the house.

Great Aunt Clary stood outside the house and looked up at the sky. The sun was high, lighting the island with warmth and the promise of new life. Nearby, Joseph was leaning on a tree, watchful, Ferny lipping at his boots. He straightened when he saw Deirdre, but she shook her head, warning him off. Ferny bounded over to her, bleating. She gathered him up into her arms.

"Let's go home, Deirdre," her great aunt said wearily.

Deirdre followed, aching for her great aunt with each step.

~*~

Shawn had wandered down the stream, still holding a couple of the bones, and into the woods separating this side of the village from the river. He knew he should take better care. If there bears had returned, he hadn't anything but his knife to defend himself. But he didn't think they'd return.

Something was off about all of this. He just wasn't sure what it was. He was an outsider, true, but in some ways, that might help him make sense of this.

Why had they killed Trevor and not hurt Deirdre? Why hadn't the bear attacked them all before Shawn had a musket? Why had it run when he hadn't fired? Had the appearance of so many men startled it? Why hadn't it run straight away?

As wrong as the inbred bear looked, perhaps it wasn't in its right mind, either.

Or, it was used to the sight of people.

Shawn stopped at the bank of the river where Trevor had died. There was still signs of where he had slipped into the water and then tried to get away from the bears.

Poor Trevor. Shawn hadn't always cared for the little man, and he hadn't always trusted him, but he'd been necessary for their escape, and Shawn was sorry Trevor wouldn't see his home again.

He didn't want to end that way. The need to get back to Philadelphia and his parents and sister was stronger than ever, even against the beauty and peace of the island. If only he knew his family was safe, he'd be tempted to remain, but if the war went in favor of the revolutionaries, he had no doubt that Tories like his parents wouldn't be safe.

Would they be imprisoned? What would become of his sister? Had she married? Would he protect her?

He sighed. No matter what the village families decided, Shawn knew he had to leave. He could draw away any militia seeking them and hope they wouldn't discover the island. And he hoped the men could figure out the mystery behind the bear attack. They were clever and had experience with the bears, generations of it. Shawn would only be in the way.

Decided, Shawn returned to the village to seek out Wallis. As he neared, he saw Deirdre and her great aunt leaving the Ballard House. He was tempted to follow, but stiff their bearing suggested that he wouldn't be made welcome.

He passed several of the younger men and boys leaving the Donaghue House. They studied him in curiosity but no one stopped to talk.

Wallis was standing with his back against one of the broad porch rails in front of the house, talking with Peter and Joseph.

"Shawn." Wallis smiled broadly. It felt like days since Shawn had last spoken to him, especially given the fact that they had been in constant company for so many months. He looked good, bathed, his beard trimmed, his bushy hair tamed back in a knot. His clothing fit, if straining across his broad shoulders. He had filled out, though not back to his old size.

Wallis' appraisal made Shawn realize that he must look normal again as well. He was clean, dressed in well-made clothing, his hair pulled back and his beard trimmed, too, though he still itched to be rid of it. He felt stronger, with three meals a day and plenty of rest in a sheltered and safe bed.

They clasped hands. "How's the ankle?" Shawn asked.

"On the mend." Wallis flexed it, then winced.

"If Mother catches you doing that," Joseph warned, "you'll get a talking to."

"Heaven forbid that should happen." Wallis chuckled. "Your mother hasn't a sharp part in her, but that makes it worse. I never thought a talking down with a gentle voice could be so humiliating."

Peter laughed. "It's hard not to feel guilty for disappointing Daisy."

"And Mother well knows it," Joseph grumbled.

"I've been hoping you'd come by," Peter told Shawn. "I wanted to assure you that no one holds you to blame for what happened. It is a great misfortune what happened to your friend."

Shawn nodded, reserved. Wallis looked from Peter to Shawn, confused, but he kept quiet, following Shawn's lead.

"Thank you for that. Has anything like that happened before?"

"Once or twice." Peter studied him far too knowingly. "What have you heard?"

"Stories. Derry and Shaw, mostly."

"Unfortunate deaths. I wish they could have been avoided."

"They couldn't?" Wallis asked. Apparently he had heard the stories, too.

Peter shook his head. "When Shaw and his wife, and my father and Joseph's grandparents first arrived on the island, they had no idea the bears were here. There was no chance to protect themselves from what they couldn't know."

"And Derry?"

"He took a risk, and it ended in tragedy."

"And no one since then?"

"Not until your companion."

Shawn hesitated. "Deirdre spoke of her father's accident."

Peter studied him again. "Yes."

"There was no sign it might have been the bears?"

"Not that was found."

"Why?" Joseph asked insistently. "Why is a past death of one of our own any interest to you?"

Shawn said the first thing that came to mind. "I've come to admire Deirdre and am sorry for her losses. It cannot have been easy for her."

"No, it wasn't," Peter agreed. "But she's well-loved and her uncle and great aunt have done well by her."

"Of course." Shawn decided he'd pushed his luck, so he changed the subject. "I'm hoping I might beg a favor."

Peter nodded.

"I'd like to return to the mainland as soon as possible. As much as I thank you for your welcome and hospitality, I'm eager to return to my family."

Peter's expression smoothed. "Of course. No doubt they miss you."

"His mother's probably knit him a bushel of socks and his sister's already got the wedding clothes made." Wallis chuckled.

Shawn could have punched him, especially given the daggers Joseph was shooting him with his gaze.

"Wedding clothes." Peter's tone was too calm. "May I offer congratulations?"

"Oh, no, not my wedding," Shawn told him hastily. "My sister's. She was affianced a few months back." Or had it been longer? He couldn't recall when he'd gotten the last letter from home.

"Ah."

"I'm not married," Shawn continued.

Peter brightened and Joseph relaxed. "You are hoping we can help you to the mainland?"

"Yes. Though we have a boat."

"A stolen boat," Wallis added. Shawn winced.

"I'd like to see it returned," he assured Peter.

"I see." Peter considered. "I'll talk with a few of the others but—"

"I can help you," Joseph spoke too eagerly, causing Shawn to wonder if Deirdre's cousin had noticed his attention to her.

"I'd welcome it."

That decided, Shawn looked to Wallis, but before he could say anything, Peter spoke again.

"The decision has been made to hunt the bears," he said. Wallis started, but Joseph didn't look surprised. "We're planning to use traps, but I was hoping we might have use of your musket. Ours are older."

"Ours are ancient," Joseph amended grimly.

Shawn hesitated, and it didn't go unnoticed.

"We'd return it to you, of course," Peter said.

"We'll help you," Wallis said, determined. When Shawn stared at him, Wallis frowned. "Those bears are a menace. We owe it to Trevor."

"To take revenge on bears?"

"No, to defend this village and its people."

Shawn regretted his hasty words. "Of course." He turned to Peter. "When is the hunt taking place?"

"We're still making plans, but in the next few days."

Shawn nodded. "Then you can count on my help."

Peter clapped him on the shoulder. "Good man. We could use someone with more experience with a musket. We rarely have call to use them."

Shawn didn't answer. He didn't care how he'd gotten his experience with a musket.

"Perhaps we can look them over," Wallis suggested. "Make sure they are in good repair."

"We keep them in shape," Joseph challenged.

"Surely so, but I've seen what a misfire can do to a man," Wallis said grimly. "I'd hate to think that I didn't take the precaution to check the weapons when I could."

Joseph couldn't argue with that.

"Ian has his father's musket," Peter said, "and Marcos has Grahame's old one. I have my father's. I'll see them brought to you along with the ammunition and matches."

"Match locks, huh." Wallis looked up a moment, and Shawn had the feeling he was saying a small prayer. Match locks weren't the safest weapons.

"You've experience with them?" Peter asked. He looked amused.

"Unfortunately."

Peter chuckled. "I'll leave you to it, then. Joseph will get the muskets for you."

The two men, one older, one younger, left them.

Wallis drooped. "Thank God." He limped up to the porch and fell heavily into one of the chairs, wincing.

Shawn laughed. "You've nothing to prove, Wallis."

"So you say." Wallis actually pouted. "I don't like to look weak."

"No one in their right minds would take you as weak. Even hobbling about, it's clear you could strangle them with one arm."

Wallis grinned. "True. I'd only have to catch them." He paused, sobering. "You're going with them on this hunt?"

Shawn nodded.

"Why? What I mean is I know why I want to, but why you? I thought you wanted to leave as quick as you could."

"I do, but I can't leave when they're in need."

"And without the musket."

"They can keep the musket."

Wallis stared at him, but Shawn only shrugged. "It will only bring attention to me. And I'd rather control when I draw attention."

"You're planning to draw the militia after you."

"It's the best way to keep them from the island."

"And if it doesn't work?"

"Then they'll come here, find us gone and only a village of simple shepherds and leave."

Wallis was silent for too long.

"You don't want to leave," Shawn guessed.

Wallis shook his head. "No, I don't."

"Who?"

Wallis didn't deny it. He actually blushed. "Her name is Hetty. She's Bernado's daughter. Marcos' niece," Wallis added.

Shawn remembered her from the women's gathering, the one who shocked everyone by speaking out on their behalf. The quips about her visits to the Donaghue House now made sense.

"Do you have an understanding between you?" Shawn asked.

"Not yet." But there was no doubt that Wallis was hoping there would be one and soon.

Shawn shook his head, but he smiled. "Then I've even more reason to draw the militia away.

Wallis stood to clapped Shawn on the shoulder, making him stagger a step. "Maybe if I get my courage worked up to talk to her father, you can stay for the wedding."

Shawn would like nothing more, but he doubted it would happen that fast, so he remained silent.

"I want to go with you," Wallis told Shawn. "On the hunt."

"You should stay here." He glanced at Wallis' ankle.

Wallis stood on it a moment, then had to sit down when the pain struck him. "I don't like feeling useless."

"You'll be here to protect the women and children."

"From the mad charge of angry bears?" Shawn could tell from Wallis' tone that he thought that unlikely.

"They believe it might happen."

"Then why hunt them?"

"They must think it worth the risk to end the threat."

"Do they even know how to hunt animals like that?"

Shawn didn't answer because he didn't know.

"Well, at least you can learn their plan and help them come up with a smarter one," Wallis said. "What with all your experience." He didn't speak wryly. He knew how Shawn had spent most of his summers.

"We never hunted to wipe out an entire pack," Shawn told him.

"No, but you were never trapped on an island with mad bears."

"Not all of them are."

"But if they keep breeding like they are, they will be."

Shawn couldn't disagree.

"McClaren." Patrick approached carrying two muskets and a shot bag. "Peter asked me to bring these." He didn't look happy about it.

Shawn couldn't help but stare at the old matchlock Patrick held out. He'd noticed it earlier at Marcos' house but thought it just a sentimental piece, not a weapon anyone would actually try to use.

"You haven't tried to fire that, have you?"

Patrick looked offended. "This was my grandfather's. He took excellent care of it, and so have we."

"Do you have any matches for it?"

"One or two."

"How old are they?"

Patrick hesitated.

"I don't mean to speak out of turn against your grandfather or you, but that weapon must be, what? Eighty or ninety years old? And it's spent the last sixty of those on an island with salt air and wet weather."

"It'll fire."

"When was the last time it was fired?"

Patrick was silent.

"We'll look it over, but my guess is that if you do decide to use it, stand well clear of anyone else."

Shawn had most likely crossed a line, but he wasn't going to let the man die from a weakened barrel because he stayed silent from politeness.

Patrick looked as though he wanted to lay in to Shawn, but he restrained himself with a control Shawn hadn't expected. "You have more experience with them," he told Shawn begrudgingly. "Peter says you'll look it over and let us know if they're safe to use."

"We will," Wallis said. "And I'm the one who's used matchlocks before." He looked pointedly at Shawn. "Mr. McClaren would never soil his fine hands with such a lowly weapon."

Shawn glared at him. "I've fired a matchlock."

"Uh huh."

"My uncle had one."

"Yeah, and that was how old?"

Shawn didn't answer.

Patrick actually chuckled. "Can I stay and see how you handle it?" he asked Wallis.

"Sure. Let's take it somewhere we won't get Daisy's porch dirty."

"That's probably a good idea."

"I'll leave you to it," Shawn said, repeating Peter's earlier words.

Wallis nodded to him, and Patrick cast him a look, but neither said anything.

Shawn wandered away from the Donaghue House, feeling at loose ends. He passed Joseph carrying two more muskets, both looking as old as Patrick's, and tried not to wince. This bear hunt was going to go very poorly with only one good musket to use. And that was only if the powder on the island was still good. They had a little powder left from what they'd brought with them.

If the matchlocks didn't work, would hunting the bears do any good? Shawn could load fast, but fast enough should a bear charge?

No. Not that fast.

He wondered if the bears climbed trees. Maybe it would be best to hide themselves and lure the bears in to traps, then fire from on high.

Strategies. It came to him as naturally as breathing. The plans, the hunt, the challenge when it went wrong. He was used to these things, but he usually knew the men with him. Or battling with. He had no idea what to expect from the villagers, not their skill or their resolve. And that was more terrifying than facing a bear charge.

But he couldn't do anything until he knew the plan. Hopefully, that would come soon, because every hour Shawn spent on the island was another hour that tried to convince him not to leave. Especially if that time was spent with Deirdre.

~*~

Deirdre was so angry with Patrick she could spit nails. How dare he talk to Great Aunt Clary that way? He didn't have near her experience on the island. He always treated her great aunt, his own aunt, like she was daft and only to be tolerated.

No more.

Deirdre stomped down the lane towards Marcos' house. She knocked harder than she'd meant to, her ire giving her strength.

Only to find no one home.

Deirdre opened the door and peeked in. "Rosa?"

No answer.

Now what was she supposed to do? It was hard to confront someone if you had to go searching for him first.

Annoyed, Deirdre left the house only to see Patrick crossing toward it. He stopped when he saw her.

Deirdre fisted her hands and stomped over to him.

"What do you have to say for yourself?" she demanded, standing nearly toe to toe with him.

He looked down at her. She saw a flitter of guilt cross his face, but then it disappeared.

"I did what I did for the sake of the village."

"You did what you did to put Great Aunt Clary in her place."

Patrick's jaw moved, but he didn't answer.

"You—" Deirdre jabbed her finger into his chest. He winced. "You think that since you are the eldest man with the Donaghue name that you can speak for us without bothering to consult with us."

"If there was another man to consult with who was of age, I would."

"Nonsense." Deirdre chewed the word out. Patrick blinked at her vehemence. "Daniel is plenty old enough, he just doesn't speak because he doesn't want to gainsay his elder brother."

"That's his choice."

"You bully him when he does speak."

"Deirdre—"

"And that whole foolishness of having to be of age. Joseph is plenty old enough to meet with the families."

"He's only nineteen—"

"And you've only got six years on him. And Daniel only three."

"He isn't twenty, and that's the rule."

"It's a stupid rule. He's old enough to take a wife, he's old enough to speak."

Patrick blinked again and took a step back. "Joseph's courting?"

"That's nothing to do with this." She jabbed her finger in his chest again. "You humiliated Great Aunt Clary. You had no right."

"I'm head of the family—"

"You're the eldest man with the name, but you aren't the eldest Donaghue. That would be Conor."

Patrick looked shocked. "Conor is a Ballard."

"No, Conor's last name is Ballard. His mother was a Donaghue."

Patrick looked as though he'd never considered that.

Deirdre crossed her arms. "We should all have a voice. It's our island, too, not just the eldest of the families."

"This is the way it's been—"

"No it hasn't. It's only become so because our numbers have grown. I heard the stories."

"What stories?"

Deirdre rolled her eyes. "Truly, Patrick, if you'd bothered to listen to Great Grandmother, or even to Miss Lizzie or Uncle Ian or anyone not a "Donaghue" on this island, you'd learn something."

"I listen," Patrick shouted, his own anger coming out. "I don't need a snip of a girl telling me that I don't. Especially a snip of a Guthrie girl." His lips curled when he said the name.

It was Deirdre who stepped back this time, eyes wide and mouth agape. "What did you just say?"

Patrick looked uncertain, then he straightened with resolve. "You heard me. The Guthries have always been a problem on the island. If Hattie Ballard had been smart and married Derry—"

"You leave my grandmother and uncle out of this." Deirdre stared at him, still in shock. "How dare you?" she repeated. "How dare you say anything against my family? The Guthries have every right to be on this island, same as you. Or do you forget that your mother didn't start here?"

"I don't need a history lesson from you," Patrick growled.

"You need one from someone." Deirdre drew herself up, even though she barely reached Patrick's nose. "You need to remember that I'm the only one on this island related to every family that settled here. Me." She pointed at her own chest. "Donaghue, Ballard, and McGregor. If anything, I should have a say in all the family gatherings, and I should have three of the votes."

"That's the most foolish thing I've heard you say yet."

"No more foolish than dismissing Great Aunt Clary simply because she's a woman." Deirdre shook her head. "I hope you can explain yourself to Rosa."

"What's that supposed to mean?"

"Rosa has some strong thoughts on what goes on around here, and I suspect you and she discuss them. How often do you vote against what she'd want? How often are you dismissing her ideas because she's only a woman?"

Patrick didn't answer. He glanced at the house, his jaw working back and forth.

"The men are not the only ones on this island," Deirdre reminded him quietly. "And all of us have earned our right to be here, and to have a say."

Satisfied she'd spoken her mind, though she wanted nothing more than to smack Patrick upside the head, she stalked off without another word. Patrick didn't try to stop her.

As she walked away, she saw Uncle John standing in the shadows of the house she shared with Great Aunt Clary. His arms were crossed and his expression was hard.

How much had he heard?

Deirdre turned toward him, but he moved back and walked toward the river. She sighed.

Patrick might have started something he'd not want to finish.

She had something to finish, too, so she left off returning home and walked toward the McGregor House and Uncle Ian.

She ran into Shawn along the way. He stopped before he reached her, and she stopped too.

And awkward silence spread between them.

Then both spoke at the same time.

"I apologize for what I said about your father—"

"I'm sorry I walked away like that—"

They both fell silent. And then laughed.

"Please," Shawn said, gesturing to her. "You first."

"Oh, no, Shawn McClaren. I get to hear you apologize first."

He grinned. He truly had a wonderful grin. It lit up his stormy gray eyes and showed off his firm lips. That beard, though. It had to go.

Too bad he hadn't been here for the early shearing. All the men on the island shaved. She smiled to think of Shawn a part of that ritual.

She chided herself. He wasn't staying. It bothered her more than she wanted to let on.

"I apologize," Shawn said solemnly. "It truly isn't any of my business concerning your village."

Deirdre stepped up to him. "Except you're here now. For a little while, at least."

"Still—"

"What did you find about the bones?" she interrupted, not wanting to hear him talk of leaving.

Shawn shook his head. "Nothing. Are you sure no one uses that area?"

"Not that I've heard." Though, given the conversation she'd just had with her cousin, it could be she just didn't know about it. "I was on my way to speak with my Uncle Ian. Would you join me?"

"Do you want me to?"

She put one fist on her hip. "I wouldn't ask if I didn't."

He smiled again. "Then, please, lead on." He swept his hand before her in such a well-practiced and elegant motion that it reminded her of how different a world he came from.

She led the way to the McGregor House. It was one of the older ones on the island, though not as old as the house she shared with her great aunt, which was original to the island. And the one that Shaw Monigal had passed away in, which is why they called it the Shaw House. It was the only trace of the name on the island since Marjorie had remarried and had lived and raised her family in the McGregor House.

Deirdre explained this as they walked. Shawn listened attentively. He truly seemed interested in the history of the island. Not everyone did, but she did. She couldn't help it. She was connect to the entire beginning by blood.

Uncle Ian was home, and he was alone. Aunt Caitlyn and Deirdre's cousin, Grace, must still be out with Grace's children, and Aiden must be out with the younger men. He and Patrick were close. Maybe Patrick was even now venting his ire to him.

"Uncle Ian is James and Marjorie's son," Deirdre told Shawn as Ian came to the door. "And they were my great great grandparents."

"Which technically makes me your great uncle," Ian said as he opened the door. He looked tired, but he offered them a smile.

"Only Great Aunt Clary insists I say that, though." Deirdre stepped up and placed a kiss on his cheek. "You know Shawn

McClaren?"

"Oh, yes, we've met." Uncle Ian and Shawn shook hands. "Come in. Though I fear you'll find only me at home."

"That's handy," Deirdre told him, "since you're the one we've come to see."

Uncle Ian looked curious, but he said nothing as he led them into the house. It wasn't large, only three rooms, but it was well appointed. James McGregor had been a woodworker and much of the furnishings on the island came from his hands. He believed that even a lowly chair should withstand time, children, and dogs.

"Tea?" Uncle Ian asked.

"I'll get it." Deirdre went to the kitchen and put the kettle over the banked coals, stirring them up.

They sat and Uncle Ian looked expectantly at Deirdre.

"Will you tell us about Uncle Derry?"

He sat back, clearly taken unawares by her question.

"It's an old story, Deirdre, and one you've likely heard."

"I've heard a few versions," she said carefully. "I'd like to hear yours."

Uncle Ian rubbed at his jaw. He had a scar along the right side from where a ram had caught him by surprise. It had happened when he was a boy. It was strange, Deirdre thought, how much she knew about everyone on the island. Even childhood stories decades old. Uncle Ian was over fifty, and she knew a few stories from when he was younger than her, including how he came to meet Aunt Caitlyn. The fiery Irishwoman had turned the island on its ears after she'd arrived, but Deirdre couldn't imagine the place without her.

Did Shawn know such stories from his family? Did they share those things on the mainland?

"My brother was impulsive," Uncle Ian began. He closed his eyes and steepled his hands. "And curious. And he didn't take well to being told what not to do. But he felt deeply and cared even deeper." Uncle Ian sighed. "He was in love with your grandmother, Hattie."

Deirdre nodded, though he couldn't see it.

"She cared for him, too, but not in the same way, and I think he pursued her too strongly and scared her off. She was a shy thing, your grandmother." He smiled and opened his eyes. "Sweet and gentle."

"How did she meet my grandfather?"

"You don't know?"

Deirdre shook her head. "Just that it was in Norfolk and that my grandfather fell in love with her the moment he saw her."

Ian's face went flat. "That's the story."

His tone told her he didn't believe it. "What aren't you saying?"

Ian sighed. "Deirdre, these things are long buried with our dead. Are you sure you want to dig up the past?"

"Yes." The certainty in her voice startled even her. Shawn was watching her, and she wondered what was going through his mind.

Uncle Ian must have as well, for he looked to their island guest. "And you? What's your involvement?"

"Deirdre asked me to come," Shawn began, then he stopped. He took a deep breath. "There's something no one's saying, or something hidden under what's being said. I don't know its importance, and I know I have no right to pry, but I can't help but notice it."

Uncle Ian nodded, apparently satisfied. He sat forward.

"After Alistaire came to the island with Hattie to wed, Derry was hurt, of course. He took an instant dislike to the man, too, which everyone figured was because Hattie was marrying him and not Derry. But Derry was certain there was something in the man's past that had driven him to marry Hattie. He didn't believe Alistaire was in love with her but using her to come here."

Deirdre couldn't help but to look at Shawn, but he was watching Uncle Ian.

"A couple years after your mother was born," Uncle Ian said to Deirdre, "your grandmother grew ill. Something in her guts twisted and went bad. There was nothing anyone could do, and she wouldn't leave the island to go to a doctor on the mainland, not that anyone believed one could help her. There was a rumor, though, that before she fell ill, she had bruises. Derry thought Alistaire had struck her."

Deirdre sat upright, stunned. "He wouldn't."

Uncle Ian didn't argue. "Derry was certain of it and held Alistaire responsible for Hattie's death. No one else spoke of it, though, but I heard rumors now and then from the womenfolk that it wouldn't have been the first time Hattie had bruises. She always claimed to be clumsy. I never saw it, myself."

"Why didn't anyone do anything?" Shawn asked. "If it was true."

Deirdre wanted to thank him for asking, because she couldn't find her voice.

"Alistaire was well-liked. And Hattie never complained. What could be said or done?"

Shawn looked down at his boots, nodding.

"Derry, though, never let it go. Alistaire's temper came out more after Hattie's, though never toward his children, and whenever he spoke of Hattie, it was with sorrow and loss. He visited her grave every day, no matter the weather. Everyone saw it as signs of his love. Derry saw it as signs of his guilt."

"What did he do?" Deirdre finally found her voice. She'd heard the stories of her grandfather's devotion to his dead wife and had always thought it touching and a sign of their love. Now, she was beginning to doubt, and she hated herself for it.

"Derry started making the trips to Norfolk. Only a few times a year, mind, with so much to be done on the island, but anytime there was need, Derry would go. He'd stay with one of the family in town. I asked him why he needed to be the one to go each time, hoping he'd admit to courting a woman, but he told me he was looking for proof."

"Proof of what?"

"Of Alistaire's guilt."

"But Grandmother died on the island." Deirdre was confused.

"Derry was certain that hadn't been the first time Alistaire had caused someone's death. Not at first," Uncle Ian said, holding up a hand to stop Deirdre's protests. "He started by only asking a few questions here and there, seeing what he could learn of Alistaire's past. He always regretted not doing so before Alistaire and Hattie had married, so he made it his duty to do it after her death. Slowly, he made discoveries."

"What?" Deirdre was on the edge of her seat.

"That's the thing," Uncle Ian said. "He only told me that he nearly had found what he needed to prove how dangerous Alistaire was. Before he could do anything more, he was killed by the bears."

Uncle Ian's voice had gone flat again.

Shawn looked up. "That's curious timing."

"My thoughts, too."

The room fell silent. Deirdre was the first to break it.

"You think my grandfather had something to do with my uncle's death." She didn't ask it. She could see on Uncle Ian's face what he thought. She recalled all his reservations in dealing with her Uncle John, how he kept himself apart, sometimes even from her.

"I think it possible."

"Why?" Shawn asked.

Uncle Ian sighed and tipped his head back against the chair. "Derry was impulsive, yes, but he was cautious. There was no reason for him to cross the river. Oh, he spoke about learning more about the bears and why they were the way they were. He used to watch them, out by the marsh, much like Elki and Tate and Lennox did. Counting them, keeping track of the ones born wrong. He didn't believe the stories of fae creatures come to torment us. I don't believe there's many that do, anymore. Father didn't. I think that's where it started. Bess didn't either, not really, but she wouldn't speak out because—"

"She was grateful to come to the island," Deirdre finished. "Briony said that Grandfather Thom didn't believe it, either."

"Really?" Uncle Ian considered the information. "I suppose I could see that. Thom was always the practical sort. But he'd hardly go against Grahame."

Deirdre and Shawn exchanged looks. Those stories were the same, at least.

"But no one said anything about Derry's death?" Shawn asked.

"They said he was impulsive and too curious. They said it was a terrible accident and showed again how dangerous the bears were." Uncle Ian rubbed his hands across his face. "They made him an example of why not to cross the river." He sounded bitter.

This was all such news to Deirdre. She knew people on the island didn't always get along, but she'd never heard such bitterness, except when Uncle John spoke about what had happened to her mother. And that she'd always thought was from grief, not true hatred. Now she wasn't so sure.

"Do you think the bears should be hunted?" Shawn asked him.

"I don't know," Uncle Ian admitted. "It is concerning that they crossed the river. They haven't done that in generations. But to hunt them out? I can't see how we can."

Shawn nodded. He looked to Deirdre. "Tell him about the bones."

Deirdre did so, explaining how she found the wallow and the bones. Uncle Ian was surprised.

"I've never heard of such a thing."

"And there was another thing," Deirdre said, recalling something that had bothered her since the bear attack. "Trevor had the wool oil all over him, but it didn't smell right."

"Had it gone rancid?"

She consider. "No, it wasn't that. I know what that smells like. It was something else. Something sickly. Was he ill?" she asked Shawn.

"Not to my knowledge. None of us were in the best of health, but I never saw signs of illness."

They all fell silent again. Deirdre heard the kettle, realizing she'd left it over the coals. She wasn't in the mood for tea, though. Not anymore. But she poured her uncle a mug and brought it to him.

"Thank you." He caught her hand before she could draw it away. "Deirdre, I know we've never been close. I am sorry for it. I've watched you grow into a fine young woman, and I think John has done right by you in his sister's name. She charged him with it, you know."

"What?" This was the first she'd heard of it.

"She was the last of his family. Your grandfather had died after she wed your father. She told John to take care of you because she was his family now. John took it to heart."

So much became clearer. Her uncle's protectiveness and care when he was normally so guarded. His attention to her learning and her health.

She frowned. "Am I why he never married?" Guilt gnawed at her.

Uncle Ian nodded without answering.

Deirdre clutched his hand as though it were her only tie to shore. How much had Uncle John sacrificed for her? His sister, his own future, his happiness. Children.

"Deirdre," Uncle Ian said gently, "John made his own choices. Don't you carry those burdens. They aren't yours."

Deirdre nodded, but absently.

The front door open and Caitlyn came in, followed by Grace and her three children.

"I should check in with Wallis," Shawn said, standing.

"Did he get Father's musket?"

"He did." Shawn smiled.

Uncle Ian chuckled. "Good luck with it." He squeezed Deirdre's hand. "Don't dwell on the past, Deirdre," he told her quietly.

"Enough of us do that, and nothing can be changed. Live your life now and look ahead."

She leaned down and kissed his cheek once more. "Thank you."

He patted her hand. "You have any need, any at all, you come see me. Derry would kick my backside if he thought I'd left you wanting." He smiled fondly. "He loved your mother as though she were his own child."

Deirdre's chest tightened and her eyes filled. She kissed his cheek again, said her farewells to a confused Caitlyn and Grace, and followed Shawn out of the house.

She stopped several feet away, her mind a swirl of thoughts and her body a twist of emotions.

Shawn touched her arm. "Will you be all right?"

"No." She looked at Shawn. "If this past is different than I've heard, what else is?"

"Deirdre—"

"I should go see to my great aunt."

"Of course." He squeezes her arm, and she offered him a weak smile.

"Thank you."

He cocked his head. "For what?"

"For being there." She couldn't explain further than that. With another attempt at a smile, she left him to return home, trying to think about her tasks for the coming evening. But all she could think was, what if Father didn't die of an accident?

CHAPTER SIX

Monday, June 3rd

The men were meeting again. Deirdre paced in front of Shaw House, crocheting as she did, pulling the wool from the ball in her apron pocket. Ferny had tried to follow her pacing but eventually gave up and was lying spread out on his side in the sunlight, napping as only lambs can nap, peaceful and playful at the same time, with twitching little legs and the occasional flap of his black tail and ears.

Deirdre knew the men were planning the bear hunt. She knew Shawn and Wallis were also there in the thick of it.

She hadn't rested easy since her conversation with Uncle Ian. She hadn't brought it up to her great aunt, though she lost count of the times that Great Aunt Clary nagged to know what was ailing her.

"Best not be pining for that Shawn McClaren," her great aunt warned. "He's leaving for parts unknown."

Deirdre had only nodded and returned to kneading bread.

Bread she'd barely touched once it was baked. She hadn't eaten much of her dinner the night before or breakfast that morning, picking at it until her great aunt chased her off to some chore. She hadn't slept well, either, plagued by questions.

What had happened to Derry? Had he been killed? Who would do that? Surely not her grandfather Alistaire. What could have he left behind on the mainland that he wouldn't want known? Did Uncle John know anything about it?

And her father, had it been an accident? If she believed her grandfather capable of killing once, he might have done so again, but he was long buried on the hill by the time of her father's death. It had to have been an accident.

It had to have been.

But she couldn't stop thinking about how her father had drown, and how Trevor had drowned, too.

It wasn't the same, of course it wasn't. The bears had gotten Trevor, and her father had lost his balance standing in the boat and tipped and hit his head. He'd landed face down in the water, unconscious. That was the belief, but no one had actually been there. They had searched for signs of the bears, but wouldn't the bears have done something to his body if it had been them?

Deirdre stopped mid-stride when she saw Marcos and Patrick walking to their house. Patrick did not look her way, and Marcos was deep in conversation with him.

She waited, hoping for some sign of Shawn, but there was none. Discouraged, she returned to the house.

Great Aunt Clary was seated in her chair under the window, sewing Deirdre a new shirt. She didn't look up. "Finished, have they?"

Deirdre sank into her chair, holding her crochet close to her. She'd started on a pair of spatterdashes for Joseph, something new to wear when he next went to Norfolk. He'd mentioned meeting a young woman the last time he'd gone, and he'd spoken with such admiration that Deirdre was hopeful he'd return and perhaps court the woman. He'd also mentioned the fancy leggings the men on the mainland wore above their shoes, sometimes lacy, sometimes plain. Joseph never spoke of fashion, which meant he was thinking instead of impressing the young woman. Deirdre had decided to help him by making him a pair, and she'd chosen on a practical stitch in a gray, sturdily-plied wool.

She didn't have the focus for it now that the meeting was over, so she set it in her work basket. And thinking of the mainland just made her ache.

"What do you think they've decided?" Deirdre asked her great aunt.

"A beetle-headed plan that'll get one of them hurt, no doubt." Her great aunt's disapproval was heavily laced with worry.

"Isn't there anyway to convince them against it?"

Great Aunt Clary finally looked up. "I expect the women who wished to have tried, but these men, once they get it rooted in their heads, are a stubborn sort. And when it comes to protecting the families, it's even more true."

"Do you think we should hunt them?" Deirdre had heard her great aunt speak her opinion at the meeting yesterday, but she could have changed her mind.

Great Aunt Clary set her stitching aside. "Child, we've lived over sixty years on this island with hardly a problem. I know," she said, holding up a hand even though Deirdre wasn't going to interrupt, "we've lost. But two losses in sixty years to the bears, when we've had more to illness and accident? The risk isn't worth it."

"But this time—"

"This time was odd," her great aunt admitted. "I've no reasoning for it. But do I think it's a sign of more to come? No."

"Why?"

"Think on what happened. Strangers come to the island—" she ticked it off on her fingers as she went, "—they shoot one of the bears, they come to this side with us, the bears find one and he's killed."

"You make it sound like the bears are intelligent."

"They've kept to their side, haven't they? Mother set the truce and they've abided it."

"What if it's because they don't need anything over here," Deirdre pressed. "The fig grove is across the river. The hogs run wild mostly on that side. They've plenty of space."

Great Aunt Clary was staring at her.

"They've had no reason to cross the river," Deirdre pressed. Her belief grew as she spoke. "They're only animals with enough sense not to work harder for food they already have. That's why they stay on their side. Not because of any truce."

Her great aunt shook her head. "This is what comes of young people always questioning. Derry was like that, too."

Deirdre stood, suddenly angry. "Everyone should stop using him as an example!"

She stomped from the house, leaving her great aunt gaping after her. She ended up on the bank of the river before she realized where her feet were taking her.

She felt terrible. She hadn't meant to lash out. Great Aunt Clary was only trying to keep her safe. But she'd taken Uncle Ian's feelings to heart, and after hearing more about her Uncle Derry, she agreed that he was much more than a caution tale. He had been a living, loving man who had lost the woman he'd loved but still tried to protect her and her daughter. Deirdre wished she had known him, but he'd died two years before she was born.

"Deirdre?"

Shawn's voice reached her. She turned to see him approaching, his expression at first one of caution, and then concern.

"What's wrong?" He came to her and reached for her hand. She let him take it, but only then did she realize she was weeping.

"I don't know." She tried to stop her tears, but it was as if his appearance made it safe for her to let go, so she did.

Shawn drew her to him, and she laid her head against his shoulder and wept for reasons she couldn't begin to understand. Too many thoughts and feelings were clashing together inside of her, challenging everything she thought she knew of her past and everything she imagined of her future.

When she finally calmed, she could feel Shawn rubbing his hand up and down her back in comfort. The sensation rooted her back into the present. Deirdre kept her head resting on his shoulder. Her arms had gone around his waist at some point, and his around hers, pressing her to him. His breath stirred her hair, and she found herself breathing when he did. It was an experience unlike anything she'd ever had, and it felt right and good. She could lose herself to this man.

Deirdre pulled away, her arms slipped from around his waist, shocked by the depth of her emotions. She'd only known the man for a week. Less than a week. How could she have come to feel so much so quickly?

Was her Uncle John right? Was Shawn somehow manipulating her?

She looked up in his stormy gray eyes and saw the same surprise and confusion.

No. He was feeling it to.

He ran his large, calloused hands up and down her arms as though she needed more comfort. Or maybe he needed it. She liked the idea that he might get the same feelings from her.

When he started to pull his hands away, she caught one. It was so unusual, a man's hands. Large with flat fingers and a broad palm. She ran her finger along it and felt scars.

"Where did you get these?"

"Musket fire."

Startled, she met his gaze.

He smiled and grasped her hand in his. "The muskets can spark when they fire. If it's a big enough spark, it burns."

That sounded awful. "Then why shoot one?"

Shawn sobered, and she saw a deep-set darkness close his gaze. "Sometimes, there's no choice." His voice was hushed and thick with regret.

She wanted to pull him to her and hold him, but that time had passed.

"What did the men decide about the hunt?" she asked. It seemed a safe enough topic, and she wanted to know. But she didn't pull her hand away. And he didn't let it go.

"They plan to lay traps around the grove, then try to lure the bears in by moving through the forests along the edge of the grove, carrying freshly butchered hog meat."

"What?" She was shocked.

Shawn nodded, looking grim.

"That's foolish and careless. Tell me you argued against it?"

"I did. Wallis, too. And Peter wasn't happy with it."

"What did Elki say?"

"That it might work against normal bears."

"These aren't normal bears."

"He said that, too."

"No one had a better plan?" Deirdre asked. "Not even you?"

"I wish I could have offered more," he admitted. "I just don't know the territory. There's too much no one knows, like where they hunt, where they sleep, how many there are."

"Elki said he counted a dozen."

"That's what they could count. It could be that not all of them were there. And we don't know where they are concentrated, or if they move as a group or individually."

"Wallis couldn't help?"

"Wallis isn't much for strategy. But he pointed out several flaws. Like hiding in a grove of trees that don't grow taller than a cabin. And getting into position without being noticed. But the others seem to think the bears aren't about in the early morning hours."

"Not typically," Great Aunt Clary said as she approached. Deirdre hadn't heard her. "But there's nothing typical about any of this."

Deirdre and Shawn parted quickly, taking a step away from one another. If Great Aunt Clary had noticed how close they'd been standing, she didn't comment on it.

Ferny trotted over to lip at Shawn's boot. He smiled and reached down the pat the lamb.

For some reason, that made Deirdre's heart swell.

"You think they'll be watching the grove?" Deirdre asked him to distract herself. She wasn't sure she believed they would do such a thing anymore.

"Wouldn't you?" Great Aunt Clary said. "Especially as the figs get closer to ripening."

"Peter and Marcos will remain behind, along with Wallis and the younger boys," Shawn told them after a moment of silence. "But Joseph and anyone older are going. They will take the fishing nets, and Elki will set heavy snares while the others get into position."

"Good God." Deirdre paled.

"They're collecting all the wool oil that's been processed," Shawn continued. "They're going to dip all the shot and arrow heads into it, and Elki is making a few spears tonight."

"What are you going to do?" Deirdre asked a little too quickly. Shawn studied her as if trying to read into the simple question.

"Help as I can." His answer was a little too innocent. Deirdre studied him in turn, but he kept his thoughts masked.

"Is there anything we can do?" she asked.

"Deirdre, you can't say you agree with all this?" Great Aunt Clary chastised.

"No, but seeing as they aren't bothering to ask us, we might as well try to be of some help."

Great Aunt Clary turned her back on both of them, her shoulders stiff and her arms crossed. "Foolishness."

"I don't disagree with you," Shawn told her. "Marcos would know how best you could help," he said to Deirdre. "I should get back to the others." He paused. "Will you stay with Wallis while it happens?" Shawn asked her. "He's feeling awfully low."

"Of course," she promised. "When is this to happen?"

"When the rooster crows." Shawn gave her a long look as though

143

he had more to say, but then he pinched his lips into a line, nodded to her and her great aunt, and walked back to the village.

Deirdre hesitated, then she faced her great aunt.

"Come along, child," Great Aunt Clary said wearily. "Let's do what we can to see them through this nonsense."

Deirdre knew her great aunt was speaking out of worry and not annoyance. Though, with Great Aunt Clary, there was usually some of that, too.

There was something Shawn wasn't telling her, she was certain. And going from what she'd learned of him these past several days, she had an idea that Shawn might take matters into his own hands to spare the others. It would be like him to do that.

She wasn't going to let him do so alone.

~*~

"How could the bears know what we're doing? What could they know about strategy and planning?" That had been Patrick's response when Shawn voiced his opinion that trying to group all the bears together for one quick kill wasn't going to work on them.

What do you know of it, Shawn had wanted to ask, but he'd bit his tongue. Wallis's look had said it for both of them.

The men in the room hadn't wanted to hear the flaws in their plan. They wanted to fix the plan into place and move on it as quickly as possible. Those men wanting to rid the island of the bears wanted it finished before anyone else was attacked. The men who had been against the hunt just wanted to be done with the entire business so they could put it behind them.

Both were dangerous ways to approach a battle, but Shawn knew speaking out wouldn't do any good. He'd seen this hardheaded determination before and had learned the only way around it was the play along and then act quickly to salvage the plan when it fell apart. But that had been with men against men. This was something entirely different.

Still, he had put his hand on Wallis' shoulder and squeezed each time it looked as though Wallis would argue against the plan. He'd made as many suggestions as he'd dared and left the house sick at heart. Wallis had returned to the Donaghue House grim and sullen because he couldn't help. The most he'd been allowed was to remain behind to help watch over the village with the older men and the boys.

Shawn kept running the meeting through his mind as he walked along the riverside. It was the only way to keep from thinking of Deirdre and the moments they had shared between them, and how he wanted more.

He pulled up short when he saw John Guthrie standing at the bank, facing him. The man's face was empty of expression, even his eyes, and it was the closest thing to seeing a living man look dead that Shawn had ever witnessed. The spot between his shoulders itched like he was walking toward an ambush he knew was coming but could do nothing to stop.

Shawn kept his expression smooth.

"You think you're good enough for my niece?" John demanded.

The man must have seen him with Deirdre. Shawn held back a wince. He'd done nothing wrong, and neither had she. Shawn knew himself. He knew he'd never take advantage of a woman. John clearly thought that wasn't the case.

"I think I'd spend my days trying."

John's jaw tightened. "You don't belong here. None of you. I said it before. You need to leave."

"I intend to."

"And without my niece."

Shawn should have been honest and told John he had no intention of taking Deirdre from her home, but he didn't know how the man would take it. So he said nothing.

John glared at him, and then, unexpectedly, he stopped. "I suppose I should at least thank you for helping us with the bears," he said begrudgingly, like each word cost him.

"I feel some responsibility for what's happened."

He expected John to agree, but the man said nothing about it.

"You think the plan is foolishness," John stated.

Shawn didn't answer.

"It's fine, I think it is, too. Elki's a fine shot," he continued, "and he can lay traps, but no one else on this island has any experience hunting anything but the wild hogs. And that's the experience they're using."

"You didn't speak up at the meeting," Shawn pointed out.

John crossed his arms, then uncrossed them. "I knew they

wouldn't listen."

"They seem to listen to you before."

"What do you see as the biggest flaw?" John asked instead of answering.

Shawn relaxed. He had the wild thought that maybe, if he could be more useful, he might win Deirdre's uncle over. Maybe if that happened, he could return to court Deirdre.

Wishful thinking, but the idea took hold and clung tight. John's argument against him had everything to do with Deirdre. Shawn needed to show him that he was a good man who could be counted on to treat Deirdre well. Helping to protect her would go a long way towards that. But he didn't relax entirely. He couldn't forget that sense he'd had of ambush.

"Location." Shawn looked across the river. "Everyone on the island seems to have avoided crossing the river. It's hard to make a strong plan without scouting the area first, or at least having some knowledge of the terrain."

John nodded, paying close attention.

"How do we know that the bears will be drawn to the grove?" Shawn asked, not expecting an answer. "Which way will they come? Where would be the best places to set traps? There is too much hurry to end this quickly. Someone is going to get hurt."

"I agree." John glanced at the village. "Here's what I'm thinking," he said, drawing closer. Shawn could smell the wool oil coming from the man. "We go through with it, but convince the others to limit it to setting and baiting traps. Then, later, we go over in groups with the muskets to check the traps."

It was a better plan. "But what kind of trap? Have you any iron ones?"

John shook his head. "There's talk of making some, but that would put off the hunt."

Shawn let out a long sigh. "Meanwhile, the village frets about the bears crossing the river to attack, which could happen." There wasn't an easy answer.

"Now you understand." John's attitude changed at once, and he crossed his arms. "You come here thinking you have all the answers, but you don't."

"I don't—" Shawn tried to defend, but John cut him off.

"We know the island. We know the bears. And we know what's

best for the ones we love. We can defend ourselves without the help of the likes of you." John turned away. "And stay away from my niece." He looked back over his shoulder as he walked away, shooting Shawn a long, hateful glare.

Once John had disappeared, Shawn leaned against the nearest tree. He gripped the hilt of his knife and thought about spears and bayonets and ambush and plans instead of how much he wanted to strike down that hateful man.

Shawn scrubbed his face with his hands.

The younger men wanted to fight. Shawn had seen it before. He'd felt it himself. He'd joined the war with vain thoughts of glory and honorable combat. That image hadn't survived his first battle. He'd lived, but so many had died.

He didn't want to see the young men he'd come to know and admire learn the same, hard lesson.

Shawn straightened, determined. He'd do what he could to help them succeed without casualties. He could do that much. He had the skill. He just needed the time.

Tonight then.

~*~

"I'm going to check in with Mathilda." It was the first excuse Deirdre could think of that Great Aunt Clary might believe. "See if there is any more wool oil to collect."

Even so, Clary eyed her suspiciously.

"That best be all you're up to."

Deirdre reassured her in as few words as possible and left before her great aunt could think of a good way to stop her. She shut the door before Ferny could follow, which might warn her great aunt that something was up if it were earlier in the day, but not this far into evening. She didn't like Ferny to be outside after dark. Not as he'd grown more curious. The time was coming when he'd have to go to the field with the other lambs and the ewes.

So she wouldn't have told a lie to her great aunt, Deirdre did go by Mathilda's for wool oil.

"All out," she told Deirdre. "They've taken the whole of it."

"Will it be enough?"

"I hope to God it will be." Mathilda shook her head before

retreating back inside her house, which reeked of wool oil. She was most likely making more.

Her word kept, Deirdre turned for Marcos's house. She didn't want to suspect Shawn of doing something foolish, but she hadn't been able to shake the feeling that he would. And, being a man of integrity, he'd see whatever it was as necessary and not foolish at all. Which only went to show how much the menfolk needed clever women to dissuade them of such notions.

Deirdre still held slim hope the women could dissuade the men from going after the bears, but with the women divided in their opinions on the subject, she didn't see much possibility.

The village would be dark soon, so Deirdre had in mind to hurry. She'd make sure Shawn was still with Marcos, make sure Patrick was still contrite over his treatment of Great Aunt Clary, and then get back home before it was completely dark. And hope she didn't run into Uncle John along the way.

Marcos opened the door. "Deirdre. Does your great aunt know you are out?"

It was a question she was getting heartily tired of, so she didn't answer.

"Can I speak with Shawn?"

"He went to speak with Wallis."

A chill of apprehension made Deirdre shiver.

"What is it?" Marcos was fair too perceptive.

"I— I'm worried about the hunt."

"And Shawn?" Far too perceptive. She nodded mutely.

"He's a good man, Deirdre, no matter your uncle's opinion. But he's not staying."

"I know."

"Would you leave?"

She wasn't expecting the question. "Maybe."

Marcos smiled. He patted her shoulder. "Take care, Deirdre." She knew he wasn't talking about going to the Donaghue House.

She bid him goodnight and made the walk. Night had settled over the island and the lamps were lit. The air was warm and humid but the breeze cool. It was her favorite time of year and she wanted to enjoy it. She wanted to take Shawn to all her favorite spots and show him the beauty of the island to chase away the ugliness. He needed to see beautiful things. He'd seen too much of horror.

Wallis was sitting on the front porch. With Hetty. They were laughing together.

Deirdre stopped. She should turn away, but she couldn't. They looked happy. Comfortable. And Hetty looked adoringly at him.

Love.

Deirdre's stomach knotted. She didn't understand why until Wallis took Hetty's hand in his.

She was jealous. She swallowed against it. Hetty deserved to be happy. So did Wallis. And she thought given the chance they could be. Would Wallis stay to be with her? Would Hetty leave to be with him?

Would she leave to be with Shawn?

Would he wish her to?

She circled the house, keeping out of sight, and saw no sign of Shawn. Was he inside? Why would he be, unless he was talking with Joseph and Daniel?

Deirdre sighed. She didn't want to intrude on Wallis and Hetty, but she needed to find Shawn. She wanted to see him now more than ever.

Making noise as she approached to porch, she smiled when the lamp light fell upon her.

Hetty drew her hand back quickly, and Wallis leaned back in his seat. Hetty's face flushed, and even Wallis looked a little embarrassed.

"Good evening," Deirdre called, stopping at the bottom of the porch. "Is Shawn about?"

Wallis shook his head. "He stopped by earlier but went back to Marcos' house."

A chill swept through her. She thought she did better at hiding it but Wallis stood, wincing against the pain of his ankle. "What is it?"

"I hoped to speak with him," Deirdre said, her voice weak.

"About?"

Deirdre hesitated, but then she reminded herself that Wallis knew Shawn better than she did. He would know if Shawn was going to put himself into trouble. "I think he might be doing something foolish."

Wallis grimaced. "Wouldn't surprise me," he grumbled. His reaction did nothing to ease her suspicions, though it did tell her that she had come to know something of Shawn in their short time together.

"What would he do?" Hetty asked.

"I don't know," Deirdre admitted. "It's just an impressed I got. And he's not at Marcos' because Marcos said he was here."

"Could be you passed him?" Wallis asked, hopeful.

Both Deirdre and Hetty shook their heads.

"Damn it," Wallis swore. He started down the porch step and stopped with another flash of pain across his face. Hetty hurried to his side.

"You can't," she told him, putting her small hands on his large arm.

"Someone needs to stop him from doing whatever he has planned."

"What might he do?" Deirdre asked.

Wallis sat heavily back in his chair and scrubbed his hands over his face. "Get himself killed if he's not careful."

"The bears." Deirdre's mouth went dry.

"He couldn't think to trap them hisself, could he?" Hetty gasped.

"He's not that foolish," Deirdre said before Wallis could, "but he'd do something to help, wouldn't he, to make sure no one else was hurt?"

Wallis nodded. "Shawn didn't like not knowing the terrain."

"Around the fig grove."

Wallis nodded again.

Deirdre straightened. "He's heading across the river." She knew it as surely as she knew the night was dark.

"He can't," Hetty argued. "It's too dangerous. And at night, too."

"I'll go stop him," Wallis said, rising again. He hid his wince better, but Deirdre was already moving.

"I will." Deirdre rushed off before Wallis could tell her not to.

~*~

Shawn didn't return to Marcos' house. He had everything that he needed with him, which was only his knife and his determination.

The couple of times he'd gone to the river, he'd marked where the two boats for the village were moored. From what he'd overheard, he knew there was at least one more, a larger boat for use in the bay. And thanks to the warnings he had received, he knew where the fig grove lay.

Shawn climbed into one of the boats. He wondered which was the one that had capsized on Deirdre's father but dismissed the thought. Instead, he untied the boat and used the short oars to propel him from the river bank and into the current.

It wasn't fierce, but it still caught the boat and moved him away from the village faster than he'd expected. He fought to keep the boat moving across the water toward the far bank. It wasn't a long distance, but by the time he reached it, the light from the village lamps was out of sight.

He caught against the bank on a bit of sunken land and grabbed hold of a thick tuft of grass to keep the boat from sweeping away. Making certain the end of the painter was tied securely to the boat, he climbed out and, locating a nearby log, tied the other end of the painter to it.

Checking that his sheath was still secure over his chest, he made for the fig grove. The nighttime made the going rougher, but he'd spent enough time skulking through the darkness that his eyes adjusted. The tree boughs weren't as thick as some of the forests he'd moved through, so the stars served as a compass. The moon was at half, which lent a little more light. He'd considered bringing a lamp but thought better than revealing his position, not so much worried about the bears but of anyone in the village seeing him and coming to investigate and getting themselves hurt.

On reconsideration, bringing a lamp might have been wiser. The bears might have stayed clear of the light. Hopefully, they weren't about.

The best place to find the edge of the grove was along the river where he had seen the fig trees, so he followed the river bank until he found the first fig trees. The figs were still green but they were large. Another week and they'd no doubt start to ripen.

As his purpose was to scout out the grove as much as he could, he turned away from the river to follow the trees. They didn't grow in any manner of order, sprouting instead wherever there was space between the older trees. He tried to keep to the thinnest growth. The grove didn't seem to be a circle, as he'd envisioned, but a strip bordered by thick grass and taller pines. He didn't know how far across the grove ran, or if the marsh was near. He doubted anyone in the village knew.

It was an important detail to know, though, so he kept following the fig trees deeper into the west side of the island, noting what landmarks he could, possible places to set traps, and anywhere to retreat to in case the entire business went badly, which Shawn was far more conscious of since Yorktown.

He didn't want a repeat of that against the bears, who would hardly show mercy. Still, he wasn't sure he believed they'd catch any of the bears in the morning, let alone kill one.

It was the low growl that was his only warning.

Taken over by instinct, Shawn threw himself aside as the bear lumbered past him. It moved at an awkward gait, but that didn't stop it from turning back.

A whistle pierced the air and the bear stopped as though confused.

"He doesn't seem to like you." John Guthrie's voice preceded him into the wan moonlight. The man was wearing his stitching and stank of wool oil, and he was carrying a bucket. "I was counting on your stupidity tonight."

Cautiously, Shawn stood. He kept a wary eye on the bear.

"What are you doing here?" Shawn asked. His mind was moving sluggishly, trying to piece together what he was seeing.

"Training."

Shawn blinked.

John reached into the bucket and pulled out a strip of raw meat. "Hog," John said casually. He set the bucket down and took an item from his pouch. As he tossed the meat to the bear, he rang a small bell.

The bear pounced on the meat and slathered over it, drool rolling from between its overly large fangs as it reached for the meat and devoured it.

"They are intelligent, to a point," John said. "The Donaghues had that right."

"You trained them?" Shawn was incredulous.

"It's taken time. Years. Experimenting with what worked and what didn't, and which bears it worked on. The others, they're smarter and avoid the village. But these—" he pulled out another hunk of meat and tossed it, ringing the bell, but this time he threw it closer to Shawn.

The bear lumbered and then leapt at it. Shawn had too good of a view of its jaw and how it ground its teeth on the meat. It eyed him with a mad gleam of expectation.

"You killed Trevor," Shawn bit out, gaze steady on the bear.

"Of course not. The bears killed Trevor. You were there," John reminded him.

"You set the bears on him."

John didn't answer.

"Why?"

"You!" John snarled, stepping forward. The bear growled in response and Shawn tensed, waiting for it to attack, his hand wrapped around the hilt of his knife. "You came here and put everything at risk."

"Put her at risk, you mean?"

"You won't touch my niece. None of you will."

"Trevor didn't—"

"He aimed a musket at her." John's tone was furious and unmerciful.

Shawn swallowed. The man was dangerous. More dangerous than he'd come close to realizing.

"So you killed him."

John straightened. "The bears killed him."

"At your command."

Once again, he didn't answer.

"Who else have you killed?"

Nothing.

"Who?" Shawn demanded. "Derry?"

John sneered. "You think you know about what goes on here?"

"How long ago was it Derry was killed?" Shawn challenged. "Fifteen years? Twenty? Were you there? Was that what gave you the idea?"

John reached into his bucket. The bear growled. Behind it, another bear whined.

Two.

John pulled out a larger hunk of raw meat. "I won't let you corrupt my niece."

"Guthrie—" Shawn put his hands up and backed away a step. The bears growled. John looked completely untouched as he tossed the meat at Shawn and rang the bell.

~*~

"This is foolish." Deirdre's voice sounded close enough to her great aunt to give her pause. "This is the most foolish thing you've ever done, Deirdre Donaghue."

But it didn't stop her. She reached where the boats were moored.

One was missing. Shawn.

Gritting her teeth, Deirdre climbed into the one that was left. She was in the act of untying it when someone called out to her.

"Deirdre! Wait."

Wallis was leaning heavily on a musket, Hetty beside him, carrying a lamp. Wallis was sweating from exertion.

"I can't let you do that," he told her.

"I'm going after him."

Wallis let out a long sigh. "Is she always like this?" he asked Hetty.

Hetty nodded, wide-eyed.

"Fine then." He limped to the boat and held the musket out to Deirdre. "For the love of God, don't drop it in the river."

Deirdre hesitated, looking to Hetty. Grim and tight-lipped, Hetty nodded.

She took hold of the musket and moved back to give Wallis room. He grumbled as he lowered himself into the boat, trying not to wince with pain.

"I'll go tell Father," Hetty told them.

"If you're sure you should," Wallis asked her.

"Yes," Deirdre told Hetty. "And your uncles."

Hetty nodded. She paused, then held the lamp down to Wallis. Wordlessly, he took it, his fingers brushing over hers as he did. A look of worry crossed Hetty's face, and then she was hurrying away.

Wallis finished untying the line and took the oars. "Were you going to row over alone?"

"Of course."

"You're as bad as he is."

Deirdre smiled grimly. "I suppose I am."

"That wasn't a compliment."

Wallis' strong strokes carried them across the river before they slid downstream too far. Deirdre felt strange holding the musket close. She'd never held one, not like this, with the intent to use it if needed. She wasn't sure she could fire it.

Wallis angled the boat so he could reach the shore. It took a moment or two for him to reach for the bank, and before he caught it, Deirdre called a warning.

"A boat," she said just before they hit it. Wallis lurched out and snagged an exposed root with an impressive show of raw strength.

"So we know where he made land," he said, grabbing the line to tie the boat to the root.

Deirdre raised the lamp. "This isn't the second boat. I haven't seen this one before." It was older and longer and had seen repairs to the hull at several points. The sight of it jabbed at an old memory, but she couldn't pull it up.

"Who else would be out here?"

"I don't know."

She handed Wallis the musket when he reached the bank and climbed out of the boat, taking the lamp with her. She dimmed the light as low as it would go without going out.

"Which way?" she asked Wallis. He gave her an odd look.

"I have no idea."

"Where would Shawn go?"

He gave the matter some thought. "If he's here scouting like I think he is, he'll circle the grove."

"It's this way," Deirdre told him. Wallis walked beside her as they followed the river bank. He was limping hard, using the butt of the musket as a crutch.

"How fast are the bears?" he asked her.

"I'm not sure." There was too much she didn't know. Too much none of the villagers knew. Deirdre hated realizing how blinded they'd all become by their fear of the bears.

Had that been Great Grandmother's plan all along? Keep the village safe on the side of the river farthest from the main land? No, that wouldn't account for the real threat that she remembered in her great grandmother's warnings or the fear when she spoke of the bears and what they could do.

But maybe someone else used her great grandmother's beliefs instead?

Great Grandfather? Had he and Thom Ballard gone along with it to keep the village unseen from the mainland?

She'd never know for certain, but she did know that everyone on the island valued their privacy from the politics and intrigues on the mainland, even Lennox, who had never fully adjusted to life on the island but swore he'd never leave it.

They reached the edge of the fig grove. "He'd follow it inland," Wallis told her. "We already know what lays along the water."

They walked the edge of the fig grove. Deirdre concentrated on listening, and Wallis was silent next to her, hopefully doing the same.

They'd left the river behind when she heard a rumbling that raised the hair on her arms and sent shivers down her back. Fear froze her in place until she realized it was coming from ahead.

The bears.

Shawn.

Without waiting for Wallis, she ran towards the sound, her great aunt's voice echoing with each footstep. "Foolish. Foolish. Foolish. Foolish."

A shadow blacker than night huddled before her, and she tripped, nearly falling, heart catching in terror, but it was only a pile of rocks.

She drew and released a quick breath. And then she heard the voice from ahead.

"You won't touch my niece."

It was her Uncle John.

What was he doing here?

"Trevor didn't—" Shawn's voice began, but her uncle cut him off.

"He aimed a musket at her." She'd never heard her uncle sound so enraged.

"So you killed him."

No. The bears killed him.

Her uncle echoed her thoughts. "The bears killed him."

"At your command."

Deirdre's breath caught. It wasn't possible. It just wasn't. But her uncle didn't deny it.

"Who else have you killed?" Shawn demanded.

Uncle John still didn't answer.

"Who? Derry?"

Deirdre went cold.

"You think you know about what goes on here?" her uncle accused.

"How long ago was it Derry was killed?" Shawn challenged. "Fifteen years? Twenty? Were you there? Was that what gave you the idea?"

A bear growled, then whined.

"I won't let you corrupt my niece."

Deirdre rushed forward, twisting the lamp key as she did.

"Guthrie—" Shawn's voice was plaintive. A bell rang, the sound echoing through the trees.

"Uncle John!" Deirdre stumbled to a stop just as two bears lurched at Shawn. "No!"

"Get back!" Shawn shouted at her even as he pulled his knife. She watched in horror as the first bear reached him, swiping out its twisted paw. Shawn dodged it deftly.

"Deirdre?" Uncle John's voice broke through her terror. He grabbed her by the arms. He reeked of wool oil and something off, something pungent and raw. She looked at him, tearing her gaze from Shawn.

"Make them stop," she pleaded.

"This is best, Deirdre," he told her. He pulled her against him, blocking her sight. "Don't watch."

She heard Shawn grunt in pain. She struggled against her uncle. "Stop, please stop!"

"I know what's best." He wouldn't let her go.

A musket shot rent the air, shocking her.

"Shawn!" Wallis' call came from behind her. Deirdre pushed against her uncle, whose grip had loosened. She dodged around him to find Shawn rolling away from a still form.

The other bear circled warily.

Spying the bucket, Deirdre lunged for it with her free hand. Her uncle grabbed her arm before she reached it.

"Get away!" Uncle John shouted.

"Let me go!" She twisted.

"Damnation, girl, listen to me."

She kicked at him. "I don't know you."

Uncle John's hold loosened. He stepped back and stared at her.

"Deirdre." He spoke agonizingly slowly, each word ripe with meaning. "Come away."

Deirdre faced the bear. "We can end this. No one else has to die." She raised the lamp, turning up the flame.

"Deirdre."

Her uncle's voice was a warning hiss. The coldness of it broke over her.

"Don't do it, Guthrie," Shawn called out, his words twisted in pain.

Deirdre turned to see her uncle standing over the bucket. He had a piece of meat in his hands.

"Come here," he demanded.

Wordlessly, she shook her head.

With a snarl, her uncle threw the meat at Shawn. The bear charged. Deirdre threw the lamp at the bear as a hulking form burst from the trees and tackled John to the ground. The lamp hit the bear's shoulder, spilling hot oil that caught fire. It howled in agony and the sound sliced through her. It dropped to the ground, trying to roll away from the pain, damping the flames as it did.

"Shawn, the musket," Wallis called.

"Let me up!" her uncle shouted, his voice muffled.

"You damned fool." Wallis pressed John into the ground. "Stay down."

Her uncle struggled, but Wallis was bigger and held him pinned. Uncle John swore vehemently. Wallis ignored him.

Shawn reached the musket.

"It's ready," Wallis told him.

Shawn raised it, took aim, and fired. The noise of the shot was deafening.

The bear jerked once, then went still. The quiet that followed was eerie, and the air stunk of burning fur.

"Get off me!" With a final thrust, Uncle John pushed Wallis aside.

"How could you do that?" Uncle John rounded on Deirdre. "We could have ended this."

"Uncle—" She didn't recognize the man standing in front of her, his face twisted in rage. "What are you doing?" She approached him.

"Deirdre," Shawn said in warning. Wallis shifted closer to her.

Deirdre ignored them both. She didn't understand what exactly had just happened, so she clung to what she knew, and that was the fact that her uncle would never hurt her.

"Uncle John, please. Let me help. We're family."

In the light of the half moon, John Guthrie's face turned toward her in disgust.

"You are your father through and through," he told her in a menacing growl. "You are no family of mine."

Shocked, Deirdre stared as he walked away, leaving her standing alone as he disappeared into the fig grove, hurt clawing at her stomach.

"Shawn?" Wallis limped toward his friend.

Shawn. The bear. Deirdre tried to shake off the despair as she hurried to him. "How badly are you hurt?"

"Scrapes and bruises."

"Are you sure?" She wanted to run her hands over him to make certain, but also to feel some warmth. Her body had gone so cold.

"Why did you even come?" Shawn turned on Deirdre. "You could've been killed."

Had she not been? Deirdre wrapped her arms around herself, unable to speak. The look in Shawn's eyes changed from accusation to concern.

"And you would have been if we hadn't come," Wallis reminded him.

They all stood silently. Deirdre looked at the still forms of the bears. The last of the flames were dying down but the stench was still strong. "Are they dead?"

Shawn followed her gaze. "Yes."

"We should go," Wallis suggested, "before any more return."

Wallis took the musket from Shawn. Shawn stepped closer to Deirdre.

"Uncle John," she said, but the words tasted wrong. Twisted and unnatural.

"I'm sorry."

Looking at him, Deirdre could see that Shawn was truly sorry. She leaned towards him and he wrapped his arms around her. She didn't weep, not like the last time he'd held her. She was too empty inside.

You are no family of mine.

She was the only family he had.

Deirdre let Shawn's warmth sooth the worst of the chill from her as she tried to blank the thoughts in her head.

"He made his choice." Shawn took hold of her arm. She let him lead her away.

"Where did you leave your boat?" Shawn asked Wallis. Deirdre could feel the vibration of his voice through his chest and it was oddly comforting.

"Not far from the grove."

"Deirdre," Shawn asked quietly. She pulled away, taking in a deep breath that nearly gagged her. But it also cleared her head.

"We need to get back to the village."

"You two go ahead," Wallis said. "I'll catch up."

"No." Shawn linked Deirdre's arm through his. "We all go together."

So together, the three walked back toward the river. No one spoke. Both men limped. Deirdre felt gutted.

"I guess we know who had this other boat," Wallis said as they reached it. "Should we take it back?"

Shawn nodded. He started to help Deirdre down into the boat with Wallis, but she shook off his arm.

"I can manage."

"I know you can."

They rowed the two boats back across in silence.

CHAPTER SEVEN

Tuesday, June 5th

The three were met on the shore by Peter, Marcos, and Bernardo, and Hetty stood nearby, her hands clasped at her chest. As soon as Wallis climbed from the boat to the river bank, she rushed to him and threw her arms around his broad shoulder, burying her face against him. Shawn couldn't hear what she said, but Wallis looked like he might burst with happiness. He embraced the small woman and whispered to her.

Bernardo helped tie up the second boat, and he stepped back as he finished. He gave Marcos and Peter a look full of meaning. Both men were grim.

Deirdre looked about to wilt.

"You should take her home," Shawn told the men. "I'll explain everything."

"No, I'll stay," Deirdre argued.

"Deirdre," Peter's voice was gentle as he took her hands. "Let's get you home. Clary is worried for you."

Deirdre's shoulders fell as she relented. She allowed Peter to lead her away, not looking back. Shawn wished she would, just once. She'd been so quiet on the trek back to the village. He knew she'd faced a terrible shock and he wanted nothing more than to comfort her, but he didn't think she'd welcome it.

"Come," Marcos told him. He eyed Hetty and Wallis. They had parted, but Hetty had wrapped her arms around Wallis' arm as if she could keep him beside her by her frail strength alone. Shawn didn't think it would take anything more than a quiet word for Wallis to do whatever she wished. His friend was looking down at the woman with awe.

Wallis was in love.

Shawn's gut twisted. He turned and followed Marcos. Bernardo stepped to the couple for a quiet word.

"I don't believe your friend will be leaving the island," Marcos told Shawn.

Shawn nodded, not trusting his voice.

When they reached Marcos' house, Patrick and Rosa were waiting. Neither of them said a word, though Patrick's distrustful expression spoke his mind clearly.

Bernardo and Peter both joined them not long after. Wallis wasn't with them.

"Tell us what happened," Peter commanded.

Shawn did. He left nothing out, not even his suspicions that Guthrie was involved in Derry's death and perhaps another's too. He didn't mention Deirdre's father by name, but no one missed his inference.

Patrick stood when he'd finished.

"Where are you going?" Marcos asked, though there wasn't any doubt.

"To find John. He has to answer for this."

"FIRE!"

The shout came from outside, and it sent all of them to their feet and racing for the door.

The blaze was easy to see in the night.

"The Guthrie Cabin," Joseph shouted.

It didn't take long for the village to reach the cabin. Deirdre was there, too, and she ran toward it, heedless of the flames.

"Uncle John!"

Shawn reached her first and grabbed her against him, dragging her back from the blazing cabin. The heat licked his skin. She struggled against him.

"He's not there," he told her. "He's not there."

She struggled a final time, then let him pull her away. The night air was cold once away from the heat.

The men and women had formed a bucket line from the nearby

stream, but it was too late to save the cabin. The most they could do was to keep the fire from spreading, but thankfully, the cabin wasn't close to its neighbors. Shawn realized it was by design. The villagers had been clever in their building.

They stood back and watched the cabin burn.

"How can you be sure he wasn't there?" Deirdre asked. Shawn still held her, his arms wrapped around her middle, her back against his chest. He could feel her ragged breathing and he ached for her.

"He was distracting us."

"Not all of us," Ian said. He approached, limping. Caitlyn hurried to him. In the firelight, it was obvious he had been struck. The side of his face was puffy and a cut trickled blood.

"He went toward the point," Ian said as his wife fussed over him. "I couldn't stop him."

"You were a fool to try," Caitlyn chastised.

"You should have taken me with you," his son, Aiden, told him, though Grace, his pregnant wife, was shaking her head.

"He was going for our boat," Wallis said. Hetty was tucked against him. He exchanged a look with Shawn.

No one disagreed.

"He's left." Deirdre pulled away from Shawn and wrapped her arms around herself. The look she gave him was hollow. She'd lost more than an uncle this night, he realized. She'd lost everything she thought she understood about him, about her family.

"Joseph, Aiden, Daniel," Peter bid, "you three stay and watch over the cabin. Make sure the fire doesn't spread."

The three young men began gathering the empty buckets to refill with water.

"Everyone else," Peter continued, looking at the collected villagers, "go back home."

"Peter—" Clary's voice was stark, but Peter interrupted her.

"There's nothing to be done tonight, Clary."

She sighed and looked a decade older. "Come along, Deirdre."

It said something that Deirdre didn't argue. Shawn reached out to brush his fingers along her arm as she passed him. She paused a moment to glance at him.

"I'm sorry," she said, her voice raw.

"You've nothing to apologize for."

She didn't look like she believed him.

The villagers made their way back to their homes. Shawn followed Patrick and Marcos.

Rosa was standing on the porch, Aileen crying in her arms. Patrick took his daughter, who wrapped her arms around his neck, and walked inside with his wife next to him.

A stab of jealousy surprised Shawn.

"Sit with me," Marcos said, gesturing to the porch. "We'll get you both back to the mainland," Marcos told him as soon as they settled. "Unless you'll change your mind and stay."

"I can't. I've put the village in enough threat. I've caused enough damage."

"I don't believe that."

"But what happened between Deirdre and her uncle—"

"Deirdre will survive. She's not a fragile girl. We all will have to face the past and all the signs we missed. It'll take time, but we have it now." Marcos rubbed his face. "At least now we have the truth. Or as much of it as we can put together."

"John Guthrie hates me," Shawn reminded him. "If he's going to the mainland, and I think we all know he is, then he'll tell them where to find me and Wallis."

Marcos frowned.

"You know I'm right."

"And you know we'd protect you."

Shawn nodded. He had the feeling they would go to nearly any length to protect their own, and for a reason he couldn't understand, they'd taken him in as one of their own.

"I've family to see to," Shawn told him, sitting back in the chair. He was exhausted and sore and heartsick. "I can't stay. And I can lead the militia off, keep them away from the island."

"They might come anyway."

"They might."

Silence followed. Shawn tried to think of how he could do what he claimed and not be caught, but he was too tired to form any plans.

"What about Deirdre?" Marcos asked quietly.

Shawn hesitated.

"She cares for you." Marcos studied him. "Do you care for her?"

"It isn't that simple."

"Her great aunt would say it is."

Shawn chuckled despite himself. "I imagine she would. But on the mainland, it isn't that simple."

"Why?"

"I put your village into danger blundering onto this island. I'm more thankful than you can know for the kindness you've shown, but I never came here with the intention of staying."

"You haven't given her cause to think you'll stay, have you?"

"No. I swear I haven't."

Marcos nodded.

"I don't want to leave her," Shawn admitted, his voice tight.

"Don't make her promises," Marcos warned him. "I don't want to watch her waiting for someone who might not return."

"I wouldn't do that to her."

"I didn't think so, but it had to be said." He put his hand on Shawn's shoulder. "We'll help you as we can."

"I can't ask for that."

"You don't have to. You're our friend."

Shawn's throat constricted, and he nodded rather than try to speak. How long had it been since he'd felt like he'd belonged? And he had to leave again.

"I'll speak with Wallis in the morning," Shawn finally said. "Find out if he wants to send word to his family." There was no question any longer of Wallis staying.

Marcos chuckled. "He'll be welcome here. He's a good man. Hetty's done well."

"I think it's Wallis who's done well."

"Most likely." They both laughed, but it didn't last.

"Patrick no doubt has his family settled," Marcos told him, standing.

"I'll sit out a while, if it's all the same."

Marcos gave his consent and went inside. Shawn sat silently, listening to the village noises even out. The smell of burning wood was still heavy in the air. He was tempted to go stand with the young men and keep watch over the burning cabin, but he was too tired to move.

In the morning, he would have to make plans to leave. But tonight, he could sit and forget the events of the day and take in the quiet of the returning peace. And dream of what might have been if he could stay.

~*~

Deirdre stood before the smoldering Guthrie Cabin. Her eyes were gritty from tears and sleeplessness. Her chest was tight, her shoulders tense, and her stomach twisted constantly. Tears rolled down her cheeks. She was so tired of crying.

Joseph came to stand next to her. He didn't speak. He wrapped his arm around her shoulders and she stepped closer, laying her head against him as they watched the smoke curl into the blue sky.

There were questions. Questions she'd never have answers for because the one man who knew the truth had gone. Where he'd gone, Deirdre couldn't know. Back to where the Guthries first came from? She didn't know where that was. She knew nothing about her family before her grandfather came to the island. Even then, she doubted she knew the truth about them at all.

"I've never been a Guthrie." Her voice was quiet, the words hushed, as if she was confessing a terrible crime.

Joseph didn't answer. For that, she was grateful.

"He killed my father."

Her cousin drew in a deep breath and let it out slowly. He was trembling. Deirdre wondered if it was from anger or grief. Her shaking came from both.

Joseph finally spoke. "He loves you."

"Not anymore."

Deirdre knew this absolutely. Any care he'd had for her she'd destroy when she hadn't sided with him. He would never forgive her, and he would never forget. Her Uncle John wasn't the kind of man to do either.

He wasn't Uncle John anymore. He was John Guthrie. And she had to let it go.

"I don't know if I can do this," Deirdre admitted. Joseph's arm tightened around her shoulders. "How do I get past it? All the lies and half-truths and betrayals?"

"You have us, Deirdre, and we love you. We're your family." Joseph turned her away from the smoking ruins of her past. "Remember what you say? You are related to every family on this island."

She smiled weakly. "Not the Fonsecas."

Joseph tsked. "Who really wants to be related to Fonsecas?"

"I heard that."

Patrick crossed to them, his expression grim.

"Well, Aileen is an exception," Joseph told him. "And Rosa. And—"

Patrick interrupted him with a light smack. Then he opened his arms to Deirdre.

She fell into them, wrapping her arms around his neck, and wept.

"You are related to everyone, you know," Patrick told her. "Remember Miss Lizzie."

Deirdre drew back. "But—"

He shook his head. "And you accused me of not paying attention. Your grandmother Hattie and she were half-sisters, remember?"

Deirdre smiled a real smile this time. "I'd forgotten."

"Who would blame you," Joseph said wryly. "We need someone whose only job is to keep track of the families on this island."

Deirdre cocked her head. "That's not a bad idea, you know."

She didn't miss that Joseph and Patrick exchanged looks.

"I know what you're doing," she told them.

"Is it working?" Joseph asked, hopeful.

She sighed. "Yes."

"Good," Patrick said, "because I already asked Mother if she could bring out all of Grandmother Ailee's papers."

Deirdre looked back at the cabin. "It was all in there. Everything the Guthries had."

"Not everything." Patrick gave her a squeeze. "Not the most important thing."

"I get it now," she said, giving him a look.

"Get what?"

"Why Rosa married you?"

He jerked in surprise as Joseph laughed.

"Where's Shawn?" Deirdre asked. Patrick bowed his head.

"He and Marcos are looking over the ship."

Deirdre's heart stuttered. "He's leaving." It wasn't a question. She'd known it would come, just not this soon.

"He's worried that your uncle—" he stopped himself and amended, "that John will alert the militia. He wants to head them off."

"Good God, he isn't going to try to surrender himself to save us?" Joseph shook his head. "Of all the beetle-headed—"

"Shawn must do what he feels is right," Patrick interrupted. He put his hand on Joseph's shoulder. "We'll help him as we can."

Joseph was still shaking his head.

"I need to speak with him," Deirdre said. Patrick nodded.

She followed Patrick, Joseph trailing behind. They made for the dock on the south end of the island, sheltered in the small cove. Marcos and Shawn were examining the small ship the island kept. It could only hold ten or twelve people, with a short mast and small sail, but it was enough to get to the mainland if the need came, and with the row boats tied behind it, most everyone on the island could leave. Thankfully, need had never come.

Deirdre came to a halt before they reached the beached ship. Marcos was talking, and Shawn was listening, but the wind caught the words before they reached Deirdre. Instead, she watched Shawn, trying to memorize him. His dark hair was tied back, though strands of it had come loose to blow across his face and get caught in the beard Deirdre itched to shave. His clothing, hand-me-downs from some of the village men, looked natural on him, as if he belonged among them.

His stormy-eyed gaze caught hers. She wanted to lose herself in those eyes. Lose herself in his arms. She wished more than ever that he would stay.

Or that she could go.

Shawn approached, dusting his hands on his trousers. He stopped before her. For a moment, neither spoke. She let her gaze roam his face, from his wide brow to his high cheekbones to where a strong jaw hid under that trimmed beard. His throat worked as he swallowed.

"I have to go." He didn't say it like an announcement but offered it as an explanation. And an apology.

"I know."

Another stretch of silence fell between them, but instead of creating a gulf, it made a bridge.

Shawn stepped closer. "Deirdre," he began, but then he stopped. He glanced back to where Marcos was watching with a grim expression.

"I understand," Deirdre said when he didn't continue. "You have to reach your family. And family is important."

His smile was weak, but it was there. "Yes, it is. I couldn't ask you to leave yours. Not for the unknown."

"I'm not afraid of the unknown," Deirdre told him, a challenge in her voice.

He chuckled. "No, I guess you aren't. I'm foolish to suggest it."

"You are foolish about many things, Shawn McClaren."

"I won't argue it."

Deirdre looked away, unable to stare into those gray eyes any longer. "When do you leave?"

"Tomorrow with the tide."

So soon. But she didn't speak. She saw Shawn begin to raise his hand as though he'd take hers, but then it dropped back to his side. "Deirdre—"

She couldn't take it anymore. Blinking against the burning in her eyes, she raised up on her toes to press a kiss to his lips. Passion throbbed through her and she wanted to wrap herself around him and convince him in any way possible to stay or to take her away with him. Anything to stay with him. He tensed as if holding himself back, and she wanted him to let go. To let the feelings building between them take over.

He cupped her cheek in his hand, his palm rough against her smooth skin. She drew back before she could break and give in to her passion and need.

Neither spoke. His gaze caught hers and held it. He dropped his hand, but he didn't turn away.

She understood. He was letting her go instead of leaving her.

So she turned, and without another look back, she walked away.

~*~

"The Stewart House." Wallis grinned. "Has a nice sound, don't it?"

"It does. When's the wedding?"

"We haven't set the date yet, but soon, I hope." Wallis clapped Shawn on the shoulder. "You won't stay for it, will you?"

"You know I can't."

"No, I don't, but you seem to believe you can't."

"Wallis—"

"No, Shawn," his friend interrupted. "This time I'll speak my mind. You're a damned fool."

"That's never been in question."

"Shut it, Shawn. I'm talking."

Shawn clamped his teeth together, surprised. Wallis eyed him angrily.

"You could be happy here. You could make a fine life, and with a fine woman to wife."

Shawn wanted to defend himself, but he kept quiet. Wallis nodded.

"You know it, but you've got this notion that you have to sacrifice yourself for everyone else's happiness. No," Wallis stopped him before he could respond, "you've always been this way. Always stepping in when it was needed. Taking the blame when it wasn't yours to take. And now, running off to give yourself up."

"I'm not going to surrender. I'm going home."

"What's the difference?" Wallis challenged. "Here or Philadelphia, they'll find you. Only here, there's an entire village willing to stand with you. Can you say that about home?"

Shawn clenched his jaw. "No."

"That's right. Everyone is going to be looking toward their own, trying to land on the right side of the war."

"My parents will need me."

"No. They won't. And the same with mine. If anything, you could be making it worse."

"I won't believe that."

"Shawn—"

"No, Wallis, you've had your say. And I won't argue it. But I can't settle here, not without knowing if my family is safe. And not without giving them a chance to know that I'm safe."

Wallis heaved out a sigh, giving up. "I'll go with you," he offered, but his heart wasn't in it. His heart was already bound to the island by a pair of pretty brown eyes and a gentle smile.

"What should I tell your parents?"

Wallis considered. "Tell them I went west."

"West?"

"You'll never be able to see them again." Shawn knew it was a given, but the words needed saying.

Wallis nodded. "Maybe that's for the best. We were never as close as you are to your family. Besides, if I'm not around, they might be able to keep their life in Philadelphia. They weren't as outspoken like your parents. They can think of me making a life in the wilderness and be free to live out theirs in Philadelphia without guilt."

Shawn extended his hand to Wallis. "I'll miss you."

Wallis looked at Shawn's hand then embraced him. Shawn returned it, feeling like a piece of himself was being gouged out. He couldn't remember a time when Wallis wasn't part of his life.

"You take care of yourself," Wallis said gruffly.

"And you. Name a son after me."

"Only if you will."

Shawn fought back a stab of longing. He gave Wallis a tight-lipped nod and left his friend before he changed his mind.

It would be so easy to stay, to make a life hidden away on this island if the militia could be countered. But he'd told Wallis the truth. He knew his family would be in danger when the patriots took Philadelphia, if they weren't prisoners already.

He had to go. He would be leaving his closest friend behind, but more than that, he would be leaving a piece of his heart on this island when he left, held by the woman with sun-touched hair and shining green eyes and a spirit that he'd never meet again.

CHAPTER EIGHT

Wednesday, June 5th

Marcos and Bernardo were readying the ship while Manny looked on. Shawn stood by, watching the waves lap onto the beach. A rough pier jutted out into the surf, and the ship dipped and rose with the motion, tied though it was to the pier. The three Fonsecas, father and sons, worked without word with a rhythm that spoke of their long experience on the sea.

Shawn wasn't ready to leave, but he couldn't put it off any longer, not if they wanted to use the tides. He doubted he'd ever be ready to leave, though. He knew he was doing the right thing, but knowledge didn't make the act any less painful. Leaving Wallis, leaving Deirdre, leaving a task half-done, for the situation with the bears was still in question. Though no one was as fearful of more deaths.

"John had trained them," Ian had told him late last night as they sat together with Marcos and Peter. "That's the assumption, at least, given what you and Deirdre described."

"I had a look at that wallow that Deirdre found," Peter had added. "And one of the boys found a rusted bell there. We think John was tying hogs in the wallow and loosing the bears on it."

Shawn had shaken his head. "Why?"

"No one could answer that but John Guthrie," Marcos had answered. "And that isn't likely to happen now."

"He'd best not return," Ian had said in a cold voice that left no doubt what he'd do if it happened.

Marcos had shared that Elki and the younger men were going to work on trapping the sick bears to make certain they wouldn't be a threat again.

"And then begin exploring the rest of the island," he had continued. "It's time to let go of the fears of the past."

"Not everyone will," Shawn had warned.

"No, but they'll understand in time."

"Or simply complain every chance she has." No one had to guess who Peter meant.

At least Shawn had the sense that the village was returning to normal.

If only he'd been able to see Deirdre one last time.

"We could delay a day," Marcos said again, coming up to him.

Shawn shook his head. If he stayed, he might never find the courage to leave. He wasn't foolish enough to think the next part of his journey would be uneventful. It might not be as unexpected as the island had been, but he still had leagues through rebel-held land to cross to reach his home.

Bernardo held the boat steady off the pier as they loaded the baggage that Peter and Ian had arranged for Shawn, supplies enough to last some while. In exchange, Shawn had left them his musket.

"Take this." Marcos pressed a piece of parchment into Shawn's hands. It was addressed to Sheridan Ballard in Norfolk.

"Peter's son," Marcos told him. "He'll help you find a ship to Philadelphia."

"I can't ask him to take a risk like that."

"You don't have to. Peter has in that letter." Marcos folded his hands over Shawn's. "You are a good man, Shawn McClaren. Let us do this for you."

Shawn swallowed hard and nodded.

"Wait!" Joseph came sliding down the dune, a bag slung over his shoulder. Shawn straightened.

"You can't come," he told the younger man sternly when Joseph reached him.

"I'm not going for you," Joseph told him.

Marcos and Bernardo chuckled. Joseph flushed. And then Shawn understood. He smiled, though he had to fight against the jealousy gnawing at him. "You've a woman in Norfolk."

"I hope so. And this is the likeliest chance to go before the supply ship arrives."

Shawn nodded. "Who am I to stand in the way, then?"

"Good man," Manny said with a nod. "But that was never in doubt."

Shawn questioned that, but he said nothing.

"Oh. Before I forget." Joseph pulled out two bundles wrapped in cloth. "This is from Aunt Clary."

Shawn unwrapped it. It was a scarf. No, one of those cowls the villagers wore.

"In case there are bears on the mainland," Joseph said wryly.

Shawn lifted the wool to his face and inhaled. It smelled of wool oil. He grinned and put it on.

"And this is from Deirdre," Joseph said, sobering.

Shawn hesitated, then opened it. A pair of spatterdashes, finally made in tight, even stitches with spun wool.

"She said she was sure they weren't near as fancy as what you'd have in Philadelphia," Joseph told him, "but that they'd serve for your journey there."

Shawn nodded, too overcome to speak. He handed the cloth wrappings out to Manny, who shook his head.

"They meant for you to have it. For mending. Lizzie slipped a huswife into your packs," he added.

Shawn laughed. "Thank her for me."

"Aye."

He and the others boarded the boat. He wished he had something to leave Deirdre in return, or at least to thank her, but what would he have said? He'd come into her life, thrown her world upside down, and would never see her again.

Best to just leave it at that.

As the boat set out, Shawn watched the island, already missing the peace and beauty of it. An ugliness had hidden among the loveliness, but he thought that was gone, now, purged with the leaving of John Guthrie and the truth revealed. Like a mending wound, the island and its people would heal. He hoped Deirdre would, too.

He saw a figure top the rise of the dunes. The wind caught her golden hair, whipping it around her face and flaring her skirts.

Deirdre raised her arm.

He raised his in return.

"We could still return," Joseph said above the ocean breeze.

Shawn shook his head, lowering his arm. He faced toward the mainland. When he glanced back, she was gone.

~*~

Shawn climbed to the pier from the fishing boat. True to their word, Marcos and Bernardo had found a place to catch a boat across the bay to Norfolk. He'd surprised himself at the catch in his voice as he bid the brothers goodbye.

Joseph had done all the talking to the fishermen. Apparently the men were not unaccustomed to the island villagers, and they shared stories, mostly of fishing, until they reached Norfolk. It wasn't difficult for Shawn to remain distant. He spent the trip standing out of the way, watching the water slip past the hull of the small ship, his mind on who he had left behind.

Norfolk was as bustling of a city as he imagined. And held by the patriots. Shawn didn't know if word had gotten so far south about his escape, and he didn't want to test it. Thankfully, with Joseph with him, he blended in. And it helped that Joseph knew where they were going.

"You'll want to give Sheridan that letter as soon as you arrive," Joseph told him as they walked.

Shawn glanced at the parchment in his hand, then he paused. "Why do I need a letter if you'll be there with me?"

Joseph didn't look at him. "Because I won't be there. I'm staying with Kenneth."

"Who?"

"Kenneth McGregor. He lives in Norfolk with his family. I stay with them when I go."

"Why him and not Sheridan?"

The younger man finally glanced at Shawn. "Iola is Kenneth's neighbor."

"The young woman you're courting." Shawn smiled in understanding, though his gut knotted with envy.

"I hope to be by the time I leave Norfolk." Joseph grinned, but it was uneasy. Shawn clapped him on the shoulder.

"I can't see why she'd refuse you."

"I'm not sure she'll want to leave Norfolk," Joseph admitted with a worried look.

"And you don't want to leave the island."

He shook his head.

"Why not figure out if she is interested in the idea of you courting her first," Shawn suggested. "The rest can come afterwards."

Joseph nodded. "Deirdre told me the same."

Shawn kept his expression calm, though even the sound of her name hurt. If Joseph noticed, he didn't say.

Joseph led him through the bustling port, past the warehouses, then skirted the heart of the city for one of the residential areas.

"I'm not going to be bringing more trouble down on your kin, am I?" Shawn asked, following Joseph along the graveled road. He was tempted to toss the letter away and make his own way north, but honestly, another attempt at traveling overland, even provisioned as he was, made him shudder. He wasn't sure he could make it into Philadelphia without help, and he was certain that he was too worn out from all he'd experienced to try to cross patrols without being seen. Not without his companions.

He missed Wallis with a stab of homesickness that caught him off guard.

"Sheridan is clever," Joseph told him. "And I know you don't want to make trouble. Just heed his word."

"And Guthrie?"

Joseph's expression darkened. "The smartest thing John could have done was take that boat as far inland as the rivers allow and lose himself in the wilderness."

Shawn agreed, but he didn't think it likely.

"What do you think Derry found in Norfolk before he died?" Shawn asked, recalling the conversation he and Deirdre had with Ian.

Joseph glanced at him again. "You heard about that?"

"Ian told us."

"Derry never told anyone if he had found something."

"But?"

Joseph sighed. "Daniel and Aiden and I were talking about it last night, what with everything coming out about John. Daniel thinks maybe Alistaire Guthrie killed someone and married Hattie to escape justice. You have to admit, the island is a good place to lose yourself." Joseph eyed him.

Shawn chuckled dryly. "That it is."

"I know this is all in the past," Joseph said, slowing, "but it still hurts that someone could live among us and hide his true self. It makes you begin to question everything you know."

Shawn faced him, taking Joseph by the shoulder. "Stop."

"What?" He looked startled.

"You've got to let it go. Yes, there will be answers you'll never learn, but life is like that. Don't let the taint in one man's soul sicken your own, and don't spend your days trying to read the truth behind every man's words. Take them as you always have, Joseph, on faith and trust unless they give you reason otherwise."

"And if they don't give you reason to think ill of them when you should?"

"Would you want to spend your days thinking everyone around you is harboring a poisoned soul, or would you rather have one man fool you and accept the others as they are?"

Joseph smiled. "I suppose you're right." He studied Shawn. "Will you do the same? Not with a man," Joseph added before Shawn could answer. "With this." He gestured around them. "With our world changing. Can you accept that it will?"

Shawn's shoulder slumped and that edge of defeat sliced across him.

"That war is over," Shawn said quietly. "And I have to accept it."

"Would you go back to fighting if it weren't over?"

"No." Shawn didn't hesitate. "I've had enough of killing and watching men die." He studied Joseph. "I wasn't fighting for the King."

"I've come to know something of you, Shawn," Joseph said. "I know whatever your reasons, they were well-considered." He grinned. "Honestly, I couldn't tell you a thing about how the king has ruled over us. Or how that might change. On the island, it never mattered."

"That might change."

Joseph nodded. "Most likely it will. But Patrick has some ideas about that."

"Does he?" Shawn was surprised.

"We'll find our way," Joseph promised. "Just as you'll find yours. And at the moment, it's right over there."

Joseph gestured across the street. The house was narrow but tall, sharing a wall with the homes to either side as though they were holding one another upright. There was no front garden, only a dirt walkway baked under the summer sun. The golden light of sunset backlit the building, giving it a more dramatic air than it deserved, though it was by no means a poor house. Sheridan Ballard was doing well for himself in Norfolk.

Shawn hitched the strap of his bag higher up his shoulder. He held his hand out to Joseph. "Thank you."

"And you."

They said nothing more. Joseph gave him a nod, turned, and walked away.

Shawn took a moment to gather himself. Finally, he went to the front door. He heard voices within before he knocked. He couldn't shake the feeling of unease, though he tried hard not to look over his shoulder to see if Joseph was still there. He missed the young man's presence. And Wallis, too. He was alone and on his own, and he didn't much care for it.

The door opened and a man older than Shawn stood on the other side. He wore a white wig in the current style, swept back and tied with a ribbon at the nape of his neck, with a couple of tasteful curls along both sides just above his ears. He'd removed his coat at some point and stood in his shirt sleeves and undercoat. His clothing and boots were of good quality. Shawn felt shabby and disheveled presented with such a man, and his time spent on the island with the informal ways of the village, plus the weeks before that on the run, made the appearance of a gentleman seem oddly out of place. But Shawn had grown up facing men of good standing, and he could play the part well enough, no matter the state of his dress.

He bowed. "Good sir," he said.

"And good evening to you," the man replied. Shawn caught a trace of accent in his voice similar to that of the island villagers.

Shawn held out the letter. "My introduction, sir, if you are Sheridan Ballard?"

"I am." The man accepted the parchment. He cracked the seal and opened the letter to read it swiftly. He started at one point, and his gaze darted to Shawn.

"You've best come inside," Sheridan told him.

Shawn did as he was bid, and Sheridan closed the door quickly behind him.

They were standing in a narrow parlor. The room was tidy, with good furnishings and a few paintings on the walls along with a cross.

A doorway opened to the right three paces from the front door, and between the two hung coats and hats from pegs driven into the wall. Several of the coats were child-sized.

A woman stepped out from the opening, a quizzical expression on her face. She had round cheeks and bright blue eyes. Her hair was hidden demurely under a clean, white mobcap with elegant lace around its gather. It was shocking to see after the free style of the villagers.

"Sheridan?"

"It is nothing, Hilda," Sheridan told her, and something in his tone warned the woman not to ask questions, but not in a way that struck Shawn as uncaring. The woman, Hilda, took no offense, merely nodding in understanding. She gave Shawn a curious look laced with worry then withdrew.

"Please, won't you sit," Sheridan said, gesturing toward the chairs and divan. Shawn set down his bag near the door and moved to one of the chairs. Sheridan lit a second lamp before joining him.

"So you've come from the island." It wasn't a question, but Shawn nodded in response. "And Father has asked that I extend you whatever assistance you may require to return north."

"He did make mention of it, yes," Shawn answered. "Though I wouldn't wish to put you in any hardship," he added.

Sheridan waved away his concern. "Father also writes that you wish to avoid the notice of the local militia." At this, Sheridan raised an eyebrow.

Shawn had a feeling it would come to this. "Yes, sir. I am no threat," he said quickly. "I'm trying to get home."

"You're a Tory." Sheridan's tone was calm, but Shawn caught the note of tension.

"I was."

"But?"

"But the war's over." Shawn wilted in his seat. "I've put my soldiering behind me. There's no longer any need."

Sheridan studied him, then nodded to himself.

"You must be weary. I'll have our girl make up a bed for you. Have you supped?"

"No, sir, but I wouldn't want you to trouble yourself."

"Nonsense. We lay a good table, and Hilda is proud of it. There's more than enough. Let me show you where you can wash. Do you need spare clothing?"

"Your father kindly saw to that."

Sheridan nodded again and gestured for Shawn to follow.

The wash room was in the back of the house off the kitchen, so the smells of roasted beef with onions and carrots set Shawn's mouth to watering. The room was small, but ample enough for Shawn's needs.

"I'll have fresh water brought," Sheridan said.

Shawn thanked him. Inside the room was a small wash basin and a clean linen towel. There was an iron hook for hanging a coat or hat. He thought at one point the room might have been a pantry cupboard. It spoke of Sheridan's standing in the town that he'd felt the need to convert the space into a washroom. Who did he entertain to make such an impression?

Fear stuttered through him. He was placing a great deal of trust in a man he didn't know. All he had was Peter's and Marcos' word that Sheridan would help him, but how long had it been since either man had seen Sheridan? What might have changed in that time?

A woman cleared her throat from the hall. She was near Shawn's age, with an unremarkable face and the garb of a serving girl. She carried a kettle by a thickly woven cloth.

"Water, sir?" the woman said.

Shawn stepped back from the basin and allowed her to pour the water inside.

"There's a cake of soap just there, sir," the girl told him, nodding to a place next to the basin. She turned on her heel before he could thank her.

Shawn shut the door. He hung up his coat and pulled his travel-worn shirt over his head. It reeked of fish and sweat. Small wonder Sheridan had tactfully asked if he had a change of clothing.

He drew out the spare clothing from his bag, kicked off his boots, and pulled off his trousers. He soaped up and sluiced off the stink of travel and boats and the last of the island, then dried himself quickly and dressed in his clean clothes.

He scrubbed his face and hands clean and dried both, trying not to think of the island, much like he'd tried all day. Had he stood on the shores that morning? It felt like a dream, the entire experience. Especially Deirdre, with those bright green eyes and her way of looking at him as though seeing to the heart of him.

He shook himself to clear the images and stave off the longing but emptiness followed. He ran his fingers through his hair, wished he had time to shave, packed away his soiled clothing and left the washroom.

The serving girl was waiting in the hall. Without word, she gestured for him to follow, and she led him through the open doorway into the dining room.

The family was just completing supper. Sheridan stood as Shawn entered, as did two young men who looked to be his sons. His wife and three daughters remained seated.

The serving girl gestured silently to an empty place at the table, which was large enough to accommodate eight. A clean place setting had been laid for him.

"I thank you, ma'am," he said to Sheridan's wife. "It is gracious of you to welcome me at such an hour." It was surprisingly easy to fall back into his old patterns of speech, though it was like putting on an old coat that no longer fit as it once had.

"You are most welcome. We are all eager for news of Sheridan's father." Her accent was lightly German. "Mr..."

Shawn hesitated for only a moment. "Shawn McClaren of Philadelphia," he said. He owed them the truth, at least in answer to their questions.

"You are a long way from home," she noted.

Homesickness nearly overwhelmed him. His parents and sisters might be sitting to their supper even now, his place at the table left empty and bereft. Did they wonder where he was? If he yet lived?

His throat too tight to answer, Shawn nodded in response.

Mrs. Ballard seemed to understand and took pity on him. "Pete, I am certain Mr. McClaren would be thankful for a drink."

The oldest boy poured him a cup of ale, and Shawn drank from it thankfully. It didn't taste like fish—a nice change from the water on the fishing boat. He had only been on the fishing boat for half a day, but he could still smell fish. He'd rather smell the marshes on the island. Or the salt breeze. Or the wool oil.

"How is my father?" Sheridan asked him, serving him what remained of the roast beef.

"He's well." Shawn smiled. "I was very taken with him. He's a man who deserves respect without demanding it. And he's wise."

"And he knows it," Sheridan said wryly. Shawn couldn't disagree.

"And the others?"

"Everyone I met was in good health."

Sheridan studied him a moment, and his wife took that opportunity to speak.

"How did you like the island?" she asked.

He noticed the children watching him avidly.

"I was only there a short time," he answered, choosing his words carefully, "but most of what I saw was lovely. It is something to behold, the village and fields, and then the beaches and marsh. I've seen nothing of its like."

"I've never been," Hilda admitted. "In truth, I've not felt the desire until recently. I think the children should see where their father comes from, and with it only being a day's travel . . ." She let the thought drift off.

"Hilda prefers the city," Sheridan said. "As do I, now. I am surprised that you saw the marshes. They are a fair distance from the village."

"We happened upon them when making land," Shawn answered, and then cursed himself silently.

"'We'?"

"My companions, who remained behind." One hopeful for a peaceful life, he thought, and another hopefully at peace.

Sheridan eyed him again. Shawn wondered what the letter had told the man.

Hilda asked a few more questions of the island and his travels. Shawn kept the answers general, not going into too many details in case he gave away more than he wished. He ate his fill, which was easy as there was more than enough food. Soon enough, Sheridan was excusing the children to prepare for bed, and Hilda followed to make a bed ready for Shawn.

"Let's retire to the parlor," Sheridan told him. He took his cup with him, so Shawn did the same.

They sat in the same chairs as before, with the lamp burning between them.

"Tell me what happened," Sheridan asked quietly.

"One of my companions shot and killed one of the bears," Shawn told him just as quietly. He knew he wouldn't have to go into more detail about the bears. "The bears came to the village and killed him." He suppressed a shudder at seeing Trevor drowned. "No one else was hurt," he added quickly when he saw Sheridan rise up in alarm. "And the bears returned across the river."

Sheridan sat back, taking in his words. "You said one of your companions," he said.

"Trevor. He's buried in the cemetery. My friend Wallis elected to stay behind." Shawn smiled sadly. "He has plans to make it a permanent home."

"Oh?"

"One of the young ladies caught his fancy. And him hers, I'd say."

A slight smile creased Sheridan's mouth. "One of the problems with living on an island," he told Shawn. "Courting can be an issue when you are related to nearly everyone."

"I could see that being difficult." He thought of Deirdre and how she'd admitted to being related to every family on the island. Would she come to Norfolk to find a husband?

The thought drove a cold chill through him that quickly turned black.

"Father asks that I help see you home," Sheridan said, "and so I will. If your name is suspect by the militia, however, we'll have to make a credible story for you, and a name to go with it. What skills do you have?"

Besides bringing trouble wherever I go? Shawn thought wryly. "I can hunt and track. I know the runnings of a city." He'd studied politics and administrating under his father, but details about population management and districting were dry and lifeless, especially after all he'd seen in the past few years. He knew he'd never return to that work. No, he'd see his family safe and then find a new way of life for himself, away from city life and politics.

Maybe on an island.

"A trapper then," Sheridan said, breaking into Shawn's thoughts. "It would be more believable than a lost city employee. We can say you were set upon by a group of natives still stirred up from the war and all your possessions were stolen, including any papers you might possess."

Shawn bit the inside of his cheek to keep from arguing against the plan. It was believable enough, but he'd always felt that most attacks by natives were well deserved. They were the ones taking over the natives' land.

"Fine," he managed to say when Sheridan glanced sharply at him because of his silence.

"I'll show you to your bed," Sheridan said, standing. "No doubt you are weary."

Shawn drained his cup and stood to follow Sheridan. He ended in a backroom on the third floor, which looked to have been for storage but had been converted into a smallish room for overnight visitors. The bed was narrow but long enough to accommodate a man of fair height. A small table served as a wash stand with a basin and pitcher that had been filled. A woven towel sat folded next to the basin. And two hooks on the wall would keep clothing off the floor, which did have a small rug.

The room was windowless, however, and stuffy in the summer heat, but Shawn didn't complain. It was enough to have a bed.

"Thank you," he told Sheridan.

The man nodded and bid him good night. Shawn found his bag had been moved into the room, and the small candle's flame gave him just enough light to see that all his things were untouched within. Not that he expected to find them disturbed, but he'd hate to lose his uncle's knife a second time.

Shawn removed his shirt and boots and blew out the candle. He lay on top of the bed sheets and stared up at the blackness.

The island would be quiet at this hour. A cool breeze would be blowing in off the ocean, fanning the curtains if the shutters had been left open. He'd smell bayberries and lavender, the salt breeze and the earthy hint of the marsh.

Closing his eyes, Shawn tried to dream of the island without dreaming of Deirdre, but she drifted through his sleep as persistently as the oppressive heat around him.

CHAPTER NINE

Thursday, June 6th

As Shawn came down the stairs the next morning, he heard voices from the parlor. The hair on the back of his neck rose and he froze in place. He knew one of those voices all too well.

"He can't be trusted," John Guthrie said with an icy tone.

"Can you?" Sheridan challenged. Silence answered. "I've had a letter from my father, John. From what he wrote, you have much to answer for."

"I don't answer to your father or anyone else on that island." Guthrie spoke with venom in his tone.

"Then why are you here?"

"Who brought you the letter?" Guthrie challenged. "I know McClaren's been here. Is he still?"

Sheridan didn't answer.

"We were close once, Sheridan," Guthrie said in a calmer voice. "Closer than cousins. Like brothers, once."

"That was before Lizbeth died. And you were the one who broke off from the family, John, not the other way around."

"You took Bryant's side!" Guthrie's roar echoed through the house. Shawn heard footsteps above him and twisted to see Hilda. He held his hand up to stop her, and she nodded, worried, as Guthrie continued.

"He seduced my sister and you stood by him!"

"Lizbeth loved him. You've never been able to see that."

"She was a girl."

"Yes, she was and they should have waited for the families' blessings, but your father wasn't going to give Bryant the chance he deserved."

"Deserved?" Guthrie laughed harshly. "Bryant was an arrogant ass who would never deserve, could never deserve, Lizbeth. She was too good for him."

"A lot of folks said that about your parents."

"Sheridan—"

"What happened to Derry, John?"

The question came so suddenly that it surprised Shawn. What exactly had Peter written to his son?

"He was killed by bears," Guthrie answered flatly.

"I don't believe that."

"I don't care what you believe."

"Don't you? Why are you here, then?"

"I came looking for McClaren." Shawn's blood ran cold at the announcement. "And I'll have him."

"I have no idea who you're talking about." The front door opened. "I'm sure you have other places to be, John."

Boot steps sounded across the floor, then paused.

"Derry wasn't killed by a bear," John said.

"John—"

"Stay out of this, Sheridan. That's the only warning you'll get."

The door slammed shut.

Shawn leaned against the wall of the stairs, weak and full of doubts. He'd brought all of this on, but it was hard to regret it completely. John Guthrie had been a cottonmouth snake hiding on that island, willing to strike when it suited him to do so. That he was involved in Derry's death, Shawn had no doubts. It was all a question of how and why, both of which most likely led to Alistaire Guthrie.

Sins of families he'd never heard of until a week ago.

Only a week? He closed his eyes. He was tired, so very tired, of running. Of worrying about his family and now about Wallis. Of worrying about the trouble he might bring into the house of anyone kind enough to offer him shelter.

He could make it easy. He could march to the local militia and give himself up. Trust that his parents and sisters could look after themselves. Swear that Wallis and Trevor were dead. And return to prison to serve out his time for choosing the wrong side of the war and being unable to accept when the war was lost. Hadn't that been why he'd truly escaped? Hoping to hear the call to arms again and rejoin the regiments?

He no longer knew.

Hilda moved above him on the narrow stairs. "Mr. McClaren?"

He glanced up at her. He had an impossible choice to make and he couldn't begin to know which the better was. Run or surrender?

Damned or the devil, he thought wearily.

"Mr. McClaren?" Sheridan called up the stairs. "You can come down. He's gone."

Shawn closed his eyes and allowed himself a moment. Hilda touched his shoulder, and when he looked up at her, she smiled. "Trust my husband," she told him quietly.

"But can he trust me?"

She didn't answer, but her smile wavered.

Shawn drew himself upright and descended the stairs. Hilda moved past him to go to her husband, who wrapped his arm around her waist. It was touching, especially since the move looked long practiced and completely unconscious.

"I can't stay," Shawn began, but Sheridan held up his hand.

"Pete, I have need of you," he called.

The oldest of his sons came into the room from the dining room. He held himself tightly.

"You heard?" Sheridan asked his son.

Pete nodded with a guilty expression.

"We'll discuss this family's need to eavesdrop at another time," Sheridan said, glancing down at his wife, who went pink but smiled to him. "I need you to go to Kenneth's and warn Joseph that John was here. Don't dawdle."

Pete nodded, grabbed his coat and hat from the pegs by the door, and sprinted away from the house. Sheridan closed the door behind him.

"I'll have Marie put on tea," Hilda said. "Breakfast will be on the table soon."

She kissed Sheridan on the cheek and left the room. Sheridan ran his hand over his chin and looked years older.

"I should go," Shawn began again.

"Yes. You should. And soon."

Shawn hesitated. Sheridan faced him. "I had enough of the story in the letter from my father to understand some of what happened in the last week, but I need the holes filled in if I'm to render you aid."

"I'm not going to ask for—"

Sheridan cut him off. "You didn't. My father did. Sit."

Shawn didn't move at once. He knew he was standing on the threshold of the choice he had to make. Run or surrender. Damned or the devil.

He'd never escape the devil if he gave in, but the damned could find salvation if he tried hard enough.

Decided, Shawn sat.

"This will take planning," Sheridan told him, "and cleverness. And speed."

"What will?" Shawn asked.

Sheridan smiled, and he looked remarkably like his father. "Stealing you out from under the fist of John Guthrie."

~*~

It was all Shawn could do not to pace. He sat in the chair as Sheridan spoke with his wife in the next room. His leg jogged up and down with barely constrained anxiety. He'd made his decision. He knew that. The knowledge, however, didn't take away his need to leave.

Selfish, that's what he was. He was putting Sheridan and his family in danger. But, God help him, he didn't want to do this alone.

When the front door opened, Shawn leapt to his feet. Joseph entered without knocking, followed by a young woman.

Sheridan met them and shook hands with Joseph.

"He's already been to Kenneth's," Joseph said without preamble. "John has."

Sheridan nodded then looked pointedly at the young woman.

"Ah, this is Miss Iola Beaman," Joseph introduced. "She was there when John came."

"Not a friendly man, is he?" Iola said with a wry smile. She was pretty, with warm dark eyes and a freckled face and an expression that spoke of easy amusement and cleverness. Shawn could see why Joseph was taken with her.

"This may not be the safest matter to involve yourself," Sheridan told the young woman, and Joseph began shaking his head in warning before Sheridan had finished.

Iola grinned at the older man. "Not safe? With all these fit men about? I can't imagine what trouble I'd come to."

Shawn liked her immediately. Deirdre would too. He wished he could be there when they met.

But no, he had to leave.

"We decided to disguise Shawn as a trapper," Sheridan told Joseph, "to help him get a ship out of Norfolk. Do you think Kenneth will help?"

"Kenneth told John in no uncertain terms that he wants no part in any of this," Joseph answered. "He made sure to include me in that little declaration, too."

Shawn tensed. "Guthrie has probably had you followed here."

"Not at all," Iola assured him. "I sent Pete with my sister, Ada. He was wearing Joseph's hat and coat, and I gave mine to my sister." She leaned towards Sheridan and put her hand next to her mouth as though sharing a secret. "Could be Ada will have her eye on your son, sir. She's a bit of a silly thing, but she can cook well."

Sheridan chuckled. "I see."

Joseph shook his head, trying not to smile. "We watched from behind the house to see if they were followed. They were, too, by two militia men."

Shawn swallowed hard. "If they're caught—"

"Nothing will happen," Sheridan assured him. "Pete and Ada will have done nothing wrong. I hope," he added, eyeing Iola.

"Oh no, sir, not a bit. I gave Ada a few coins, and Pete is escorting her to the confectionery. She tends to overindulge in sweets. But she is a very good cook," she repeated.

"We'll have to put together clothing for Shawn without Kenneth's help, then," Sheridan said, rubbing his chin.

"If we might suggest," Iola began, then she prodded Joseph in the ribs.

"Right. Iola had an idea as we walked over. I think it's a good one."

"Oh?" Sheridan didn't look hopeful, but Shawn had seen the power of a young woman's cleverness. He came forward.

"I'd like to hear your idea, Miss Beaman."

She smiled at him with a gleam in her eyes. "There's a ship leaving with the morning current," she told them.

"How do you know this?" Sheridan asked, surprised. Joseph looked on with pride and amusement.

"I sent my friend's brother to inquire. He owes me a favor," she explained, "on account of my introducing him to his betrothed. As I was saying, there's a ship, and, with your assistance, sir, my friend's brother will purchase a berth aboard. Then he'll leave on it."

Sheridan and Shawn looked at her.

"I should say," Iola amended innocently, "that Mr. McClaren will be on it, only not as himself, but as Mr. Hathaway Bivens."

"Your friend's brother," Shawn said. Iola nodded.

"And my friend, Betsy, will be there to see her brother off."

"She will?"

"She owes me a favor too, for introducing her brother to his betrothed. Her father wouldn't let her court until the eldest son made a good match."

"It must be a good match," Shawn said.

"Oh, yes, they are all very happy with the arrangement."

"This could put him into some trouble," Sheridan warned her.

"Hathaway is accustom to trouble," Iola said with a wave of her hand. "And his father is used to getting him out of it."

"You may not understand the whole of it," Shawn began, but Joseph interrupted.

"I explained everything to Iola. She understands what's at stake."

"And Mr. Bivens?"

"Hathaway thinks it's a fine game," Iola told him.

Sheridan was looking unhappy, but Iola and Joseph were full of enthusiasm.

Shawn turned to Sheridan. "What do you think?"

"I think Mr. Hathaway Bivens is going to give his wife-to-be a great deal of trouble in their lives."

"She's looking forward to bringing him to heel," Iola assured them. "So consider this a wedding gift to them both. He gets one last bit of mischief and she gets to rail him for it. They'll both be happy."

Shawn couldn't help but laugh at that. "You've convinced me, Miss Beaman. If Mr. Bivens is willing to risk his good name—"

Iola chuckled.

"—then I will accept your plan." He faced Sheridan again. "John might be watching at the docks, especially any ships leaving for the north."

"That's the best part," Joseph told them. "The ship Iola means to send you on is going south."

Which was how the next morning, Shawn walked to the docks with a young woman he'd never met on his arm.

Iola's plan was simple, but brilliant. He'd take the ship to Charleston, then hire another going north. It would take longer to reach Pennsylvania, but it was a safer route then trying to hire a ship north from Norfolk with John Guthrie and the militia watching. Sheridan had given him money enough to return to Philadelphia, with extra for room and board should he need to stay in Charleston.

He was dressed in one of Pete's suits, which had been quickly altered by Iola and Hilda to fit him, as he was broader than Pete, but not as tall. He carried a satchel from Sheridan with a change of clothes, none of which came from the island except for the cowl from Miss Clary. The spatterdashes from Deirdre, he wore over his trousers and boots, which were a pair of Hathaway's that his sister, Betsy had brought with her.

If Guthrie was watching for him and recognized the stitching of the spatterdashes, so be it, but Shawn was going to wear them even with the risk. It was all he had of Deirdre.

He had left Sheridan's house with Pete in the early hours before dawn and hidden in a shed near the Bivens house, tucked in a corner, and had awoken with a crick in his neck. Joseph and Iola had stayed through supper, waiting for Pete to return so they could sneak back to their own houses. Before they left, Iola had given him a hug.

"Take care, Mr. McClaren, and wish your family well from me."

"I owe you more than I could repay."

"Nonsense. I'm sure you'd find some way to repay me if you could." She'd left him with Joseph.

"That's quite a young woman," Shawn had told Joseph, who was staring the direction Iola had gone with a love-struck look.

"Yes." He faced Shawn and held out his hand. "I wish you a good journey."

Shawn hesitated, then held out his own. In it was his knife in its beaded sheath.

Joseph stared at it. "I can't accept that."

"Yes, you can." He pressed it into the younger man's hand. "With my thanks. And, if you will," Shawn paused, and Joseph spoke before he could go on.

"I won't pass any word from you to Deirdre," he told Shawn solemnly. "Let her go on with her life and you go on with yours."

Shawn had swallowed hard, but he had nodded.

Betsy drew him to a halt. "There be your ship," she told him, her Irish accent thick.

"Thank ye for seeing me to it," Shawn told her, drawing out his own Scots-Irish as thick as he could make it. It made her smile, dimples appearing in her cheeks. She raised up and leaned toward him. He thought for certain she meant to kiss his cheek, but just before she could come close enough, she stopped.

"Good voyage, sir," she told him. "And much luck."

"Thank you."

Betsy turned and walked away, glancing back once to give him a little wave. She clasped her hands behind her back and went with her head held high and a jaunt in her step.

Who knew women could be so clever? Or so bold? Or so devious.

Shawn sighed. He was thankful for it. Hopefully, Sheridan and the others would come to no trouble for helping him. He owed them more than he could repay, no matter what Iola had said. Shawn was in their debt. Somehow, he'd find a way to settle it.

In the meantime, he had a ship to catch, and a home to return to.

Moving with confidence he didn't entirely feel, Shawn walked to the ship, trying to keep his thoughts toward the future and not dwelling on who he was leaving behind.

CHAPTER TEN

Monday, June 10th

"How long did Joseph say he'd be gone?" Wallis asked. He and Deirdre and Hetty were sitting on the porch at Shaw House. Wallis was staring at the wool tangled between his fingers as Hetty calmly unraveled it.

"He didn't," Deirdre answered. She was stitching absently on a new pair of spatterdashes, these for Joseph, while Hetty tried to teach Wallis how to stitch. That wasn't going well, but Wallis was determined, and Deirdre admired him for it.

No one spoke of Shawn or if he'd made it safely from Norfolk. Deirdre refused to believe that he didn't. She imagined him on a ship, sailing for Philadelphia and his family, and going on with his life.

As she had to go on with hers.

"When Joseph goes back, though," Deirdre said, lowering her stitching to look at the couple, "I'm going with him."

"What does your great aunt say?" Hetty asked.

"I'm tired of waiting for everyone else to decide for me. I'm going and that's that."

Wallis chuckled. "I'm looking forward to watching anyone try to stop you."

Deirdre stared at him, then she laughed. "I'll make sure to have the discussion near an open window, then, so you can overhear."

Hetty shook her head.

"There's a ship!" Claude and several of the other boys, who had taken to watching for Joseph's return, ran through the village.

"A ship!" Paden echoed. Dogs raced after them, barking.

"Why are those dogs barking like the end of times is coming?" Great Aunt Clary slammed back the door to the house.

"Claude says a ship is here," Deirdre told her, standing. "I'm going to go meet Joseph at the dock."

"You do that. And get those boys to stop shouting and carrying on."

Smiling, Deirdre left the porch. She was eager to hear about Joseph's trip to Norfolk and his visit with the woman he hoped to court. And, of course, to learn that Shawn was safely away.

It ached to think of him, but she was muddling through it. She was thankful to have met him, to know that there might be a time she'd find a man she'd want to marry. It wasn't going to be Shawn, and she had to accept that, no matter how it hurt. She had to move past everything that had happened.

As Uncle Peter had told her, it would take time. There was so much she had to work through. For now, she was simply trying to live in the moment.

She crested the sand dune. And stopped.

That wasn't a fisherman's boat. There was no way Joseph would have hired a brigantine. And even if he had, it wouldn't be lowering an oar boat carrying so many men.

Militia.

Deirdre turned and ran back down the dune, her skirts gathered in her hands out of the way. The dogs saw her when she reached the village and began chasing her, barking once again.

"Claude!" she shouted as soon as she saw the boys, "fetch your father!"

Claude looked surprised, then nodded and raced toward the Lacour House.

"What's going on?" Patrick hurried towards her.

"Militia." She grabbed his forearms to steady herself. "They have a ship. They're coming to the island." Her heart was pounding.

Patrick's jaw worked back and forth. "Go get Rosa. I'll pass the word."

"Wallis—"

"We knew this would come, Deirdre. We have a plan. We keep to it."

33333333333333

Deirdre nodded, forcing herself to calm, and they parted, Patrick towards the dock and Deirdre toward Marcos' house.

Rosa was standing on the porch with Aileen in her arms. "They've come?"

"We haven't much time."

"I'll pass the word."

It was gratifying to see how quickly the village could move when motivated. Wallis disappeared. The women gathered in front of the main houses to spin or stitch or finish chores. The older children were sent to tend the sheep and the younger stayed with their mothers.

Deirdre went with Hetty to Marcos' house with their stitching. Rosa had brought out her wheel and let Aileen play in front of the porch. Ferny bounced over to her and the little girl squealed with delight.

"All will be well," Deirdre comforted Hetty quietly. Hetty nodded, tight-lipped and clearly upset.

"I thought Aunt Clary would be with us," Rosa said as she started treadling her wheel.

Deirdre glanced back at the house but saw no sign of her great aunt.

"Trust Great Aunt Clary to go her own way," Deirdre said. She tried not to fret, but there was no telling what her great aunt might do. At least she'd agreed with the need to protect Wallis. No one in the village was going to let him be captured.

They heard Patrick's voice growing closer.

"There they are," Rosa whispered. The women stopped their work to watch the militia enter the village.

Honestly, they weren't much to look at. Their uniforms were more of a haphazard collection of wool coats dyed the same shade of blue and tan trousers, with a variety of shirt colors and hats. The eight men carried muskets with bayonets, however, and shot bags and powder horns.

The man obviously in charge was the only one in an actual uniform. He wore the same shade of blue coat, this with brass buttons, and pale trousers with a white shirt and undercoat. He had a tricorn hat with a blue braid. He did not have a musket, but he had a pistol and saber hanging from his belt. He was younger than she would have expected to be in charge.

Then again, Shawn had been younger, too, and obviously in charge. Or had that been simply his natural ability to take the responsibility of leadership.

Patrick and Conor were with the militia, with Patrick doing the talking.

"We don't care for intruders," he was saying crossly. "Especially unexpected ones."

"My apologies, Mr. Donaghue," the leader said, "but under the circumstances it did not seem wise to announce our intentions."

"Because of this fugitive."

"Exactly."

Patrick stopped and crossed his arms. "And we tell you he isn't in our village."

"I do wish that I could take your word for it, sir," the officer said, and he sounded as though he did wish it were so. "We have had a clear report of his presence, along with possible others."

Patrick didn't reply.

"I trust you will allow us to conduct our search?" the officer asked.

"Fine. But be warned, lieutenant, we won't think kindly of any of our people being mistreated."

"That won't be an issue, sir. I give you my word." And with that, the lieutenant turned and gave a terse command. His men separated into pairs and spread through the village, Conor trailing after.

"I'd like to meet some of your fine people," the lieutenant said to Patrick. "With your permission."

Patrick nodded unhappily, his arms still crossed.

The lieutenant looked to where Deirdre sat with Hetty and Rosa and approached. "Ladies." He removed his hat. His black hair, somewhat ringed by his hat, was pulled back by a tidy ribbon, and his blue eyes caught Deirdre's and held. He was a handsome man.

Deirdre blushed when his gaze lingered.

"My cousin," Patrick said pointedly, "Deirdre Donaghue."

The lieutenant bowed, much like Shawn had, but without the flourish. "Miss Donaghue."

"My wife," Patrick continued, "and her cousin Hetty Fonseca."

"Mrs. Donaghue. Miss Fonseca."

Did Deirdre imagine it, or did the lieutenant's gaze dart back to her.

"You're looking for a fugitive?" Deirdre asked.

"Yes, miss. Have you seen strangers in the village?"

"I have."

Patrick stiffened and the lieutenant looked at him with consternation.

"Are they still here?"

"No, sir."

Hetty sniffled and ducked her head.

"Miss Fonseca?"

"I'd take it as a personal favor if you'd leave my cousin be," Rosa told the lieutenant with a trace of sadness.

"I do apologize, madam, but I must ask questions." The lieutenant knelt down before Hetty. Deirdre was impressed by his courtesy. "Have you seen the men in question, Miss Fonseca? Let me assure you, in no way are you in any trouble. You may speak freely."

"He—" Hetty's voice broke, and Deirdre knew it wasn't feigned. Hetty was so worried for Wallis. "He said he'd marry me."

The lieutenant drew back, clearly shocked.

"And then he left the village," Rosa bit out.

"We gave him our hospitality," Deirdre said, her hands on her hips, "and he repaid it by wooing dear Hetty before he left."

"I am so very sorry," the lieutenant said to Hetty. He stood. "Do you know where he might have gone? And if anyone was with him?"

"The one," Patrick answered, "McClaren, left several days ago."

"Did he say he'd return?"

Deirdre bit her lip and looked away.

"Miss Donaghue?" The lieutenant's voice was full of sympathy. "Did he make you promises?"

"If you are suggesting—" Patrick began angrily.

"It's all right, Patrick," Deirdre told him. She straightened. "No, Mr. McClaren was kind and decent. He made no mention of having any intention of returning here again."

"He said he wanted to return home," Rosa added.

Two of the militiamen approached. "Sir, we found the burnt cabin, just as was reported. And two of the three oar boats."

"We only have two in use," Patrick said to the man darkly. The man tried not to quell under Patrick's stern gaze.

"We were told there were three," the lieutenant explained.

"It might have been the older one. We never use it."

"But it's missing?"

Patrick shrugged. "We never use it, so no one's checked on it."

"Where does the river let out?"

"Near the marsh," Patrick answered.

"Could a man hide in the marsh if necessary?"

"I suppose. We've never gone there."

"Why?"

"No need."

"We have all we need on this side of the river," Deirdre added, smiling. The lieutenant's expression relaxed.

"But I suppose he might have crossed the river," Patrick said. "There's the fig grove. And forest, we think. And the marsh."

The lieutenant nodded.

Two more militiamen approached. "We've searched all the houses but this one and that one there, sir." The man nodded toward Shaw House.

A screeching voice came from in front of Shaw House.

"Come into my home uninvited, will you!" Great Aunt Clary chased a militiaman around the corner, one of the old muskets in her hands.

"Oh, dear lord," Patrick muttered.

"I'll do you one for invading our village." She held up the musket to aim. Deirdre and Patrick both sprinted forward as the lieutenant gave a sharp command to his men to lower weapons.

"Aunt Clary!" Patrick reached her first and grabbed the musket from her. "What are you doing?"

"He broke into my house," Great Aunt Clary screeched. "Woke me from my nap. I'll give him a good switching, I will. Deirdre, go fetch my switching stick."

Deirdre didn't move. Great Aunt Clary didn't have a switching stick.

"That won't be necessary, madam," the lieutenant said quickly as he approached. He glanced at the militiaman.

"No one inside, sir." He was rubbing his head. "She hit me with a broom," he admitted.

Deirdre covered her mouth to keep from laughing.

"You get going!" Great Aunt Clary demanded. "We don't want nothing to do with your war."

"The war is over, madam," the lieutenant told her. "We were

looking for a fugitive from it.”

“Ain’t no one here running from any war. Deirdre, where is that stick?”

“I don’t believe that will be necessary,” the lieutenant answered. He was trying to hide his own smile.

“You don’t, do you, now? How old are you, boy? Humph. Boys playing at soldiering.” Great Aunt Clary put her hands on her hips and walked back toward the front of the house, muttering about beetle-headed young men and their foolish notions.

“I apologize for my great aunt,” Deirdre told the lieutenant and the militiaman.

“Think nothing of it. We should have ascertained the house was empty first.” He gave his man a pointed look. “If we could inspect your home?” he asked Patrick, who nodded curtly, still holding the musket, the end pointed toward the ground.

The militiamen were quick at their work and reported finding nothing out of the ordinary.

“Of course you didn’t,” Patrick snapped.

“I hope you left everything the way you found it,” Rosa told them. The men nodded quickly.

“Where would be the best place to put in on the other side of the island?” the lieutenant asked Patrick, though his gaze darted back to Deirdre.

“I suppose the southeastern shore,” Patrick said grudgingly.

“But you must take care for the hogs,” Deirdre warned him. “They don’t like intruders any more than my great aunt does.”

The lieutenant studied her. “Does that mean that you are not so opposed to visitors?”

Deirdre opened her mouth, then shut it with a snap. There was no doubting the lieutenant’s meaning. He gave her a smile, which made him even more handsome.

Deirdre knew Rosa, Hetty, and Patrick were staring at her. She struggled to find something to say.

“I apologize,” the lieutenant said before she could think of anything. “That was out of line.”

“Not at all,” she told him, then closed her mouth again. What was she doing?

He smiled again, then faced Patrick. “The southeastern shore. Good. We’ll leave you to your peace, then.”

"There's biting flies in the marsh," Rosa warned him. "They come over here sometimes."

"Thank you for the warning."

"And watch out for the bears," Deirdre added.

"Bears?" The lieutenant frowned.

"The reason we don't go over there," she said. "Aside from having what we need here. The bears—" Her voice caught. It was still too close, everything that had happened with her uncle and the bears.

"They've killed men," Patrick finished.

"Recently?"

He nodded. "One of your fugitives. He's buried on the hill if you want to take him back with you," Patrick added coarsely.

"That won't be necessary." To his credit, the lieutenant took the suggestion without offense. He sighed. "Bears. They're a threat?"

"Always."

"You don't think they'd kill him," Hetty gasped. Rosa reached over and took her hand.

"Wallis knew about the bears, Hetty."

Hetty look unconvinced.

"If I might," Deirdre said, drawing away from the others. Patrick and the lieutenant followed. "They had to arrive on the island somehow," she said quietly.

"It could be that he plans to return the same way," the lieutenant finished. "How long ago did he leave?"

"I'm not certain."

He looked at Patrick.

"Last I looked for him, he was gone."

The lieutenant's eyes narrowed. He studied Patrick, then Deirdre.

Deirdre's mouth went dry. They'd all agreed not to lie except by omission, but she couldn't bring herself to admit that Wallis had only just left the village. It was too likely that the lieutenant would call for a more extended search, if he wasn't already planning to, and Wallis wouldn't have had time to reach the rock shoals near the north shore.

His gaze stayed on her and she tried to look confident. Finally he nodded. "Very well." He said the words as though he was accepting their lack of an answer. "I understand," he added, still looking at Deirdre.

She ducked her head. She couldn't help it.

"I hope you will forgive our intrusion," the lieutenant said to Patrick.

"I'll try."

"I don't think you have to worry about us returning," the man continued, which made Deirdre look up in surprise. "Unless we might be made welcome," he said to her.

"I—" Deirdre stammered. He meant to come to see her.

Her.

And maybe court her.

An officer.

She didn't know what to think.

Patrick glanced between them. "We might," he said slowly. "With an understanding between us."

"Of course."

Deirdre swallowed, feeling shaky.

"Miss Donaghue." The lieutenant bowed again before turning towards where his men were assembling.

"Wait," she called before thinking better. He faced her. "I don't know your name."

He smiled again. "Lieutenant Warren Grant."

"Thank you for your courtesy in all of this, Lieutenant Grant."

"Of course."

With a final smile, he turned away. Deirdre rejoined the others to watch the militia depart the village, Patrick going with them.

"What was that about?" Rosa asked as Deirdre sank back into her chair, stunned.

"I think— I think he means to court me."

Hetty and Rosa stared at her. "You didn't give him reason to do so, I hope," Rosa said.

"I'm not sure."

"Deirdre," Hetty gasped. "We can't keep hiding Wallis every time an officer comes to the island."

Deirdre sighed. "Of course not. So, I suppose I'd have to go to him. If I was of a mind to."

"And are you?"

Deirdre didn't answer. Instead, she stared off in the direction of the mainland.

CHAPTER ELEVEN

March, 1783

Shawn sat in the parlor before the hearth, staring into the dark recess. A single candle burned at his elbow on the table next to the upholstered chair. He was clean. He was well fed. His beard was gone, his hair trimmed and combed, and he was wearing clothing made for him that had been recently washed.

None of it had eased the burdens weighing down upon him.

"Shawn?"

His mother came into the parlor, carrying an oil lamp. The light was far too harsh, and he squinted.

"I am sorry, darling." She put the lamp on the table by the door and came to sit in the chair next to him. She'd aged in the time he'd been gone. Sorrow darkened her gray eyes and white touched her honey-colored hair, but she was still lovely and her smile for him was still sweet. "Can you not sleep?"

"I think all I've done the past months is sleep."

His mother looked at him skeptically. "You can't fool me, Shawn. I know you haven't slept more than a few hours each night." She reached over to take his hand. Hers was small and pale in his. Deirdre's hand had been tanned and calloused.

"Won't you speak to me?" The plea in his mother's voice tore into him. "You've hardly told us anything of how you came to be home with us. I know you've seen awful, terrible things, Shawn, but don't feel like you must keep it all bottled inside you to spare my sensibilities. I grew up in Beryl's Hollow, if you'll recall."

"I remember."

"Then please, son, unburden yourself. It does you no good keeping these memories buried."

Shawn frowned at the cold hearth. When he spoke, he meant only to tell her of how devastating the defeat at Yorktown had been and how difficult the imprisonment that followed. But then he was speaking of the escape, of running overland in hiding, of finding their way to the island.

It all came out. How Deirdre had found him, how the villagers had taken him in, and how he'd left it all behind to return home. He left out what had happened with Guthrie and the bears, though.

Silence followed as his voice fell quiet. He felt empty, but freed at the same time. He'd been keeping these memories buried for over half a year, and it was good to give them voice.

His mother still held his hand in hers. He didn't quite dare to look at her.

Without speaking, she rose. She gave his hand a slight squeeze, then she left the room.

Aching, Shawn stared into the hearth, feeling chill. He should have known better.

His mother returned. She set a wooden box onto the table. It was the size of one of the books his father kept in the library, but made of plain wood fitted together with grooves at the corners. Simple leather hinges held the box lid in place, and a metal clasp kept it closed.

Shawn leaned forward, watching his mother as she ran her fingers lovingly across the surface.

"My grandfather made this box for my grandmother. It is said that she kept it by her bedside until the day she died." She drew back. "Open it."

"What's inside?"

His mother didn't answer. Uncertain, Shawn loosened the metal clasp on the box and raised the lid. Inside were letters, folded carefully and laid one atop another.

"I don't understand."

"I didn't know my grandmother," his mother said, "but Father shared with me the stories she used to tell him. Some of those stories were about a friend living on an island. I thought they were simply tales for children until he gave me this box with the letters. I read them all. They were sent from that island."

"From an island. It couldn't be the same island." It just wasn't possible. But a doubt nagged at him with one name. Donaghue. The same last name his great grandfather had carried.

"Look at the letters."

Carefully, Shawn drew the top letter from the box and unfolded it. The handwriting was small but elegant. Someone learned had written these. He looked for the signature at the bottom.

His heart constricted. It was signed Ailee Donaghue.

"They met during the crossing from Ireland, your great grandmother Elsie MacClayne and Ailee Donaghue," his mother said. "That was when Elsie was carrying your grandfather, Jack."

"How is this possible?"

"I stopped asking that years ago."

The way his mother was looking at him made Shawn nervous. "You said you'd read the letters. What did they say? About the island?"

"More than you did. Shawn, what did you see there? What haven't you told me?"

He swallowed hard. He could still feel the weight of the bear atop him, feel the claws digging into his back, feel the hot breath upon his neck.

His mother took his hand again. "Tell me. Are the bears real?"

Slowly, Shawn nodded.

His mother's hand tightened over his. "Dear God."

He realized what Ailee Donaghue must have written about the bears. "It's not like you might think, Mother. They were only bears."

He told her the story of landing on the island, of the bears and John Guthrie.

Silence fell over them while the candle flame danced. Shawn's gaze was fixed on the letter in his hand. On the small, pinched writing.

It wasn't possible.

His great grandmother and Deirdre's great grandmother.

"Did she ever go to the island? Your grandmother?"

"No. She wrote her friend often and received letters in return, but Father said that after they parted on the ship, they never saw one another again."

Had his great grandmother paced the floor, anticipating another letter? Had she known what life was truly like on that island?

And who wrote to tell Ailee Donaghue of his great grandmother's death? She had died before his own mother was born. How many years did Ailee live, grieving for a friend who would never write again?

He thought of Wallis, living the rest of his days on the island, never knowing what would become of his parents.

He thought of Deirdre, of his last sight of her on the dunes.

"I can't go with you to Nova Scotia." He placed the letter back into the box.

"Shawn—"

"I'm sorry, Mother. I can't."

She smiled, and in the candlelight, she looked years younger. "Oh, my son. I was going to say that I already knew you wouldn't come with us. You would never be content running away again. I know your father doesn't consider it running, but we are. We'll make a good home in Nova Scotia, your father and I, and your sister and Gordon. They have little Muriel to consider now, after all. We'll make a fine life. I know it. But you… you were never one to run away from a fight, Shawn. All those summers spent with your cousins at Beryl's Hollow—you don't think I knew they treated you like a cast-off? But you went back every year. You were eager for it. I think you liked proving that you could keep up with them no matter what. And you'll do that again."

He was speechless. He'd run away, he wanted to say. He'd spent months running. He was still running.

"I can't say I won't worry for you," she admitted, and he saw tears sparkling in her eyes, caught in the gleam of the candlelight. "It would not be good if you were captured again. But I have faith in your skills. I know you'll take care." She reached up to touch his cheek. "I couldn't be more proud of the man you've become. And this country will need good men like you now more than ever."

Shawn leaned forward, and she held him. It was the closest he'd come to feeling like he was home, wrapped in his mother's embrace.

Reluctantly, he pulled away.

"Where will you go?" she asked. "Back to the island?"

"I can't stay there. Once I leave here, word will get out. Father told me today that my name came up in the assembly."

"He could try to get you clemency."

"And ruin your chances for Nova Scotia? No, I won't risk it. And I won't draw the villagers into this again, either. Wallis understood that when I left. It's why I told his folks he'd gone west."

"So you'll go west?"

"I think so. It'll give credence to what I said about Wallis."

"But you'll go to the island first?"

He looked at his mother, his throat tight. "Why?"

She tried to hide a smile, but he saw it. "Wallis might want word from home. And I thought you might want to share these with Ailee Donaghue's family." She touched the letters.

"I couldn't take these."

"Yes, you could. You will. They should be returned to her family." His mother grew sober. "I can't take them with me. They don't belong to me." She stood. "There's something else I want you to take, too."

"What is it?"

"When the time comes. When will you leave?"

He drew in a deep breath. Eagerness had chased away the last of his doubts. Eagerness and hope. "Soon."

CHAPTER TWELVE

April, 1783

Norfolk was exactly what Deirdre had imagined, and nothing like it at the same time. People, buildings, bustling port—those she expected. The diverse dress and accents, the smoke, the stench—those she hadn't anticipated in the least.

It was the people and the smells that got to her the most. The people were fascinating. She'd always enjoyed when someone brought a wife- or husband-to-be to the island and heard them speak and saw how they dressed. Elki and Mathilda had been the most interesting with their French and Iroquois upbringing. The town was like that nearly every place she turned. English, French, Irish, and Native accents surrounded her. The clothing varied just as much, with fancy breeches and long-tailed coats and tricorn hats resting on white wigs, to buckskins and beads. The women were no less extreme, from lovely skirts and blouses to homespuns.

At least Deirdre didn't feel too out of place in her own homespuns. She wasn't sure she liked having to wear the lace-frilled cap that her Aunt Daisy had insisted on. Mathilda had braided her hair and wrapped it around her head before Aunt Daisy tied the cap over it. Great Aunt Clary had given her a lacy shawl to wear over her best dress and apron, her copper spiral shawl pin curled through the delicate stitches to keep it in place. Nessa had given her a straw, flat-brimmed hat to wear and dressed it with bayberry leaves and lavender buds. The stockings were scratchy, though, and the shoes pinched.

Deirdre wished she could slip a few of the lavender buds free to hold to her nose. The stench was unbearable. From the fish and manure odors to the tanners and butchers stench, Deirdre thought that she might lose her sense of smell altogether. How could anyone stand it?

"We'll walk from here," Patrick told her. She'd accompanied him and Joseph on the fishing boat, and she'd held up very well on the water, though Joseph had warned her she might feel unsettled. She'd take that single stench of fish over this miasma of stink any day.

Perhaps staying on the island wasn't such a bad thought.

"I still don't see why you won't stay at Kenneth's with me," Joseph said as they walked, their bags thrown over his shoulder.

"I'll be there often enough," Deirdre assured him. "But Hilda invited me to stay with her and Sheridan, and her letter was so kind, I can't refuse. Besides," she added with a wry grin, "you'll be so busy trying to think of the right words to ask Iola to marry you that you won't even notice I'm not there."

"Not true." Joseph sniffed. "I need someone to help me come up with the right words."

"I'm sure Kenneth and Patrick will be more than happy. They've actually proposed before. I've not had the pleasure."

Patrick chuckled. "I'm still not sure if I was the one to propose or Rosa was."

"A little of both?"

"Are you going to see Lieutenant Grant if he calls on you?" Joseph asked.

Deirdre didn't answer at first. She had grown fond of Grant over the past months. He'd written her letters and had met with both Patrick and Joseph when they'd visited Norfolk, and they'd returned bearing small gifts from him. She was wearing the gloves he had sent, pretty pale blue cotton ones trimmed with tea-dyed lace that came to her wrist. She thought they'd look even better with crocheted lace instead of tatted.

She fiddled with the lace at her wrist, and Patrick caught her at it.

"Deirdre, if you aren't sure you want his attention, just say so."

"That's it, I'm not sure." She drew in a deep breath. "We've only spent that brief time together on the island, and that when he was hunting for Wallis. His letters are polite, and I enjoy reading them, but I'm not sure I should have accepted the gifts."

"Grant isn't an idiot," Joseph told her. "He knows trinkets aren't going to win you. I think he just wants the chance to try."

"If I were to marry him, I'd have to leave the island."

"Yes, you would," Patrick said.

"And there would be times he'd be away, or that we might have to move even farther from the island, with him an officer."

Patrick nodded and Joseph frowned.

"I know I've talked about leaving," Deirdre said, "but I always imagined leaving with a husband to be together, not spending time far apart."

"It would be a sacrifice, but if you cared enough for him, you'd be willing to make it." Patrick stopped in front of her. "Deirdre, don't make a match only because you want to leave the island. If Grant isn't the one for you, then I'll keep bringing you to Norfolk until you do meet the one."

"And what if I've already met the one?" her voice was small and she felt frail admitting it. She hadn't spoken about Shawn in so long, keeping him like a secret treasure close to her heart, one that, each time she brought out, caused her longing and heartache, but she kept doing so.

"Shawn isn't coming back," Patrick said sternly. His expression gentled. "I'm sorry, Deirdre, but it's time to put that behind you."

She nodded mutely.

Patrick looped her arm through his and they began walking again.

"I have an idea," Joseph said. "Why don't Iola and I take you for a walk to meet with the lieutenant? That way, we'll all be together and it won't be so strange. You could tell him you'd like to try being friends before anything else."

Deirdre brightened. "Yes, I like that idea."

Joseph looked pleased to have made her happy.

When they reached Sheridan's house, Deirdre was thankful to find that the worst of the stench had gone, but when she saw how closely the houses were built, right next to one another, she shuddered.

"How do they live like this?"

Patrick chuckled. "Sheridan likes the company. He says that he and the neighbors get together often, like a small village, sharing meals and celebrations together."

"Can't they do that without living on top of each other?"

"I think it's fun," Joseph said with a faraway look. "I'm looking forward to it."

"So you still mean to do it? To leave the island?"

He nodded, sobering. "I do. If Iola's father hasn't changed his mind about me working for him."

Deirdre fell silent. She couldn't imagine the island without Joseph, but she knew things changed. They'd changed so much in the past year she could hardly keep pace.

Patrick knocked on Sheridan's door. It opened almost at once.

Sheridan smiled when he saw them. Deirdre remembered her cousin as an eager, energetic young man, but the older man greeting them was far different, with his coat and breeches and white-powdered wig.

"Patrick, Joseph, come inside. Deirdre." Sheridan paused to look her over with a happy smile. "You've grown into quite the young woman."

"She's quite at that," Patrick muttered.

Sheridan laughed. "So I've heard. Come in." He shut the door behind them. "I have a bit of a shock for you all, especially you, Deirdre."

Deirdre looked at him in confusion, and Sheridan nodded toward the interior of the parlor. She turned, expecting to see the lieutenant.

It was Shawn.

Silence fell over the room, and her breath caught as she took him in, hardly daring to believe him real. Gone was the rough-dressed, bearded, and unkempt man from the island. In his place stood a gentleman, clean-shaven, well-dressed, his tricorn hat in his hand and a look of wonder on his face. His eyes, though, were the same stormy gray and were fixed on her as though he were memorizing every part of her.

"Shawn." His name came out breathless.

"Deirdre." Shawn blinked and seemed to remember himself. He swept into a bow that, this time, fit his stature and dress with such ease that Deirdre caught herself about to curtsy.

"Patrick. Joseph." Shawn greeted them both, looking hesitant. "It is good to see you well."

Patrick was the first to recover. "And you. Though, seeing you is a surprise, since we didn't think it would happen again."

"Yes." Deirdre finally found her voice. "Why are you here?" The question came out rudely, and Deirdre knew it, but the awe and shock of his appearance had twisted quickly into anger. "You were going home."

"And I've been home," he answered. "My family is safe. They are leaving for Nova Scotia soon."

"I've never heard of it."

"I hadn't either."

"So you're going to Nova Scotia, wherever that is, too? And just happened to stop here along the way?"

Shawn had the nerve to chuckle. "No. They're going north, out of the states. Many of the loyalists are, those that can't go to England."

"I hadn't realized it was as bad as all that," Patrick said with concern. "I hope they are being well-treated."

"For the most part." Shawn's expression grew shadowed. "Those who are cooperating, at least."

"Does your being here mean you aren't cooperating?" Patrick challenged.

Shawn looked down before answering. "I can't go north."

"Why?" Deirdre demanded. She took a step toward him.

His gaze met hers. "I had to know if I might have a chance with you."

Deirdre's chest tightened as chills raced through her. "A chance at what?"

He took a step toward her. "At making a life together."

"And if I've already chosen a life with someone?"

Shawn jerked back as if she'd struck him. "Have you?"

"No."

He relaxed, drawing in a deep breath.

"But there's someone wishing to court me."

"Who?" he demanded harshly with narrowed eyes. If she didn't know him better, she'd think he would fight the lieutenant for his chance to court her.

Did she know him better? After only a week in each other's company almost a year ago?

Shawn saw her hesitation and stepped back. "You're here to see him."

"I'm here to see my family. And," she confessed, "maybe him." She played with the lace on her gloves, and Shawn followed the movement. He pressed his lips together as if to hold back words.

"What?" she asked.

"Nothing."

She straightened, putting her hands on her hips. "Out with it."

"Were those a gift from him?"

Her arms dropped and she tugged at one of the gloves self-consciously. "And if I say yes?"

"Then I'll give you finer ones."

"You will, will you?"

"Yes."

"And if I don't want finer ones?"

He grew thoughtful, then smiled. "Then I'd give you a gift you'd truly appreciate."

"Oh? And what do you think I'd truly appreciate?"

Shawn turned from her to a satchel resting by one of the chairs in the parlor. He set aside his tricorn and drew out a parcel wrapped in cotton cloth and tied with a silk ribbon. Wordlessly, he held it out to her.

Her hands shaking, Deirdre accept it and untied the ribbon around it. She unfolded the fabric and her breath caught, nearly choking her.

Linen, finely woven, with an elegant and elegantly stitched roses lay amid the fabric. She let the fabric fall as she took hold of the linen, spreading it out.

It was a shawl. A magnificent, pale linen shawl worked with stitched roses sewn onto the fabric. The lacing around it was the same she'd envisioned putting on her gloves, only made with such delicate thread with much more skill than she possessed. Gently, she touched the delicate lace, then the fine linen.

"It belonged to your great grandmother," Shawn said, his own voice thick.

Deirdre stared at him in shock. "What?"

He stepped forward, hesitant. "Ailee Donaghue crossed the ocean with my great grandmother, Elsie MacClayne. They became friends. Elsie gave her a spiral shawl pin her husband, my great grandfather, had made for her, and Ailee gave her this shawl. The one she had worn for her wedding to your great grandfather."

Deirdre touched the spiral pin in her shawl. Shawn caught seen of it and his eyes widened in shock.

"How do you know all of this?" she asked.

"I have letters that Ailee wrote to Elsie."

Deirdre's mouth opened, but no words came out. She heard someone approach behind her.

"We have letters, too," Patrick said in awe, "from Elsie to Ailee."

Shawn smiled. "My mother thought it might be so. She insisted I bring the letters to you."

"Why would she do that?" Deirdre asked.

"Because she said they belong together to tell the story of the friendship between two great women."

"I can't believe this." Patrick moved to one of the chairs and sat heavily.

"I couldn't at first either," Shawn said. "I chose that island by chance. I had no idea—"

Deirdre interrupted. "Why the island?"

"What?"

"Why choose the island? Any island? How did you know they were there?"

Shawn frowned. "My grandfather made mention of them. He was fond of geography and made us sit with him for an hour or two a day when we visited, quizzing us. He told about the barrier islands and how a man could live a fine life on one. That's what made me think of them."

"This… this is incredible." Patrick ran his hands over his face.

"But you didn't know we were on that island?" Deirdre asked.

Shawn shook his head. "I recognized the name Donaghue, though, but I've known others by that name."

"Who?"

"My great grandmother's husband, for one. Niall Donaghue."

"Niall—" Deirdre's breath grew short. "He was my great grandfather's brother. And," she continued, remembering the family names she'd worked on so meticulously, "he was married to a woman named Elsie."

"Yes."

"Oh lord." She found the other chair and sank into it, the linen shawl clutched to her chest. "We're related."

Shawn laughed. "Not a bit."

"But—"

He came to kneel in front of her. "My great grandfather was Jacky MacClayne. He died at sea during the crossing. Elsie married Niall later. But you do have relatives, several of them, back north. They mostly live in a place called Beryl's Hollow."

"We're not related?"

"We're not related."

"So . . ." She glanced at the shawl in her hands. "You said this was my great grandmother's wedding shawl."

"Yes." His voice was gruff.

She eyed him. "Are you trying to tell me something, Shawn McClaren?"

"I thought I'd been clear enough."

"No, you said you wanted to know if there was a chance for us to make a life together."

"That's what I said, yes." His brow wrinkled. It was adorable.

"There are lots of ways that could happen," she told him archly. "You could move onto the island and we'd be in the village together. Or I could move here and we'd both be in Norfolk. Or—"

"Deirdre."

"Yes?"

"Marry me."

She was silent, but only for a moment.

"Are you asking or demanding?"

"Which would have you saying yes?"

"Asking," Patrick answered for her. "Unless you've forgotten she's a Donaghue."

Shawn smiled. "No, I haven't forgotten." He took her hand in his. "Will you marry me, Deirdre Donaghue?"

Thrills chased through her and she could hardly catch her breath to answer. "Yes, Shawn McClaren, I will."

Shawn stood, drawing her up with him, and wrapped his arms around her. She leaned against him, once again overcome by the sense of him around her, sheltering but seeking comfort from her at the same time. She laid her head on his chest and listened to the rapid beat of his heart. It was the most comforting sound in all the world.

"I believe you forgot an important point," Patrick interrupted, standing. Shawn drew back to look at him in question. "Asking permission to marry her? I am the head of the Donaghue family—"

"Patrick!" Deirdre turned on him, and he backed away, raising his hands. Shawn caught Deirdre before she could catch Patrick.

"Of course I give permission," Patrick quickly, with amusement.

"As if I needed any sort of permission," Deirdre told him crossly.

Patrick laughed. "Of course you don't. I suppose," he said thoughtfully, "we'll have to build another cabin. Unless you mean to live in Shaw House with Aunt Clary."

Shawn frowned suddenly. "I can't stay."

"It's fine," Patrick told him. "We have the matter with Wallis cleared up. He's taken Hetty to wife, and they are living in the cabin Joseph had started."

"Stewart House." Shawn nodded, looking pleased. "It does have a nice sound to it."

"He's been more than helpful to us," Patrick said. "The state has wanted an accounting of the island, so we've had to deal with the politics of it all. He's good at it. Taught me quite a bit."

"So it's safe for you to stay here," Deirdre said, but she felt the bite of guilt. Lieutenant Grant had been the one to arrange clemency for Wallis, though it had meant the island becoming an official part of the State of Virginia.

But Shawn was shaking his head. "I left Philadelphia on false pretenses. They'll be looking for me again, at least until everything is settled with the treaty with England, and there's no telling how long that will take. I won't put your family in threat again." He rubbed the bridge of his nose. "I didn't think this through. I'm sorry, Deirdre. I don't want to force you to run, too."

"Run where?"

"West. There are settlers heading across the Cumberland Gap to make homes west of the mountains. There's a river, a large one, that I thought to cross. I can't legally purchase land, not in my name, so I thought to go where the surveyors haven't been yet."

"That sounds dangerous," Patrick said, crossing his arms.

"It will be. Deirdre—"

She laughed. "You men."

"I don't see what's to laugh about," Patrick told her sternly.

"Don't you? Of course, you would be fixed with tradition, wouldn't you?" She waved her hand at her cousin as though shooing him away and faced Shawn. "It's simple. We get married on the island." It felt so natural to speak of marriage to Shawn, like it was always going to happen. "We can't marry anywhere else or Great Aunt Clary will hunt us down and drag us back by our ears."

Shawn chuckled. "I can see that happening."

"But then, we go west, like you said."

"Deirdre—"

"But we don't have to go as west as you thought, because you'll be able to purchase land."

"Deirdre—"

She laid her fingers over his mouth to silence him. "You'll be able to purchase land because after we're married, you'll take my name."

He gaped at her. Patrick did, too.

"Patrick is the one who officiates all the legal contracts on the island, aren't you, Patrick?"

He nodded.

"So when he submits our names, you'll be a Donaghue."

"You want me to take the Donaghue name."

Something in his tone made her pause. "Well, yes."

"And claim to marry another Donaghue?"

"Of course not. Patrick will list me by my other name."

The name hung between them, stark and rife with past betrayals.

"It was my mother's name, too," she said quietly. "I won't be ashamed of it."

He took her hands. "Nor should you be, Deirdre Guthrie."

Shawn pulled her to him. Her heart pounded again as she looked up into those stormy gray eyes, eyes she hoped to one day see looking back at her from their child. She could see her and Shawn working together, side by side, to make a new home, to raise crops and animals and finally, children. They'd teach them of the families they had left behind and tell the story of two women and their friendship that had somehow, across the years, brought Shawn and Deirdre together.

"I love you, Deirdre," Shawn whispered to her. "I'd run to the devil and back again if I could be with you."

"You don't have to run anymore, Shawn," she promised. "This time, we're going forward to make a new life, not run from an old one."

His arms tightened around her.

"I love you," she told him, each word full of gratefulness. Eagerly, she lifted to her toes. Shawn met her, and the kiss, their first kiss, was a promise of love and passion and a lifetime of friendship. And probably more than a little adventure.

As long as Shawn was there to share it, Deirdre was ready.

GENEALOGY

Ailee & Grahame   James & Marjorie   ??   Thom & Bess
Donaghue   McGregor   Ballard
| | | |
Jack   &   Nancy   Alistair &   Hattie
Donaghue   McGregor   Guthrie   Ballard
| |

Bryant Donaghue   &   Lizbeth Guthrie
|
Deirdre Donaghue

~*~

Jacky & Elsie MacClayne   Bruce & Tavey Vance
| |
Jack "Little Jack" MacClayne & Sally Vance
|

Ellie MacClayne & James McClaren
|
Shawn McClaren

Village Residents

April 1783

The Donaghue House
Daisy Donahgue
Deborah and Daniel

The Ballard House
Peter Ballard
Conor & Blair
Annabel

The McGregor House
Ian & Caitlyn McGregor
Aidan & Grace
Shannen, Allison, and Brendan

The Fonseca House
Lizzie & Manny Fonseca
Lucio & Mary Margaret
Maggie, Neddy, and Nola

Shaw House
Clary Donaghue
Deirdre

2nd Ballard House
Tate & Nessa Ballard
Rona and Jayme

The Smyth House
Lennox & Briony Smyth
Paden and Maisy

2nd Fonseca House

Marcos Fonseca
Patrick & Rosa Donaghue
Aileen

3rd Fonseca House

Bernardo & Mathilda Fonseca
Ewen, Taylor, and Annie

The Lacour House

Elki & Robert Lacour
Mona and Claude

The Stewart House

Wallis & Hetty Stewart
Shawn (1 mo.)

Deirdre's Kerchief
Designed By Laurinda Reddig

Yarn:

Approximately 6 oz /400 yds Sport Weight yarn. Sample on cover used 1 skein each Camano and Chehalis, 100% East Friesian Wool (4 oz/280 yds per skein), grown in Chehalis, WA, worsted spun by a mill in Montana.

Available from the Ewe and I Yarn Shop in Chehalis, WA, home of the Black Sheep Creamery, making cheese from the milk of the same sheep sheared for the wool.

http://www.eweandiyarns.com/
https://blacksheepcreamery.com/

Notions:

K/6.5mm hook for Kerchief or size needed to obtain gauge
Tapestry needle

Gauge:

Rows 1-6 on K hook = 3" tall from bottom point to center of top edge by 5 1/2" across top edge, unblocked

Pattern Notes:

• When working "into next" V-st or 2dcV-st insert hook in chain-2 space of the V-st or 2dcV-st.

• When joining rounds, work sl st into 2 loops of the top of beginning chain.

Special Stitches:

V-stitch (V-st) – Dc, ch 2, dc in indicated space or st.

2 Double Crochet V-stitch (2dcV-st) – 2 dc, ch 2, 2 dc in indicated space or st.

KERCHIEF PATTERN:
Worked from the point up. With K hook, ch 4.

Row 1 (RS): Work in fourth ch from hook (2dcV-st, 1 dc), turn. (Triangle begins with one shell, increasing one half shell every row to shoulder)

Row 2 (WS): Ch 3 (counts as first dc here and throughout), V-st in first dc, ch 1, sc in next 2dcV-st, ch 1, (V-st, 1 dc) in top of turning ch, turn.

Row 3: Ch 3, 2 dc in first dc, sc in first V-st, 2dcV-st in next sc, sc in next V-st, 3 dc in top of turning ch, turn.

Row 4: Ch 1, sc in first dc, *ch 1, V-st in next sc, ch 1**, sc in next 2dcV-st; Rep from * to **, sc in top of turning ch, turn.

Row 5: Ch 3, 2dcV-st in first sc, [sc in next V-st, 2dcV-st in next sc] across to last V-st, sc in next V-st, (2dcV-st, 1 dc) in last sc, turn.

Row 6: Ch 3, V-st in first dc, ch 1, sc in next 2dcV-st, ch 1, [V-st in next sc, ch 1, sc in next 2dcV-st, ch 1] across, (V-st, 1 dc) in top of turning ch, turn.

Row 7: Ch 3, 2 dc in first dc, sc in first V-st, [2dcV-st in next sc, sc in next V-st] across, 3 dc in top of turning ch, turn.

Row 8: Ch 1, sc in first dc, [ch 1, V-st in next sc, ch 1, sc in next 2dcV-st] across to last sc, ch 1, V-st in last sc, ch 1, sc in top of turning ch, turn.

Rows 9-40: Rep Rows 5-8 eight times.

Row 41: Rep Row 5.

Row 42: Ch 3, (dc, ch 1, dc) in first dc, ch 1, [sc in next 2dcV-st, ch 1, (dc, ch 1, dc) in next sc, ch 1] across, sc in last 2dcV-st, ch 1, (dc, ch 1, 2 dc) in top of turning ch, turn. Do not finish off.

Edging:

Rnd 1: Ch 1, sk first 2 dc, 2 sc in each ch-1 sp across, 2dcV-st in top of beg ch of Row 42; Working down first side, in last st used on each row. [sc in top of dc at end of next row, 2dcV-st in sc at end of next row, sk next row, sc in top of beg ch of next row, 2dcV-st in top of last dc of next row, sc in sc at end of next row, sk next row, 2dcV-st in top of beg ch of next row] 5 times, sc in top of last dc of next row, (2dcV-st, ch 2, 2 dc) in same ch as Row 1 to form corner; Working down second side, [sc in top of beg ch of next row, 2dcV-st in top of last dc of next row, sk next row, sc in sc at end of next row, 2dcV-st in top of beg ch of next row, sc in top of last dc of next row, sk next row, 2dcV-st in sc at end of next row] 5 times, sc in top of beg ch of next row, 2dcV-st in top of last dc of last row, join with sl st in first sc.

Rnd 2: Sl st loosely in each sc across top edge, [sc in next 2 dc, 3 sc in next ch-sp, sc in next 2 dc, sk 1 sc] across to corner, [sc in next 2 dc, 3 sc in next ch-sp] 2 times, [sc in next 2 dc, sk 1 sc, sc in next 2 dc, 3 sc in next ch-sp] across, sc in last 2 dc, join with sl st in first sl st. Finish off and weave in all ends.

For more information about Laurinda's crochet designs, please go to: www.recrochetions.com

For the photographs of the finished kerchief or to purchase a PDF of the pattern, which includes Deirdre's Summer Mitts please go to:

https://www.ravelry.com/patterns/library/deirdres-kerchief-and-summer-mitts

A Special Preview of

THE KENTUCKIAN

THE DONAGHUE HISTORIES
BOOK FOUR
BY C. JANE REID

WHEREIN MY STORY BEGINS

In the autumn of 1836, south of Boonesborough, Kentucky, I learned I'd killed a man.

"Hollis!" Burr Bradley rode for all he was worth, which wasn't much given his cataracts and the old horse he'd borrowed from a neighbor. I'd come off the Otter Creek trail onto the old Boone's Trace when I heard Burr shouting my name. The old hunter rode the hard-trotting bay as his name said, a burr in its mane.

"Burr Bradley, what are you doing riding at this time a day?" The sun had sunk well into the trees and after a long day on the trail, me, my mule Tennessee, and my dog were all eager to reach Burr's little cabin. My old bones were aching from the coming cold.

Burr reined the horse in. "Hollis, you can't be here."

"I'm a bit early this year, but I am here." I tried to jest, but it fell flat. Burr's appearance was alarming. He rarely rode anymore. "What are you doing here?"

"I came to warn you," he huffed, out of breath. "They're looking for you."

"Who's looking for me? And how did you know to find me here?"

"I had it from the Davies boy that Widow Green's eldest son told the constables you'd left her farm four days back. They think you're taking the Kentucky River trail, so they ain't expecting you for another day, which gives you time."

"Time for what? Why do they think I'm taking the Kentucky River trail? Burr, what in the devil is going on?"

"Hollis—" He leaned down in the saddle to focus his filmy eyes on me. "Constable Bridger says you killed a man."

I'd never heard anything more absurd from Burr Bradley, and I'd heard all his stories. "Nonsense," I told him. "Where is the constable? We'll get this cleared up."

Burr nudged his horse in my way when I would have walked forward. Tennessee tossed her head and pinned back her long ears at the old bay horse.

"This ain't no jest, Hollis. These men are dead-set against you, and they mean to have you."

He was serious, more serious than I'd ever seen him except when he spoke of the time the Shawnee besieged Boonesborough.

I'd gotten quiet, and when I got quiet, Dog got alert. He raised his tawny head and perked his loppy ears as if trying to overhear us.

"Who do they say I killed?"

"Zachariah Wells' boy."

Cold washed over me, and my breathing hitched.

Burr reached down to take me by the shoulder. "I knowed you didn't do it, Hollis."

"I saw Zachariah Wells not three weeks ago. His son is dead?"

"Kilt dead, yes."

"When?"

Burr hesitated. I took him by the arm. "When, Burr?"

"The night after Zachariah says you stopped by."

"I stopped by at the Olneys that night."

"And that's what they told the constable."

"So why do they think it was me? How was he killed? Why was he killed?"

"Hollis, you need to get off the trace."

"This doesn't make any sense, Burr. Take me to the constable and I'll—"

"No!" Burr's shout cut through the shock. "Hollis, you know how Constable Bridger works."

I did indeed. I still dreamt of the Chickamauga Cherokee man kicking as he strangled from where he'd been strung up from a hickory tree.

"This makes no sense," I said again.

"You need to go to ground," Burr advised. "Stay off your usual trails. Go somewheres no one would think to find you 'til we get this cleared up."

"Burr—"

"And for God's sake, Hollis, get out of them buckskins. You don't want to look so much like yourself. Folks mark that sort of thing nowadays. Grow a beard. Ain't natural you don't keep one anyway. And get rid of that mule."

The look I gave him told Burr what I thought about that last suggestion.

"Fine, keep the mule but ride her at least. Everyone who knows you don't think you can ride. Maybe I should take Dog with me."

"Dog stays where he is," I told him. "Burr, I know Bridger and I aren't breaking bread in friendship anytime soon, but I can't see how he could think me a killer."

"You need to get a move on," Burr urged me.

"I'll head to Sally's—"

"Don't you go anywhere near your sister," Burr growled. "Or your brother neither."

I glared at him. "You know I'd never do anything to put them in harm's way."

"Don't get wrathy on me, Hollis, I knowed it. But those are the first places Bridger went looking for you, and he's sure to have asked neighbors to watch both farms."

I heaved a mighty sigh. "This is beetle-headed. I did nothing wrong."

"Then it won't take long to clear up. Now git. Might be someone followed me."

"Burr—"

"Just git, Hollis! Curse your hide, git!" He tugged the horse around and set his heels into it. It took off in that jarring trot, leaving me standing off the old Boone's Trace more confused than ever.

"C'mon, Tennessee." I aimed her back down the Otter Creek Trail and whistled for Dog. I'm not the sort to turn and run, but it was easier to pacify Burr when he was in this mood by agreeing with him instead of arguing with him.

He mentioned Widow Green's eldest boy. Widow Green's old station lay only two days back up the trail. I'd known Widow Green and her three boys for years. They'd tell me all they'd heard.

Still, as I doubled back along the Otter Creek Trail, I tried to wrap my head around Burr's news.

I couldn't quite grasp that Stephen was dead. Lord, Delia must be hurting. And Zachariah, what must he be feeling? Stephen was his only boy. Zachariah had only his three girls now.

Who would kill Stephen? And why did the constable think it was me? True, there was no love lost between Constable Bridger and me, but I didn't think him the sort to blame me out of hand. Then again, I'd seen his brand of justice before.

If Bridger thought I'd killed the boy, then Zachariah must have told him about our visit. Good Lord, did Zachariah think I'd do his boy harm? Had I offered him any sign that I could do such a thing?

Follow Hollis Donaghue's story in
The Kentuckian, coming Spring 2019

ACKNOWLEDGEMENTS

I must once again first thank my family for supporting me when I was lost in writing. I'm sure, however, that my children, Kate and Liam, won't think that they sacrificed anything because it meant more video game time for them. My husband, T.C., offered countless backrubs, forced me to take breaks to play Sea of Thieves, and generally was there when I needed to whine.

My mother was invaluable in her help with dishes and laundry and several meals. And Ash the dog was full of snuggly love whenever I was in need. The cat, Kiwi, completely ignored me.

As always, I'm grateful to my dearest friend, Laurinda Reddig, for starting me on this journey with the Donaghues. I am also very thankful for my wonderful friends, Mercedes and Katherine, who cheered me on or plied me with chocolate when I needed it.

Special thanks to my beta readers, Laurinda, Jane, and Jeanette, my lovely proofreader Nancy, and my amazing cover designer, Cheri Lasota of Author's Assembler. I am also indebted to my fellow local authors, who listened to me moan, sympathized when the story fought back, and celebrated when I'd made my daily word count. Carolyn, Cheri, Christina, Sarah, Tina, Gina, Bonnie, Amanda, Irene, and Katherine, you are the best.

Thank you to Blizzard Yarn and Fiber in Vancouver, WA, for being so supportive. Friendly Local Yarn Shops and the folks who run them are amazing. So are local coffee shops like Di Tazza and Hidden River Roasters, both in Camas, WA. I have left permanent seat marks from the hours spent there in my favorite spot with my favorite drinks.

Especially, though, thank you, Readers, for nagging me until this was done. The next one won't take nearly as long. Promise.

THE AUTHOR

A lifelong writer, C. Jane is excited to combine her interest in history with her love of crochet in a series of stories blending romance and mystery. Her first novel, *The Secret Stitch*, book one of the Donaghue Histories series, was released in March 2016, followed by book two, *The Sojourners*, in July 2018. Both stories follow the life of a Scots-Irish immigrant woman attempting to survive in the New World in 1721. She also published a collection of her poetry, *Barded in Poetry*, under the pen name Cari Reid, along with *The Soldier Poet*, a historical novel inspired by actual events during WWI.

She lives in the Pacific Northwest where she is part of the Ficstitches Yarns team, a quarterly crochet kit that features the continuing saga of the Donaghue family, along with a historically-inspired crochet design by her friend, Laurinda Reddig, and includes hand-dyed yarn and a handmade accessory, all themed around the story.

You can find more information about her work, including a bibliography of research material and a sign-up form for her newsletter, on her website:

www.cjanereid.com

THE
SECRET STITCH

THE DONAGHUE HISTORIES
BOOK ONE
BY C. JANE REID

There be dangers in old, untouched places . . .

September, 1720: One month ago, Ailee Donaghue married a stranger to save herself from scandal. Now aboard a ship bound for the New World with ninety other Scots-Irish, she has no idea what she'll be able to offer her new husband. She's a horrible knitter, a bad cook, and can barely be trusted with a sewing needle. She is determined to help her new family thrive, but she is completely unprepared and fears she'll only be a burden. Can she face the challenges ahead with a man she barely knows and dangers that threaten her from unexpected enemies? Or will the friendships she makes along the way prove to be her salvation?

~*~

This first book in the Donaghue Histories begins the saga of the Donaghue family. Each book follows the next generation of the family against the backdrop of the developing New World and features strong women, historical detail, the evolution of crochet along with a crochet pattern by designer Laurinda Reddig.

THE SOJOURNERS

THE DONAGHUE HISTORIES
BOOK TWO
BY C. JANE REID

That woman will bring shame down upon us...

The New World is no place for a penniless widow. Elsie MacClayne's choices are few: remain with the other Scots-Irish immigrants to become a burden on her friends or search out her cousin, Connor, who has already made Pennsylvania Colony his home. Elsie longs to make a life for herself and her unborn child, but old prejudices are still alive amongst the colonists, and she is looked upon with either pity or distrust.

What I did was inexcusable...

Niall Donaghue had anticipated his brother's arrival in the New World, but he hadn't expected Grahame to arrive with a new wife. Anger and jealousy drive him to make a mistake that costs him not only Grahame's trust but the chance to pursue his own hopes for the future. He is forced to set aside his ambitions for the sake of his aunt and their livelihood.

Can Elsie find the courage to withstand the threats around her and claim her place in a foreign land? Can Niall find the will to ask for the forgiveness he longs for?

THE
SECRET STITCH
A CROCHET COMPANION
BY LAURINDA REDDIG

A Crochet Companion features nine historically inspired designs based on *The Secret Stitch*, the first novel in the new series by C. Jane Reid, tracing the evolution of crochet. Each design is named for a character from the story, with quotes that inspired that accessory.

Patterns feature:

- 2 shawls, 2 capes, 2 cowls, a bag, hat and mitts
- Stitch diagrams and tutorials for right- and left-handed
- Alternatives to make each one your own

Ficstitches Yarns

Every craft lovingly handmade tells a story. Ficstitches Yarns Crochet Kit Club takes creating to another level by offering crochet patterns along with hand-dyed yarn, handmade accessories, and fictional stories, all bound together in a theme of romance, history, and the coming-together of friends.

Be one of the first to receive the latest book in the Donaghue Histories series by C. Jane Reid, along with a crochet design from designer Laurinda Reddig and a handmade accessory, both inspired by the story, along with hand-dyed yarn from an indie yarn dyer. So much more than a yarn club, each element of these kits is an adventure, with a little bit of mystery and a whole lot of fun. Preorders open quarterly in January, April, July, and October.

For more information about the crochet kit club that inspired the writing of this novel and its companion crochet book, please go to:

www.ficstitchesyarns.com

50505237R00144

Made in the USA
Middletown, DE
26 June 2019